CAPTIVATED

BETHANY-KRIS

Published by Bethany-Kris

www.bethanykris.com

eISBN 13: 978-1-988197-62-3

Print ISBN 13: 978-1-988197-63-0

Cover Art © London Miller
Cover Photo © Michael Stokes
Editor: Elizabeth Peters
Cover Model: Antoni Bialy

For all the buried women—gone far too soon. And for the ones still dying slowly. You are not alone.

CONTENTS

ONE

THERE WAS NOTHING quite like being strapped in while speeding through the clouds in something that might as well have been a *tin can*. It was no wonder that it was practically impossible to find bodies after a plane crash, all things considered.

Christ, his thoughts were morbid today.

"You really don't like flying, do you?"

Joseph Rossi hated that his discomfort was this obvious. Mind you, it was his father, but still. He took great pains to keep his outward appearance at undecipherable levels. It was a talent of his.

Or shit, it should have been.

He fingered the rosary, a gift from his uncle, Tommas, at his First Communion, around his throat, and wished it would give him the peace he usually found in it. The church had become somewhat of a sanctuary for him.

No matter the kind of shit he did—or how much blood stained his hands when the daylight broke over the horizon—those doors were still open. The church still welcomed. His priest was still there to listen.

He was the *worst* kind of sinner.

It never seemed to matter.

Damian didn't miss Joe fidgeting with the rosary. Frankly, his father never missed very much anyway. Eagle-eye, and all.

"We'll only be another thirty minutes," his father said.

Joe shot Damian a look from the side that he hoped screamed at his father to just stop before he started—

"Take a deep breath," Damian added.

And there he goes.

"Don't use that voice with me," Joe muttered.

Damian raised a single brow high, and regarded his son. "What voice?"

"That one—the one you just used. The one with the *tone*."

It unsettled Joe for more reasons than he cared to explain. Mostly, though, because it wasn't like his father to be a gentle kind of man in his speech. Soft-spoken, and quiet, sure. That was just Damian's way because he didn't need noise to get the job done, or to do violence.

A lot like Joe.

No one ever saw them coming that way. Yeah, he was definitely the worst kind of sinner.

"Hand to God, Joe," Damian said, shaking his head," I have no idea what you are talking about."

His father looked sincere, too. That was the thing about Rossis, though. They could look innocent as fuck, but at the same time, be planning some way to slit your throat the first chance they could … if they had a reason to.

Men like them—criminals; *Mafiosi*—all needed an edge to stay on top where this life and business was concerned. Joe's edge just happened to be a hell of a lot like his father's edge once used to be. He was the man in the shadows doing what needed to be done to protect the organization and family. Damian had once done that, too, except he traded his hitman-style in for a cushier seat as the Chicago Outfit's underboss.

Funny how that worked.

"That tone you *just* used," Joe said as the plane finally settled out of the turbulence. Jesus, he could actually breathe again. "You know exactly what I mean, Dad. It's the same tone you used to use on Cory and me when we were kids, and you wanted us to admit to something we had done wrong. Now, you use it on Monica because it doesn't work on us anymore, and she's the only one who hasn't caught onto your shit."

And Joe only blamed his sister's trusting nature on her age—being a decade younger than his twenty-one years, she had a valid excuse for being gullible.

Damian's lips twitched with the ghost of a smile. "You sure about that?"

There it is again.

Joe opened his mouth to speak, but his father held up a single hand and let out a short laugh. It was only the amusement and mirth in Damian's eyes that kept Joe quiet for a moment. Sometimes, he just let his father have his moments. They all needed them occasionally.

"You're right," Damian said quietly, "I do know which tone you mean."

"Great—stop using it."

"Glad I could distract you long enough to prevent you from ripping the armrests off your seat, however."

Joe blinked.

Huh.

He had removed his death grip from the armrests. At least, for now.

"I know you hate flying," Damian murmured, staring out the port window.

He really did. More than he cared to admit. It was an unjustified fear, and just about the only thing in life that did scare the hell out him, but that didn't make it any less real to him. Like the universe was coming around to kick Joe in the ass with a sarcastic smirk to remind him that he was just as fucking human as everybody else.

"We could have drove to New York," Joe said. "Damn, I would have drove for you."

Damian's gaze drifted toward his oldest son, and he smiled a little bit. "It's amusing."

"What is?"

"That you feel like when another family calls—a family with bigger pull and more control than yours—that you have the option to *make them wait.*"

Joe stiffened a bit in his seat. "I didn't—"

"That's exactly what you're saying, and you know better, son."

Just like that, the easy banter between a father and son was lost. In its place was the unspoken code of made men, and the mafia life they were surrounded and suffocated by. It was never-ending. All the rules, the expectations, and everything else that came along with being men like them.

Usually, he didn't mind.

Joe didn't know anything different.

"You're twenty-one," Damian said, never turning his attention away from the window as he spoke, "and so I will give you a pass for putting your own wants before someone else's. But you're close enough to twenty-two, Joe, that I can't keep giving you passes."

Clearing his throat, Joe glanced down the first class aisle at the flight attendant starting to make her rounds again. She was too far away yet to hear their conversation. No doubt, his father knew that, too.

Damian knew *everything.*

"No offense," Joe started to say.

"Whenever someone starts a sentence with that statement—"

"It's usually going to offend someone. Yeah, let me talk."

Damian waved a hand as if to silently say, *Get on with it.*

"No offense," he repeated, "but you didn't even tell me what we were coming to New York for, Dad. You just said the Marcellos needed something, but not what, or why I needed to come along. You expect me to know everything just because? I'm not a goddamn mind reader."

"Business," Damian said simply, "when the Marcello family calls, it always means *business.*"

And Joe knew … He'd grown up his whole life being told—everybody bent to the Marcellos, but they didn't fucking bend for anybody else. So was their right being who they were, and having what they did.

No mafia organization remained on top by playing nice with others.

"No, I won't be long, Lily," Damian said. "I won't miss Mon's game."

In the backseat beside his father, Joe ignored the buzzing of his own phone. He didn't need to pick it up and look at it to know who it was.

Cory, likely.

His younger brother—by only a year—was dying a little because Joe was in New York for this mysterious *business*, and Cory had to stay at home. He was not in the mood to listen to his brother whine or bitch about it, so he just opted to not pick up the phone at all. It would be nicer to listen to Cory rant about that, anyway.

"You got it, sweetheart," Damian said. "Love you, bye."

Not a damn second after Damian hung up the phone with his wife—Lily, Joe's sweet-natured, good-hearted mother—he snapped at his son, "Joe, stop that goddamn fidgeting."

It was almost like his father had been watching him the whole time through his phone call, and knew the closer they were getting to the Marcello mansion, the worse his fidgeting had become. Joe's hands stilled in his lap instantly.

Joe scowled at his father. "I'm nervous, all right."

"Be nervous, but stop the jittery bullshit."

"Easy for you to say, Dad."

Damian smirked, but he didn't hide it fast enough for Joe. He still saw the grin before his father turned his head, and stared out at the cars they passed. It kind of struck him then at how content and comfortable his father seemed in a state that was not in any way theirs—at least when it came to the business side of their life. Going into the territory of another family could sometimes be tricky. Like navigating alligator infested waters. A person might think they were stepping on a rock, and before they knew it, they were in the mouth of an alligator.

Yeah, just like that.

Maybe it wasn't the same for his father, though. He often made trips to visit other organized crime families to do deals, or make peace. Despite how intimidating his father could be at first glance, Damian was charming when he made the effort to be. And doing good business and keeping peace *was* one of his many jobs as the underboss for Joe's uncle, Tommas.

Really ... he worried about fucking this up for his father. It was the first time Damian brought Joe along for a meeting of this caliber, and it kind of put him on edge. He was always the one in the shadows, never the one stepping up to take center stage.

He didn't like that.

He wasn't the type.

"Dad?" Joe asked.

"Yeah?"

"Cory would have been better for this, not me."

There, he said it.

Let his father make of that what he wanted.

Damian sighed, and looked at Joe. For a short while, the two simply stared at each other in silence. He took in the almost-perpetual smirk his father wore, the strong jawline, and sky-blue eyes, and felt like he was staring into a reflection of his oncoming older years. Even their hair was the same shade of dark brown, although Damian toted a bit of salt color behind his ears, and Joe liked to keep his cut in a high-fade style.

Still, his father stayed silent. More often than not, that was Damian's way of getting one of his sons to speak. It worked far better on Cory than it did Joe.

Joe liked silence, after all.

And right now, he had nothing to say. He said what he said.

"I know Cory would have had more fun maybe," Damian finally said.

"Exactly."

That was also evident by the phone in Joe's pocket that had *finally* stopped ringing for two goddamn minutes.

"But you're in a position where you could use a bit of education on the rules of other families," his father added, shrugging. "And as someone once told me, Joe, comfort zones are reserved for weak men who are afraid to try something new. I want you to succeed—you chose this life, son. Don't shy away because you prefer to hide away."

Joe frowned. "I hate it when you do that."

"I know."

Smug asshole.

"How much longer?" Joe asked.

Better to change the topic—he wasn't going to get anything else from his father in this conversation, clearly.

"Actually, we're almost there."

Damian hadn't been exaggerating, thankfully. It was only ten minutes of driving later, and the car pulled in front of a gated driveway. Once the gate was opened for them, a long and winding driveway lined with tall trees led them to a stop in front of a mansion that was probably large enough to house a small army.

He took in the manicured grass, carefully placed cobblestones in the driveway, and the large marble pillars holding up a grand entrance for cars to drive under. Their car parked off to the side, instead.

Wealth.

The place screamed wealth.

Joe had just slid out of the car—still taking in the Marcello estate with fresh eyes—when the front door of the mansion opened, and a group of young women fled onto the marble steps one by one. Five young women, actually.

Marcello daughters?

Principessas?

Did the Marcellos have that many daughters in their family?

Joe didn't really know.

He figured it didn't really matter anyway, and besides, his attention had caught something far better to focus in on. Like the young, willowy woman hanging back a little from her group of friends. Her hazel gaze caught his, and something struck him still and silent when she refused to drop his stare. Confidence wafted from the tall, gorgeous woman. Her dark blonde hair hung in loose waves that flicked over her shoulder when she turned her head a bit to keep staring at Joe even as she rounded the back of the waiting SUV.

Goddamn.

Joe wasn't one to notice women. He liked a good time once in a while when the mood struck him, but he had far more important things to focus on in his life. Not like his brother, Cory, who liked to have a different female on his arm every weekend.

And yet, Joe found it damn near impossible to look away from the hazel-eyed, blonde woman with the bow-shaped lips, and dancer's legs. She had to be a dancer given the way she walked like the ground was made of clouds, and her toes barely touched the cobblestone in her flats before lifting back up again. Quick, carefully taken steps with a posture that spoke of beauty and grace.

All the other ladies wore skinny jeans, and heels. But not her. She wore a flowy summer dress that spun wide with every step she took.

Still, she kept staring.

So did he.

What was her name?

And why couldn't he breathe normally again?

"Joe," Damian said loudly.

Joe snapped out of his daze just as the unknown woman reached for the backdoor of the SUV, and looked over his shoulder to find his father staring at him. He couldn't even pretend like he hadn't been gawking like a foolish boy caught with his prick in his hands. He didn't even try, either.

"Yeah, Dad?"

Tires squealed before the SUV quickly pulled out of the circular drive, and headed down the winding path out of Joe's sight.

Damn.

Who was that woman?

"Find something you like?" Damian asked, smiling in that way of his.

"Uh …"

Fuck.

Damian cocked a brow.

Joe cleared his throat.

Jesus.

Maybe he should have acted like he hadn't been staring.

"The last one—you were watching her," Damian said.

Joe spun around to face his father completely, and tried to laugh it off. "So, what if I was?"

"Since when do you stare like that?"

"I don't."

His father nodded like he knew exactly what was running through Joe's mind.

He wanted to know the woman. Who she was, and what made her so bold as to stare at a man she didn't know from Adam like she liked what she was seeing.

"Leave it alone, Dad," Joe said.

"I didn't say a thing."

"You're thinking it."

Joe didn't need to be told.

He knew.

"No, I'm thinking that I should give you a heads up," Damian said.

"What's that?"

Damian grabbed Joe by his shoulder, and turned them both to face the entrance of the Marcello mansion. During Joe's little daze, it seemed someone else—or several people, actually—had come to stand out on the marble steps.

Three men.

Dressed in black three-piece suits.

Side by side.

Even from this distance, Joe could see the resemblance between two of the men, and easily guessed this was the infamous Marcello brothers. One of the three were adopted—or so the stories went. The men waited for Joe and Damian to come to them, and not the other way around.

"That girl, Joe," his father said slowly as though he wanted to make sure his son heard every single last word, "is Liliana Marcello."

Joe grimaced.

A visceral reaction he couldn't even *try* to hide. Not because that deterred his interest in her, but rather, because he knew it was going to make it that much harder on him.

Liliana Marcello.

Daughter of Lucian Marcello.

Principessa of the family underboss.

Shit.

Nothing good ever came easy.

"Oh?" Joe asked.

He tried to sound unbothered.

He failed like a fucker.

Damian laughed. "The man on the left end is her father—the other two are her uncles. She's a year younger than you. Lucian is intimidating as hell. Don't let him know you think so, however."

"Thanks?"

Why did that come out like a question?

"That's a start," Damian grunted as he gave Joe a hard pat on the back. "Best way not to fuck this up, Joe, is not to act like a *cafone*. That is something you're incapable of doing. I know because I raised you this way. Do you want to know that girl?"

His head said to keep his mouth shut.

The rest of him didn't listen.

"Maybe," Joe said.

Because *yes.*

He did want to know her.

Damian nodded in the direction of the men waiting on the steps. "Start with her father."

"Great." Moving forward in step with his father, Joe asked, "Shit, they don't call her Lily, do they?"

Lily, like his *mother.*

Oh, damn, that thought just made his dick shrivel—

"No," Damian murmured, "and as far as I can recall, she has always asked to be called Liliana."

Oh, good.

There was his dick again.

"Also, I might have been wrong about the age thing. I believe she's the oldest, actually. A year older than you, not younger. How do you feel about an older woman?"

Joe gave his father a look. He was doing that annoying fucking thing again. He needed to *stop.*

"Got it," Damian muttered at the look on Joe's face, "now fix yourself."

"Damian," the man in the middle greeted, "and company. Good to see you, old friend."

"Dante," Damian replied, taking the hand the Marcello boss offered. "Gio, Lucian; nice to see the two of you. Theo says hi, Gio."

Gio—or Giovanni—Marcello grinned. A sight that threw the man's features back a good fifteen years in a blink. "How's Chicago, D?"

"It's good. You should visit more often."

"Unlikely," the quiet man said.

Lucian.

Liliana's father.

Lucian's gaze drifted over Joe momentarily as though he was studying him. Although for what, Joe had no fucking clue. He still didn't even know what in the hell he was here for to begin with. Just as quickly as Lucian gave him that appraisal, he moved his attention back to Damian when Joe's father spoke.

"You're never going to get over that little incident from years ago, are you, Lucian?" Damian asked.

"I don't kill one of you every time someone from the Outfit comes into my city," Lucian replied, "and so if I were you, I would take that as a win."

Damn.

Seemed this man didn't pull any fucking punches.

"We do consider that as a win, actually," Damian returned easily.

"Play nice, Lucian," Dante said. And then to Damian just as quickly, he added, "We should take this conversation inside. The girls were heading to the store for ... well, junk food and whatever else. I don't think we need to be on the steps discussing business when they get back shortly."

"Agreed," Damian said.

As they climbed the last couple of steps, and the Marcello mansion was opened to them, Lucian Marcello glanced back at Joe with a grin that came off as altogether cold, and just a little bit sly. Joe rarely found himself put on edge by someone else. He just wasn't the type, and he was usually the one with his linebacker size, towering height, and silent nature to make people feel nervous.

This change was strange for him.

Entirely unsettling.

"Welcome to New York, Joe," Lucian said, his smile fading in a grim line, "I certainly hope you're worth the amount of money I am about to pay for you."

What?

"Fair warning," Damian said as he took a seat across from the large oak desk Dante rested behind, "he doesn't know why he's here. I figured it best to let him in on the secret when it was needed."

Joe shot his father a look from where he stood in the corner—the other chairs in the room were already taken, and only a seat with the back facing the window remained. He was not a stupid man, and he was not about to put his back to a window in a house he wasn't familiar with, not to mention around men he wasn't sure if he could fully trust.

Dante glanced over at Lucian, asking, "Do you want to start this, or should I?"

"You're the boss, brother," Lucian replied.

"And this is—"

"You're the boss."

Joe stiffened a bit as the two men passed a look between each other while everyone else stayed quiet. He could never imagine interrupting his boss without some kind of action for disobedience, but clearly there was a different kind of relationship with these brothers. They were made men, sure, but family still held a firm line where it counted.

Dante nodded, and pushed his chair back just enough to open a drawer in the desk. Pulling out a file, he tossed it on the desk, and then gestured to Joe. "Go on, pick it up, Rossi."

He moved away from the wall with footsteps that didn't make a sound, and plucked up the folder. Opening it, he scanned the contents, and then flipped through the items inside. Pictures of older men stared back at him—details of them, and their life. Their careers, too.

One, a politician—George Earl. Republican senator for the state of New York. Joe remembered him winning by a landslide during the last election.

Another, a Chief of Police for the city of New York. A man by the name of Martin Abraham. Joe didn't recognize him as well as the first man, but his title was more than enough to make Joe hesitate.

Fuck.

Already, Joe was not liking where this was going. The only reason he would be given a file like this with marks inside was to rid the world of them. He could make a business out of being a hitman, if he wanted to. He wasn't stuck with only work in Chicago, but that's where his loyalty and family were at the end of the day. So, he only willingly offered his *services* to his family.

After all, that's just what he was good at. Like his father had once been, too.

"These look like prospective marks for me," Joe said.

"Because they are," Lucian said from his chair.

Joe flipped through the pages again. "Shit, you've even laid out details for me the way I like …" He passed his father a glance, adding, "Which tells me this has been in the works for longer than I actually was aware."

"Yes, well …"

"I don't hire out my services," he said quietly. "I work for the Chicago Outfit only."

"You will in this circumstance," his father said quietly.

Joe's jaw flexed at that comment. "No offense—"

"*Joe.*"

"Don't give me that rhetoric again, I mean this to be fucking offensive."

Damian sighed. "Then don't color it up with useless nonsense. Just *say* it."

Joe passed a look at the quiet, waiting men. "Maybe I shouldn't right now."

"What, son? Just say it, Jesus."

Fine.

"I'm not going to work for them just because the Outfit is still trying to get on friendlier terms with the Marcello family. Beyond that, look at these names, Dad." Joe dropped the file into his father's lap, and quickly retook his place in the corner before he added, "*Very* high fucking profile names. A politician? Chief of Police? That's asking for trouble, and it's not the kind of shit I want to be stepping in. It looks like someone else's shit, to be honest, and they're probably not even going to give me the decency of telling me what kind of shit before I step in it."

"On that, you're correct," Dante said, finally stepping into the conversation. "We're not going to tell you why we want these men dead. We will tell you why we want *you* to be the one who does it."

Christ.

Joe's molars were going to crack from the way he was clenching his jaw so goddamn tight. "Try me, but don't assume it will make any difference to what I already said."

Gio chuckled from the couch. "Damn, Damian, I like him. He's … got balls."

Damian scowled. "Usually, he's quieter than this."

Dante went on speaking to Joe as though the other men weren't conversing at all. "These men need to go for reasons we're not willing to disclose. However, that shouldn't be important to whether or not you're able and willing to do the job, not to mention, how much we're going to pay you to do it. What is important is that you come from Chicago, not New York. You, Joseph, have never even been in the presence of our family properly. Not been pictured with any of our made men, or our women. *Nothing.* Invisible, essentially, which is exactly what we need. We cannot afford for attention to be put on our family for these hits, although we assume we'll get some spotlight anyway just because. Nonetheless, with nothing to find by way of connections, we'll all make it out unscathed."

Joe was barely listening because he was now staring at his father. "Give me *one* reason why I should agree to take on this job when you know I have only worked for Chicago."

"I can give you two, actually."

"Try me."

"The thing we talked about outside, for one. Might want to be here a while. It could help with that, you know."

Ah, yeah.

Liliana.

He heard his father's unspoken words. Although frankly, working for her family like this might put a serious fucking dent in those plans. Not to mention who her goddamn father was. Shit could never be simple for Joe.

"And for two?" Joe asked.

"Because I am asking you to take it, Joe," Damian said, "and not for any reason you might assume, but because sometimes, we lend a hand when it is desperately needed. There was a time once when you started taking on marks because you wanted to remove those who did not deserve to breathe the same air we did—maybe it's time to get back to that place for a while."

His rosary felt heavy around his throat.

Like a noose, almost.

"Asking me, or telling me?"

"Asking," his father murmured.

"What was it they called you, Damian?" Lucian asked, quietly jumping into the conversation again. "Back when you did all the dirty work for the Outfit, I mean."

Damian grinned a little. "Ghost."

"Hmm."

"And you?" Dante asked, glancing up at Joe. "What do they call you?"

He didn't want to answer.

He was going to have to take this job, anyway. His father asked, and something inside told him it was the right thing to do even if he didn't have all the details.

"Well?" Lucian pressed when Dante didn't.

"Shadow," Joe said.

"Pardon?"

"When the Outfit wants someone gone," Joe clarified, "they send the Shadow."

Because he moved quietly, as though he wasn't there at all. Because he blended in with the crowd, and was never really seen. Because in darkness, and in the shadows, he was the most dangerous.

There, he felt the most normal, too.

Strange how that worked.

"Five million for both," Dante said, "and they both have to be successful hits. We're not particularly working on a tight deadline, either. We've been briefed that you can take a while to make sure … everything is good and clean."

"Half in my account by tonight," Joe returned.

Dante nodded, and waved a hand toward the door. "Done … now, you should probably acquaint yourself with the mansion, as this is where you'll be coming to brief or get orders. Have a look around, and if you see my mother, say hello. She enjoys guests."

Great.

TWO

"JUST COME OUT this weekend," Cella said. "What's *one weekend* going to hurt?"

Liliana's younger sister always liked to dangle that rope to her as though she seriously thought it was going to work. It never did.

"Gordo would kill me," Liliana replied. "If he knew the shit I was about to shove into my mouth, he would have a fit. Imagine him finding out I was drinking and partying all weekend when I am supposed to be resting in prep for next week."

Cella and her two friends—mutual with Liliana, too, really—piled out of the SUV. "You're no fun anymore, Liliana. All you care about is dance, and that company."

"That's not true, but I worked hard to even get my spot in that company. I have the chance to be the lead dancer *again* for the upcoming production, and I don't want to piss off my—"

"Whatever."

Catherine, their cousin, rolled her eyes in the front seat when the door slammed. "She's dramatic today."

Liliana would tend to agree. "I think she misses me being available all the time."

"Maybe."

Fact was, even before Liliana had gotten her spot in the Wylder Ballet Company three years ago—a couple of years later than most of the dancers in the company, as some of the people there liked to point out—she still hadn't been able to spend every waking moment with her sister. From the age of ten, her focus on ballet had been a huge part of her life. She didn't want to do anything her parents tried to put her in for extracurricular activities.

Then, ballet was on the table.

God, she *hated* it at first. Despised it, really. But she watched all the ballerinas come into the studio to work, and something about them was amazing. They were beautiful, graceful, and strong. Sylph-like in their *pointe* shoes, and moving across the floor as though they were completely weightless. Like fairies with their hair tied up in perfect buns, and their soft pink or flat black leotards.

Liliana had been young enough—and dumb enough—to think she should be able to do ballet just like them, and that was where the frustration came in. And then she nailed her first *en pointe* and she got it. She finally understood why doing the work, learning the craft, and earning the praise, was a far better reward than anything else.

She respected ballet.

She worked hard for it.

Cella didn't understand, and Liliana didn't know how to explain it to her sister. Cella was two years younger than Liliana's twenty-two, and she was just trying to have the time of her life. She was living her *best life*.

Her sister didn't realize that Liliana was trying to do that, too. They didn't have to be doing the same things to reach a similar goal, or to be happy.

What did it even matter?

"Maybe she'll be out of her mood by the time we get upstairs to the theater room," Liliana grumbled.

Catherine pushed out of the SUV with a laugh over her shoulder. "You know how Cella is—that's unlikely."

Tell me about it.

Liliana's gaze scanned the driveway of the old Marcello estate as Catherine headed for the mansion. She didn't see the same black car that had been parked off to the side when they first left for the store.

Or the gorgeous man she couldn't stop staring at, either. The man with the sky-blue eyes, and dark hair. Just his size alone should have been enough to make Liliana a little hesitant considering he was built like a linebacker with the height to match, and an almost blank expression, but still ... she had stared, and couldn't seem to stop.

Which was altogether strange for her, considering ... Liliana didn't take notice of men anymore. At least, not ones she would consider strangers. She wasn't as trusting as she once had been. Life taught her to be wary, in a way.

And yet, she wondered about him.

Who was he?

"You coming?" Catherine called.

"Yep."

Liliana shook off the curiosity still burning in her gut, and headed after her cousin.

Before long, the two were inside the mansion, and heading for the upstairs where the theater room was situated. Her grandparents owned the mansion—no one lived there but Antony and Cecelia, most of the time. Still, Liliana liked to visit them as much as she could. Usually, she brought along others like her sisters, cousin, or a friend.

It gave the place some noise. Life, even. And her grandparents *loved* to entertain. They never complained, and even welcomed it.

So was the Marcello way.

Upstairs, Liliana could already hear the laughter coming down the hall from the theater room. Catherine shot her a sly smile.

"Maybe Cella is in a better mood," she said.

Liliana shrugged. "Maybe. I'll be right in. I need to use the bathroom first."

"Okay."

Disappearing into the closest bathroom—one of probably twenty in the large, two-wing monster that was the Marcello mansion—Liliana didn't actually need to use it. She pulled out her phone, and checked for any messages or missed calls.

The director of the Wylder Ballet Company could be particular. To say the least. While he didn't mind giving Liliana the weekend to rest and relax in preparation for the coming weeks of grueling practice, and long hours of training, his mind was like a switch.

He could flip his decision back in a snap.

Just like that.

Finding nothing waiting on her phone to say Gordo had suddenly up and changed his mind about Liliana's weekend, she counted her lucky stars, and considered it a win. Shoving the phone back in her pocket, she headed out of the bathroom, and damn near crashed into what felt like a fucking brick wall the second she left the room.

Liliana couldn't have caught herself from falling even if she tried. For all her balance, strength, and grace … none of it helped very much when she ran headfirst into something as unexpected as—

"Careful there," came a dark, rich voice.

Like a bass rumbled with his words.

Like a melody colored up his chuckles.

A strong arm had caught her easily—just one, it seemed he didn't need two—and righted Liliana to her feet probably before she even realized what had happened. Pushing her wild waves of dark blonde hair back out of her face, she blinked.

And came face to face with *him*.

The mysterious man from earlier in the driveway.

He was not quite the same as he had been earlier, though. Getting a closer—*really* up close and *personal*, considering how she was balancing herself by putting her palms to his chest, and was close enough to feel his warm mint-scented breath wash over her face—look at him was bad for her insides.

Bad, because he was gorgeous. More so than she realized. Bad, because her stomach clenched, and her palms felt sweaty already. For a second, she tried to make her voice work, but nothing came.

The dark lines of the man's face were shadowed by the hall, but it only added to the appeal of his square-cut jaw, strong cheekbones, and inviting grin. He was taller than her five foot eleven by at least six inches or *more*. She had to wonder if he played football, or rugby, because under her fingertips, his chiseled-from-stone muscles jumped from her touch.

Jesus.

"You okay?" he asked.

Liliana nodded quickly. "Yeah, sure."

"It's Liliana, right?"

She blinked.

He grinned deeper.

"*Right?*" he pressed.

"Liliana, yeah, but if you call me Lily, I'll probably gut you."

Might as well get that right out in the open and over with. She expected a bit of surprise in the man's eyes at her warning, but he actually tipped his head back and laughed. And sweet Christ, that laugh of his was *dangerous*.

The sound made her breath catch.

The sight made her heart race.

"Good to know," he said.

Laughter echoed from down the hall—her cousin, sister, and friends voices followed right after. Conversation about the movie they wanted to pick, or something like that. It didn't really matter.

"Ah, that's what I was trying to find," the guy said.

Liliana's brow dipped. "Pardon?"

"I heard noise, but this place is so big that I couldn't find out what it was or where it was coming from. I think I got lost."

She pressed her lips together to keep from smiling. "Well, the mansion is pretty big."

Liliana had a good mind to ask him what exactly he was doing at her grandparents' mansion, and why she had caught sight of her father and uncles waiting for him and the other man before she left with the girls. She didn't ask any of that because if the guy was in any way connected to her father and uncles' business in the mafia, he probably wouldn't tell her anyway.

Besides, sometimes it was better *not* to know.

That's what life as a Marcello *principessa* had taught Liliana. It was also pretty quick to teach her that even men who weren't connected to the life were their own particular brand of dangerous when it came right down to it.

"I bet your friends are wondering where you are," he said.

It was only then that Liliana realized how close and alone the two were in the dark hallway. Sure, someone might hear her shout if she needed to, but none of that had even factored in to her usual cautiousness.

In fact, the last thing she felt in that moment was unsafe.

"They probably are," she agreed.

"Would you do me a favor first?"

"Shoot."

He cocked a brow, and shrugged one large shoulder like it wasn't a big deal before he said, "Give me directions to the downstairs—I don't want to miss supper later. I hear that's rude, and I'm going to be around for a while. I would hate to make a bad first impression and all."

Liliana laughed, but not for the reason he probably thought. The last thing he did was make a bad first impression.

Far from it.

Joseph Rossi.

That was his name.

Or Joe, rather. It seemed no one actually used Joseph when they talked to him, and instead, simply called him Joe.

Liliana hadn't even gotten Joe's name before Catherine had popped out of the theater room upstairs, and shouted for her to hurry the hell up. Dinner came two hours later, and Liliana was—strangely—happy to find that Joe hadn't been lying.

He sat directly across from her at the table. His attention was on the conversation flowing around the table between her family, and the girls' friends. More than once, though, Liliana caught him glancing her way, too.

And not a quick glance.

No.

A *lingering* one.

Especially when he thought she wasn't looking.

"I hope Damian made his flight," her uncle—Giovanni—said before he shoved in a mouthful of food.

"He did—let me know a few minutes ago," Joe said.

His gaze dragged away from Liliana as he spoke, and she couldn't help but glance down at her plate and smile. It seemed like no one else at the table noticed their occasional glances, and for the moment, she was grateful.

Oddly, Liliana still found herself wishing his attention was back on her instead of on other people at the table. She opened her mouth to make sure exactly that happened, too.

"And where do you come from?" she asked.

Although, she was pretty sure she knew the answer. His last name was enough of a hint to say he probably hailed from Chicago—or more specifically, he came from the Chicago Outfit. Another criminal organization much like the one her father and uncles were involved with.

Liliana got what she wanted.

Joe's attention came back to her.

"Chicago," he said. "You couldn't tell by—"

"Your accent?" she interrupted with a sly grin. "Actually, the last name gave it away."

Throats cleared around the table, and Liliana could almost feel the eyes turning in her direction at her statement. Apparently, she was getting a little close to waters she probably shouldn't be talking about. The men of her family never actively discouraged the women to discuss business, or *la famiglia*, but it was always a big no-no at the dinner table.

That had never changed.

"I've never been to Chicago," she said.

Joe lifted a single brow high. "We have a big lake. Lots of crime. Good food."

Liliana nodded. "And you, too."

"Pardon?"

"It has you."

Joe matched her grin, then. "That it does."

A beat of silence passed before down the table, her uncle, Dante, said, "Joe, we will have everything set up for you tomorrow to make your stay in New York comfortable and quiet. I'm sure you understand why we would rather be the ones to do it than have you go on record anywhere."

Liliana's brow furrowed.

Quiet?

What did that mean?

Her confused thoughts drifted away as she glanced back at Joe, and realized something just by the expression on his face. Or rather, the lack of expression. He had suddenly—in nothing more than a breath and blink—reverted to his neutral, passive state.

His gaze gave nothing away. No warmth, or interest. Some might even look in his eyes in those moments, and think the stare was cold or hard. His posture became a bit more rigid in the seat, and when he spoke again, his tone was flat yet concise.

"Sounds fine," he said.

"Good," Dante replied.

Even when Joe's attention came back to Liliana for a brief few seconds, his expression and posture didn't change. It was as though he had dropped his defenses and pretenses with her during their exchange, and just as quickly, shifted back to someone else entirely.

Certainly not the same man she had met upstairs in the hallway with his charming nature, and boyish grins. Sure, he had the same dark, sexy, and mysterious appeal now. Just for two entirely different reasons.

Yet, Liliana had to admit ... she was just as curious about this Joe, too. What made him like this, and why? Was it the men at the table—was he like them, too?

Oh, yeah.

Her curiosity about Joe Rossi dug in under her skin, and suddenly refused to let go. It only burrowed deeper the longer they sat at the table, and she continued to stare at him. She was pretty sure her attention wasn't going unnoticed by others, but she didn't really care.

It wasn't like her father was the type to hold her back when it came to men, or dating. He simply asked her to be careful, but he never stepped in.

Or he hadn't before ...

"Do you dance?"

At the quiet question Joe posed, bringing Liliana out of her thoughts with a bang, the rest of the table quieted. Or at least the people nearest to them quieted down while they waited for her answer. She could plainly see the way her sister's gaze darted between the two of them curiously, a lot like her cousin, too.

A little too interested, maybe.

The men at the other end of the table were too busy discussing something in hushed tones with their gazes locked on each other to notice what was happening a few seats away.

"I do dance," Liliana said.

"Ballet, I bet," Joe murmured.

She swore she *felt* his words reach out and touch her like the softest stroke.

"How did you know?"

Joe's smile deepened into a sexy smirk—just like that, his defenses and mask dropped once more, and she was given a glimpse of *him*. "The way you walk."

"The way I walk," she echoed.

He nodded. "It's telling."

"And how do I walk?"

"Like the ground is air, and you're floating on it. Ballet dancers have a unique kind of grace. Mesmerizing, really." Joe leaned back in his chair, adding quieter, "Some might say it's even alluring."

Funny.

That's exactly how she would describe him, too.

"Well, how did dinner go?" Jordyn asked.

She gave Liliana a quick pat on her cheek—she had only come with her father to grab some stuff from her old room for her apartment before she was heading out.

"It went ... well," Lucian said.

Liliana didn't miss the way her mother's gaze darted in her direction. "Really?"

Lucian came to a stop in front of Jordyn, and reached for his wife before pulling her into a tight hug that engulfed her mother. Liliana almost looked away simply because the action seemed so personal and affectionate, but she didn't.

Her parents wouldn't care, anyway.

They had never hid their love.

And it was a *beautiful* love.

"I promise," Lucian murmured, "you know me."

"I do," Jordyn said. "Did John show up?"

"No."

Liliana stiffened at the mention of her older brother. Four years older than her, John was ... well, her brother was a lot of things. Diagnosed with bipolar at seventeen, she knew that things were not simple for John in his life. Nothing was easy for him.

He hadn't made things easy for them, either, growing up. To say the least. His mania had manifested in ways that both terrified her, and hurt her.

Mostly, emotionally.

He could be nasty one second, and violently angry the next. He might say something so cutting, the words felt like knives slicing through someone's heart.

And then he would be good again, as though nothing had ever happened. It just made for a difficult and complex relationship, as far as that went.

Liliana loved her brother, though. She just found it easier to love John from a distance so that they could both see each other a little more clearly. She didn't want to hurt him, or worse, hate him for things he couldn't control. And she worried if she pushed too much, or stayed too close, that was exactly what might happen.

"Andino must know where he is," Jordyn said.

Lucian sighed heavily, and scrubbed a hand down his jaw. "I assume so, yes."

"Assuming isn't good—we need to *know*."

"Gio said he was going to get ahold of Andino tonight, anyway. We need them both for tomorrow."

Liliana came to lean against the kitchen island, and gained both of her parents' attention when she asked, "What's happening tomorrow?"

Her father graced her with a smile that usually distracted people. She wasn't the type to fall for it. Jordyn gave her husband a look before she made a beeline for the entryway to leave the kitchen.

What was that all about?

"Nothing you need to be concerned about," Lucian replied easily once his wife was gone.

"And yet, I asked, Daddy."

Lucian gave the ceiling a look as though he were searching for the heavens before saying, "Just business, sweetheart."

"Joe?"

Her father stiffened a bit.

Liliana didn't miss it.

"Dante said at dinner that tomorrow they would set Joe up in the city. He comes from the Chicago Outfit, right?"

Lucian chuckled, and patted his daughter on her cheek as he passed. "You're too curious for your own good, Liliana. Let it go, sweetheart. You have much more important things to focus on with the ballet company now. Worry about that."

"Nice deflection."

Her father shrugged as he pulled open the fridge, and produced a beer before spinning around to face her. "So be it."

"So, you're not going to tell me anything about him at all?"

"Who, Joe?"

"Yes, him."

Lucian popped the top off the beer, and took a swig before saying, "There's really nothing to tell."

"Why's he in the city?"

"No particular reason."

Mmhmm.

She didn't know if she believed that.

"He seemed … nice," Liliana settled on saying.

She didn't think her father would appreciate her saying all the other things she also thought Joe was—sexy, gorgeous, killer smile, beautiful eyes, and dangerously alluring to her senses. Those were not the kinds of things fathers appreciated from their daughters.

"Nice is one way to put Joe Rossi," Lucian agreed.

"But again, *why* is he here?"

This time when Lucian passed her by, he patted Liliana on the top of her head with an affectionate touch. As though she were a small child again, and his greatest pride and joy. He always used to do that when she was a little girl.

Oh, she had idolized her father.

Loved him.

Adored him.

Still did, really.

Lucian never failed her.

A lot like her ma, too.

"Liliana, in New York, Joe does not exist," Lucian said as he headed for the doorway of the kitchen where her mother had disappeared to, "and it will do you well to remember that for a while."

"Doesn't exist?"

"That's what I said, sweetheart." Lucian ticked a finger over his shoulder, adding, "I always take care of things, even if it takes me a while to get to it—don't forget that, Liliana."

What in the hell did that mean?

THREE

WHAT WAS SUPPOSED to be only a day for Joe to get settled into New York with whatever the Marcellos wanted to provide him, turned into a week. Not that he minded—this was their show, after all, and he was just there to do a job for them when they wanted him to.

Nothing more, nothing less.

If they wanted to fuck about and extend their timeframe, then that was on them. As long as he still got paid, even if he still wasn't one hundred percent sure on this job, then he didn't care very damn much about the rest.

Besides, the week with no calls allowed Joe to do his favorite thing.

Roam, and people watch.

New York wasn't all that different from Chicago, for the most part. Chicago was windier, and he recognized the streets better. He felt more at ease in Chicago—maybe a sense of protection that came with being an Outfit *principe*. It always followed him around there. New York didn't afford him much in that sense, but at the same time, he liked that about it. He enjoyed that he could move almost freely with very little interference or worries.

Here, nobody knew him. Or … nobody that he ran into, anyway. It allowed him to move within the crowds without actually being seen, and visit places he hadn't been before. Since he didn't have any expectations on him, he allowed himself the privilege to explore and get comfortable in the city.

And then that had to end.

Like all good things.

Stepping into the small Brooklyn café, Joe did his cursory look at the bustling business. His gaze drifted over the people sitting in the booths, and at the tables in front of the windows. A line up of at least ten people between two cash registers was moving fast, it seemed. The place was modestly decorated with the usual cliché style of a café—coffee deco all the way.

Still rather comfortable, though.

Nobody paid any attention to the man in the leather jacket, and dark aviator sunglasses that stood just beyond the door. Joe glanced down to see he was standing on a latte-decorated welcome mat.

Figures.

How fucking cute.

The mat, that was.

Not the people.

Joe didn't see anybody he recognized sitting at the tables, even though this was the address that had been texted to his phone the night before with nothing more than a time attached. Since the only people who knew he was in New York were his immediate family, his boss, and the Marcellos … he figured he could safely narrow down who was calling him in.

The Marcellos, that was.

Figuring he might have to stay a while since nobody was there yet, he stepped into line behind what seemed to be the faster of the two cash registers, and waited. A good five minutes passed before he was finally able to order.

Black coffee in hand—he couldn't stand the taste when it was sweetened or creamy—Joe took a seat at the very back of the café. A few gazes came his way as he passed people by, but he didn't pay them any mind.

People stared for one of two reasons.

His impressive size.

Or they liked the way he looked.

Either way, Joe didn't much care as long as people didn't try to actually *engage* him beyond the staring. He wasn't much for chitchat, and certainly not with people he didn't know. He much preferred to watch people, anyway.

That was more interesting to him.

Settling into one of the far tables, Joe leaned back in the chair and kicked his feet out to crisscross his leather boots at the ankles in the aisle. While a little rude as there was still a table to his left for someone to sit in—a small two-chair table—that was kind of the point. He didn't want someone sitting next to him.

Too close.

Too bothersome.

It was practically impossible to blend in when someone was staring you right in the face. Or, that's what Joe found, anyhow.

Joe sipped on his black coffee, and enjoyed the bitterness sliding down his throat. Behind his dark aviator sunglasses, the many people inside the bustling café had no idea that he watched them. He found human behavior fascinating sometimes.

There was a man watching an Anime show on his laptop two tables down. A couple at a booth by the window were arguing about something even though they tried to keep their faces a reflection of calm. The employees moved in sync with one another, leading Joe to believe they had worked together for quite a while and were quite comfortable in their routine. Despite the café being a bustle of constant activity, the place was still pretty quiet.

Joe kind of liked it here.

The ding of the entrance bell drew Joe's attention to the front door. At the sight of the two men who came into the café, he straightened a bit in his chair. A man like him, in the business he dabbled with, could tell when someone was connected just by the way they entered a room. Their posture, even. Or perhaps the way they stopped to let their gaze take in their surroundings before choosing what to do next.

And even if none of that hadn't been the first thing on Joe's mind about the two newest patrons, he still knew who they were just from sight alone.

Johnathan and Andino Marcello.

Cousins that rarely ever seemed to be apart for very long, or at least, that's what Joe had been told about the two. Marcello *principes* given both men had fathers who owned two of the highest seats in the Marcello Cosa Nostra.

Some might even call them mafia royalty. Joe didn't know if he would. People considered him mafia royalty, too, but he wasn't exactly very fucking fond of the title.

He killed people for a living.

He didn't wear a fucking crown while he did it.

Over the years, Joe had run into the two Marcello cousins when they occasionally came to Chicago for business. The Marcellos were known for sending others to do their business for them when it came to organizations they didn't particularly like, or had problems with.

The Marcellos had long since had problems with the Chicago Outfit. An incident from decades back that put a rift between the two, although some kind of peace had been made that allowed the two to do business.

John was likely a Capo now—who knew if Andino was, or if he was still working his way to that position. It was inevitable, though.

Andi—as Joe knew he preferred—would be a Capo eventually. Like his father had once been before moving up in *la famiglia*.

So was the way of their life.

Soon, the Marcello cousins found Joe sitting in the back, and came his way. They didn't even bother to make an order before coming for business. *Perfetto.*

"Joe," John greeted as he neared the table.

"John," Joe returned.

Neither man offered their hand, and Andino was the first to take a seat. John followed right after.

"How long has it been, man?" Andino asked.

Joe shrugged. "A year, maybe. Last time I saw you two—one of you was dragging the other one out of a club."

John nodded appreciatively. "Truth."

Andino chuckled. "Couldn't have John causing trouble in Chicago."

Yeah, Joe didn't know very much about that, so he just moved on to the next topic at hand. The elephant in the room, so to speak.

"You called me here—what do you need or want?"

"It's for you, actually," John returned.

The older of the two men pulled a few items from the inside pocket of his blazer, and slid them across the table. A phone—a sleek, black burner by the looks of it. A hotel key with a tag that told Joe exactly which business he would be staying at, and a folded up piece of paper.

John tapped the phone first, saying, "Burner only. It's safe—we have a hacker who will regularly monitor and scrub it when needed."

"All right."

"Turn your phone off, and leave it that way until you're done in this city."

Joe shrugged. "My phone is at home. I grabbed a burner before I left the city, anyway. I didn't know what I was coming for, and I don't like to take chances. Only a few people have the number."

John and Andino passed a glance between one another.

Andino spoke up first. "Use that one for your family, then. Ours for us."

"Sure."

John moved to the next item; the hotel key. "The boss—"

"Dante."

"Yeah, the *boss*."

John's maybe.

Not Joe's.

Still, respect was important, so Joe said, "The boss, yeah."

"The boss has a permanent room at the Waldorf Astoria hotel in Manhattan that he and his wife like to use on occasion. They don't expect to need it anytime soon, so he figured you might like it for your stay."

"Under his name?"

"Do you think he's that stupid?" John returned.

Joe smirked. "Had to ask."

"It's safe."

Picking up the piece of paper—the last thing on the table—Joe unfolded the paper at the creases, and looked at the statement in front of him. "I hadn't checked my account to see if he paid like I told him to, but half of the money is in my account now."

Andino nodded. "Time to get to work, I guess."

"What did George Earl and Martin Abraham do to the Marcellos that your boss is willing to have them both whacked?" Joe asked. "And mind you, lots of people die because of affiliations to the mob. I know this better than anyone. Not usually people who are this high profile, though. That spells bad news, you know?"

John cocked a brow.

Andino's face went passive.

"Your job is to do what you're told," John replied quietly, "and not ask questions."

Yeah …

Because that didn't make Joe suspicious *at all*.

Jesus Christ.

What was going on?

Joe scanned the Manhattan Waldorf Astoria hotel room with an appreciative eye. Apparently, the Marcello boss didn't like to cheap out when it came to places he stayed. The cost of this suite likely ran in the tens of thousands a month, if Joe had to guess.

He wasn't complaining.

Rich, expensive tapestries and rugs gave the main room a nice decorative touch. A white leather chaise rested near the window with an afghan blanket tossed over the back. A loveseat and chair made up a sitting area in front of a flat screen television that nearly covered an entire wall. Gold chandeliers hung from high ceilings, and glinted from the lights.

In another room, he found a small kitchen and dining area. Beyond that, a private bedroom with a four-poster bed, and an attached bathroom the same size as most of the other rooms. There was even a safe hidden behind a mirror in the bedroom, although it was tightly closed.

Joe didn't have any interest in that, anyway.

Coming back out to the main room, Joe dropped his bag onto the loveseat, and moved toward the windows. Staring out below, he found the Manhattan street was busy. Lots of people, and lots of shit happening.

Nothing unusual.

Good for him, though.

If his goal was to stay under the radar during his time in New York, then Manhattan was a great place to be. A melting pot of people and tourists, it was unlikely anyone would be able to pick his face out in a crowd.

He would go ahead and count the view and room as a bonus.

At least for now.

"Home sweet home," Joe muttered.

Turning away from the window, he shrugged off his coat, and reached for the phone sitting on a nearby decorative table. Since he was already here, he might as well make a call down to the dining room and get his dinner—

It was only the ringing of his own phone that stopped Joe from making that call. And not the burner phone that Johnathan Marcello had dropped off earlier, but his own that he brought along. Moving to the couch where he dropped his bag, Joe found the phone, and took a quick look at the caller ID before he bothered to pick it up.

D, it read.

His father.

Joe picked up the call with a, "Hey, Dad."

"Son. Why aren't you answering Cory's calls?"

"Because you fucking know what he wants," Joe replied. "And what he wants is to be here with me, and not in Chicago where he needs to stay while I get this done."

Damian sighed. "He's driving me crazy."

"Better you than me."

Only a dry chuckle answered Joe back.

Truth was, he loved his brother to the ends of the earth and back. Only being a year apart in age, the two had practically grown up like twins might. Constantly together, and stuck at the goddamn hip. Joe was a little more reserved than Cory, but sometimes that worked out, too. He looked out for his brother, and kept him levelheaded. Cory, on the other hand, pushed Joe to take a few risks once in a while.

It … worked.

Yeah, that was a good way to put it.

"I'll give him a call," Joe said after a minute, "but he's still not coming here. You know Cory wouldn't be able to keep his head down, and not draw attention to himself."

"Not even if he *tried*," Damian grumbled.

It was funny.

Because it was true.

"Oh, is that Joe?" he heard his mother say in the background. "Give me the phone, Damian."

"Lily, I am trying to—"

The phone crackled before his mother's voice came on the line, and her sweet, happy tone made Joe smile. Out of everything back in Chicago, he probably would end up missing his mother the very most.

Italian boys and their mothers.

It was all true.

"Joe," his mother said, "I miss you."

"You, too, Ma."

"New York is being nice to you, isn't it?"

His mother didn't even try to hide the underlying threat in her words. It was as if she would personally make her way over to the state if she thought someone was fucking with her son. Any of her kids, really.

His mother probably would, too.

"New York is treating me fine," Joe assured.

"Better be. Try to have fun—bring me home something nice."

"I will, Ma."

"There, you talked to him, now give me the goddamn phone, Lily," Damian muttered in the background.

"Love you, *bye!*"

That was all he heard from his mother before his father was back on the line once more. Joe rolled his eyes at the absurdity of it all, but that was just his family. That was his mother, and she was never going to change.

Her kids were everything to her. Even now that two of them—Joe and Cory—were grown men, and out on their own, none of that mattered to his mother. She liked to baby them, and keep them as close as she possibly could. Or, at least as much as the two would allow.

Frankly, Joe and Cory didn't have much of a choice. Their father made sure of that—Lily complained about anything, and Damian fixed it. That included her sons when she thought they weren't coming to visit her enough, or whatever the case may be.

It was what it was.

Joe learned not to fight it.

"Oh, good," Damian said quietly, "Mon is distracting her for five minutes."

Lily, he meant.

"Say hey to Monica for me," Joe said.

"I will later."

His little sister—and youngest sibling—was accustomed to Joe coming and going a lot of the time. He wasn't even sure if she noticed he was gone, to be honest. She didn't say much about it, but she always liked when he came back after a spell of being gone, and took her out to do whatever she wanted for an entire day.

Something else his father demanded.

Family was important.

Always.

"How's it going there?" Damian asked. "Any news?"

"The Marcellos have me settled in now."

"How so?"

"Phone; hotel; money. A car is on the way for me to use, too. Not sure how long they want me to be here, or how long this is going to take, rather, but they're making sure I am comfortable for the duration. Have to respect that. Usually, it's me figuring that shit out when I go underground for a while."

Damian whistled low. "Taking care of you, then."

"Too bad that doesn't exactly make me feel any fucking better about this whole thing, though."

"I beg your pardon?"

"A Senator and a Chief of Police—it's a little concerning, Dad, that's all. And by the sounds of it, there's some kind of problem or reason the Marcellos want them gone. Mind you, a fucking reason they can't be bothered to explain to the rest of the class, so I might have to dig into that myself."

"Don't go digging into the Marcello family's business. That isn't your place, Joe."

Not his place and not able to do it were two very fucking different things, though. Joe didn't say that out loud to his father, however.

"You know how I feel about these kinds of kills," Joe muttered.

At least, if Joe understood why a person had to die, and they had earned or deserved the death, he didn't feel quite as guilty the next time he went into confession. Or even when he had to pray, and ask for his own forgiveness.

Fucked up, sure.

But that's how he was.

A killer with a goddamn conscience.

Lucky fucking me.

"Point is—they likely already have attention from whatever issues they have with these people," Joe said, "and that means the Marcellos will be the first people looked at when the marks are dead."

"I don't think they care. They chose someone outside of their organization for a reason. They did explain that to you."

"Yeah, but—"

"Joe, it is literally none of your business why they want to do this. What is your business is that it is done, and you follow their orders while they are paying you to do so, and nothing more. Do you understand me?"

"Who knocks off two high profile figures like that, huh? Tell me."

"Tommas did it once."

"When was that?"

"Years ago," Damian replied, "back when he first took over."

"And how long did the attention and feds stay on the Outfit's ass?"

Damian laughed—a bitter sound that echoed in Joe's ears. "Longer than you care to know, son. Pretty sure if there was still a Public Enemy Number One, your uncle would own the fucking spot."

Technically, Tommas was a cousin of Joe's ... but he grew up calling the man his uncle, and that wasn't going to change.

"You know I don't like to make a hit like this," Joe said. "And it's not even *one*, it's fucking two. It kind of feels like they might be playing with fire, and I don't want to be the hand that gets burned in the process. That is all I am saying."

"You're there to do a job, Joe."

"Quite aware, yeah."

"So, do it."

His father hung up the phone.

That was that.

The last thing Joe wanted to do was be called to the Marcello mansion at just after ten in the evening. And yet, here he was.

"Joseph, correct?"

The old Marcello who greeted Joe at the grand entrance of the mansion was the man who owned the place—Antony. The man's kind smile belied the fact that Joe—like most *Mafiosi*—had heard all the stories of the infamous Antony Marcello, and just how creative and dangerous the man could be when crossed.

"Antony," Joe greeted, "nice to see you again."

"Oh, I'm sure we'll be seeing more of each other." Antony waved a hand, and said, "Come, my sons are waiting for you upstairs."

Joe's brow lifted. "All of them?"

"Two—Lucian, and Dante. I think Giovanni had a thing tonight. He doesn't like to miss his wife's special days."

"Understandable."

Joe followed behind Antony silently as the man led him through the mansion. Despite having explored a week earlier, Joe still didn't feel familiar enough with the place not to get lost again. And wouldn't that be just fucking grand, too.

"You'll have to say hello to Cecelia for me," Joe said. "I'll probably miss her."

"Little late for her, yes," Antony said. "My wife likes to sleep early when she can."

At the bottom of the stairs leading into one of the upper wings, Antony turned to Joe with a shrug.

"I assume you can find your way from here, can't you?"

"I can," Joe said. "Thanks."

"Good. I don't feel like climbing stairs tonight. Keep the noise down to a minimum. Remind my sons if you need to."

Joe thought to scoff at the idea of him telling any made man *anything*, but the look on Antony's face told him the man was damn serious. He chose to keep his sarcastic comment to himself.

"You got it," Joe said.

Antony waved two fingers over his shoulder, and then he was gone, too. Joe took the stairs two at a time, and barely made a sound. He found the same office he had visited the last time he was at the mansion, and stepped up to the open doors. Inside, the two oldest Marcello brothers stood next to a window, and overlooked the back property as they talked quietly between one another.

Too quiet for Joe to hear.

Apparently, they didn't hear him, either.

That wasn't exactly unusual.

Joe cleared his throat, and tampered down his urge to smirk when the two men spun fast on their heels to face him. "Sorry, but I didn't think you wanted me to stand here and listen to the two of you mutter on."

Dante cocked a brow. "How long *were* you standing there?"

Lucian, on the other hand, stayed silent.

"Long enough to see you, and let you see me," Joe said.

"He is *just* like his father," Lucian said quietly to Dante, although never looking at Joe directly. "Same thing, I swear."

Joe scowled. "I can hear you."

"That was the point," the man returned.

Dante ignored the exchange between the two, and waved a finger at Joe. "Come in, and sit down. Or don't sit—whatever the hell you prefer. We have a problem."

Great.

"I don't like the sound of that," Joe said as he moved further into the office. He didn't take the offered seat, but that was only because he preferred to stand when bad news was delivered.

"Sit where we do, and then we'll talk," Lucian muttered.

"What?"

Lucian gave Joe a pointed look and said, "Exactly."

Right in that moment, Joe decided Lucian Marcello was probably the most dangerous out of all the Marcello brothers. The man was like whiplash, and he wasn't very fucking easy to figure out. Which meant it would be hard to predict any of his upcoming moves, and he probably liked to keep it that way.

Yeah, dangerous.

But …

Joe respected those kind of men, too.

He was one, after all.

"That problem—what is it?" Joe asked.

A look passed between the two men, and Joe felt the strangest urge to ask them to knock that shit off. The short amount of time he had spent in the Marcello brothers' presence was enough to tell him this silent conversation thing was a regular occurrence.

And he didn't like it at all.

Lucian resumed his spot beside the window, while Dante moved behind the desk, and took a seat. Joe stayed in the middle of the room right where he was, and didn't move.

"Well?" he asked.

"One of our men was found dead in his apartment today," Dante said.

Shit.

Joe rocked back on his heels, and stuffed his hands in his pockets. "Sorry to hear that."

He didn't know the guy—Dante hadn't even given a name—but it didn't matter. Death was death, and death still deserved respect. Or so Joe had been taught growing up. A good man apologized and showed the proper respect for someone passing, as long as that person was deserving of it.

Dante nodded, and glanced over at his brother. "Beaten to death, it seems. We only found out when he didn't check in with Lucian as he should."

"Why would he be checking in with Lucian?" Joe asked.

"He's my oldest daughter's enforcer," Lucian said quietly.

Joe stiffened a bit. "Liliana."

"Yes." Dante scrubbed a hand down his jaw, and leaned back in his chair. "So here is where our problem becomes apparent—we believe this might be connected to the little issue we hired you to take care of."

And there it was.

Joe took the opening. "And why do you believe that?"

He shouldn't have thought the two men would be so naive as to fall for his little trick. They didn't even think about stepping into the trap, really.

"That's not your concern," Dante said quickly, "but it puts us in a bad position. We now have a woman without an enforcer, and since it may be connected to the rest, we have to consider other things."

"So, get her a new enforcer," Joe said, cocking a brow.

One part of him thought, *Why the fuck is this my problem?*

The other part thought, *Have somebody on that fucking woman right now.*
He didn't know what to think of himself right then.

Lucian passed Joe a look that felt dead as the man said, "It's not that easy. Liliana is a grown woman, and well into her own life. While she isn't a silly girl running around New York unprotected, I have done my very best to let her live as normally as possible. It is the very least she deserves, considering everything. And that includes her guards. She never sees them—should she see them, she doesn't recognize them. I don't want to concern my daughter when she has a stressful few months coming up with her ballet company, and everything else on her shoulders."

"And what does that mean, exactly?" Joe asked, looking to Dante for an answer.

"It means," Dante said, "that we were hoping you might take on the task of guarding Liliana from … a respectable distance for the foreseeable future. At least, until we figure out how to handle what just happened, and whether or not it is related to other things. Should she see you, it won't concern her all that much. She seemed to get on quite well with you, and that's a good thing. Of course, we won't want you mentioning to her that you are guarding her."

To say the least.

Joe kept quiet.

Dante continued with, "She recognizes all of our other enforcers, and she doesn't need to be getting anxious or worked up."

"Why would—"

"Will you guard her, or not?" Lucian interrupted sharply.

Jesus Christ.

It wasn't even a question for Joe.

He barely had to think about it at all.

"I will," he said.

The relief between the two other men in the room was palpable, but Joe still didn't understand why. There was a hell of a lot going unsaid in this arrangement, and he didn't like that very goddamn much.

It didn't seem like there was much he could do about it, either.

"And what about my marks?" Joe asked. "How long do you want me to fuck around before I move in on them?"

"Plans have to change sometimes," Dante said.

"Clearly."

The Marcello boss gave Joe a look that quieted him instantly. His smart mouth was probably going to get him killed one day, but frankly, there was nothing he could do about it. This was why he liked to stay quiet—it was everyone else who made him *talk*.

"We will have you take care of the marks when we are ready, and things are in place for it to happen properly," Lucian said, "but for now, your mark is my daughter, and you need to keep her alive."

Alrighty, then.

FOUR

THE DRIVER OPENED the back door of the SUV with a smile, and offered a hand to help Liliana down from the high vehicle. Still a little wary about why she was even there to begin with, she took his hand and let him help her down.

Besides, she had lived as a Marcello long enough to know that when someone was sent for her, it would be entirely useless for her to refuse. They were typically told to give no information, and answer no questions. Rather, they were directed to drop whoever off wherever they had been told, and nothing more.

It wasn't often it happened.

Today, the man picked Liliana up after her training was finished at the studio. He had been waiting outside—a recognizable face as he was an enforcer who often followed her father around—and leaning against his car with a smile.

And with orders to take her to the Marcello mansion.

"Are you going to be taking me home after?" Liliana asked him.

The man nodded. "I'll be waiting when you're ready."

"Great, thanks."

Frankly, she was ready to go now, and she hadn't even gotten inside the house yet. A full twelve hours of training was more than just physically taxing, it was emotionally exhausting. Her feet ached—they needed to be cared for, and soon. Her muscles needed a good soak, so they wouldn't be terribly sore in the morning.

Given she had been brought *here* first, and not home to her apartment in upper Brooklyn, it was unlikely that she would get enough time to take care of her body, and sleep long enough not to be tired tomorrow.

Win some, lose some.

That's how the saying went, right?

Liliana supposed the quicker she got inside the Marcello mansion, and figured out what was going on, then the quicker she could get back home and relax. She had to practically drag her tired legs—and stiff back—up the marble entrance to the mansion.

The man posted at the door gave her a nod before opening it, and stepping back. "You will find your father in the upstairs office, Liliana."

"Thanks."

So, it was Daddy who called me in.

It was only lately that her grandparents had begun posting enforcers at their doorstep, and usually only at night when the sun went down, or if they were having a big party and needed extra precautions. They didn't typically have the guards so close, but they also didn't like it being pointed out, for whatever reason. Age, she supposed. No one liked to feel like someone else thought they were incapable, or something like that.

Liliana was half way to the office—just coming up to the top of the staircase into the upper wing of the mansion—when a familiar face greeted her.

At the sight of her, he instantly grinned. A sexy, yet still sweet grin that accompanied the way his gaze drifted over the comfortable flats on her feet, tight leggings, and the long-sleeved body suit she hadn't gotten the chance to change out of. Usually, she would do that once she got home.

He didn't hide his staring *at all.*

And her heart skipped.

Joe.

"Back again so soon?" she asked him.

Joe laughed, and gave a half-hearted shrug. "Seems I am going to be around for a while."

Was she supposed to complain about that, or something? Because she couldn't find a single reason to do that.

Not at all.

"Good," Liliana said.

"Is it?" Joe asked back.

"Is it, what?"

"Good, *Tesoro.*"

Treasure.

Liliana felt a familiar heat climb up her throat, and threaten to color her cheeks with a pretty red. She used to be a shy girl who blushed at every little thing. Somehow, she had grown out of the trait over the years, and she was grateful for doing so.

Yet, here she was with this man about to turn into a teenager again who flushed and tittered at every little compliment he gave her. Add in the way her stomach did the strangest clenching and flipping whenever he stared at her, and yeah ...

She was *screwed.*

"I think it's good," she said.

"And why is that?"

Liliana tried to play her interest off because that seemed easier than stumbling over her words to admit she was curious, and interested in him. "Guess we'll find out, huh?"

Joe laughed *again*.

That sound—the look of him when he tossed his head back and let loose—was intoxicating. Liliana had seen firsthand how this man was able to flip his switches back and forth when it came to other people. She watched him shut off, and shut down like it was nothing. Warm to her, and then cold to someone else in a blink.

So, when she was able to get a glimpse of him like this?

Free, defenseless, and happy?

She liked it *a lot*.

Sobering from his laughter, Joe crossed his arms over his broad chest, and gave her another once over with his gaze. The action caused his white T-shirt to strain against his muscles in the best way, while the veins in his forearms and strong hands stood out even more.

Liliana had her *thing*.

All women had their things when it came to men, and what they found attractive. Apparently, she had more than just one thing because she suddenly had the strangest fucking urge to feel those hands of his grabbing ahold of her tightly while she traced the veins in his hands and arms with her fingertips.

Preferably naked.

Wow.

She went there fast.

"Dancing today?" he asked.

"Training," she clarified, hoping how turned on she was didn't come through in her voice. "But basically, yeah. I dance six times a week, and sometimes seven. Really just depends on what's coming up, and what's happening."

"What would you have done, if not ballet?"

Liliana blinked at the unexpected question. People never asked her that—she knew why, too. Everyone just always assumed when they heard that she was a professional ballerina that dance was all she had ever considered as a path in her life. It was probably all she had ever known, and she didn't fault them for that way of thinking.

She kind of adored Joe for asking something *different*. He was different, so it shouldn't have been that much of a surprise to her.

It still was.

"A nurse," Liliana said, "and it still might be an option once this career gives out."

A brief frown flickered across Joe's face before he schooled his features. "Why would you think this career would give out, sweetheart?"

"Even the best ballerinas can't dance forever."

"Teaching. Mentoring. Owning their own studio. There's lots of options."

Liliana nodded. "There are, but I spent the first three years after high school trying to get in with the company I am currently at, and going to school all at the same time. A demand of my father—if I couldn't be a ballerina, then I had to have something else to fall back on. I never got to finish school, so ..."

"Because you got the spot in the company," Joe assumed, and rightly.

"Exactly. I learned something about nursing, though."

"Which is what?"

"After all the world gave me, it's nice to give a little back."

"So, a nurse, then?" he asked.

"Someday," Liliana said.

It was another dream of hers. It wouldn't mean her name would be in lights, or that a whole theater full of people would be enamored with the way she floated from one side of the stage to another, but it did mean fulfillment. A kind of fulfillment she had not yet been able to find as a ballerina.

"Sometimes, that's how life works," Liliana said vaguely.

"I get that."

Joe didn't press her for more details about her strange statement. She thought right then and there to ask the man to dinner, or even for a coffee, but it was the sound of footsteps echoing from down the hall that stopped her from asking anything at all.

Her father, and uncle, it seemed.

In a blink, Joe's entire demeanor changed. He reverted back to that stone-still statue with little expression, and no clear emotion as he regarded the oncoming men. He still looked like the same man, and his woodsy scent was still lingering with every breath Liliana took in, but it was clear he put on a different mask depending on who was around.

She didn't take that as a sign he disliked the men of her family, either, but rather ... that Joe was probably more like them than she knew.

Liliana had come to learn that all made men acted in similar ways when other made men were around to see it. She didn't know if that was because they wanted to keep business separate from their personal life, or because the mafia demanded those kinds of things.

None of it mattered, anyway.

Liliana saw Joe.

She had *seen* him.

That was enough for her.

"You're heading out, Joe?" Dante called.

Joe nodded, and then passed Liliana a quick look, too. "Until the next time, Liliana."

"There will definitely be one."

She would make sure of it.

Liliana turned to greet her father, but still took the chance to glance over her shoulder at the same time. She caught sight of Joe's broad back as he took the stairs two at a time with his hands stuffed loosely in his pockets like he didn't have a care in the world.

And then, he was gone.

"I wondered when you were going to get here," Lucian said.

Liliana turned back to her father. Her uncle gave her a small smile before he too headed down the stairs to the main floor of the mansion's largest wing.

"Is something wrong?" she asked.

Lucian's warm smile belied the fact that there might be something for her to be concerned about. "Not at all, *mia ragazza*. Why would you think that?"

Uh …

"Because you had a driver pick me up from the studio, and bring me here without as much as a phone call. You only do that when something's up."

Lucian shook his head, and shrugged. "No, I just haven't seen you all week, and your mother was getting worried. I told her I would *make sure* you were fine."

Liliana laughed. "By dragging me two hours away to the mansion?"

"Yes, well …"

He sounded both amused and nonchalant at the same time. She could only laugh again.

"Well, I am *fine*," Liliana said, "as you can see. Pass the message along to Ma, and tell her I will be at church on Sunday for her to see for herself."

"You better be," her father joked.

"So, seriously, nothing's wrong?"

Lucian reached out, and grabbed his daughter. He pulled Liliana in for a quick, tight hug that almost took her breath away. Still, she relaxed in his embrace, and a familiar comfort seeped into her bones.

"Everything is perfect," he said, dropping a quick kiss to the top of her head, "and everything is going to stay that way—I promise."

"Wow, I can't believe you actually got out of the studio this week to spend more than five seconds with little old *me*," Cella teased.

Liliana shot her sister a look. "Are you back on that again?"

Cella rolled her eyes upward, and smiled in that joking way of hers. It made her look like their mother when Jordyn was trying to play tricks on them—albeit, their mother had never been very good at following through because she would just start laughing her ass off.

"I just miss you, Liliana," Cella said.

"I know."

"But you did get time away to spend just with me, so *yay!*"

Her sister did a little happy dance on the sidewalk, and gained the attention of several passersby. Some of the people gave them a strange look—how often did you see a girl dancing on Fifth Avenue like a crazy little wild child, anyway?

"Stop that," Liliana muttered, trying hard not to laugh. She grabbed her sister's arm, and tugged Cella back into her side to get her attention focused on what they were currently doing. "You're drawing attention."

Cella preened. "I know, that's the whole point."

"Well, let's *not.*"

"You're a ballerina, Liliana. Your whole job is to be beautiful and graceful on stage, all the while keeping an entire audience's eyes on you. So …"

"Yes, but we're not on a stage right now," Liliana countered, "we're on a sidewalk in the middle of Fifth freaking Avenue."

Her sister only laughed, but she didn't try to do another crazy dance routine to give the gawkers a show. Soon, the two sisters were on their walk again, and nearly at the salon where they both had appointments for the day.

Cella, for manicures.

Liliana, for a foot treatment.

God knew her feet could use it.

"We should bring Lucia the next time," Liliana said. "I bet she's feeling left out at home."

Their *far* younger sister sometimes liked to tag along for their girls' day out, but she never actually spoke up and asked to go. That didn't stop Liliana from feeling like shit whenever they left their younger sister behind.

"She went to the movies with John, according to Ma," Cella said, shrugging. "I called and asked."

"Huh."

"Yep."

Liliana stared into a storefront window as they passed, and wondered out loud, "Do you ever feel like she got a longer end of the stick with John?"

"Uh …"

"I just mean … she kind of never had to deal with the bad shit from John, right, not like we did. And so, she doesn't have the same kind of issues we do when it comes to him."

"I love John."

"Me, too," Liliana quickly said.

But the history they shared with their older brother was still very real, and a little too raw sometimes. It was just easier to deal with those feelings from afar.

"I'm actually really glad Lucia has a good big brother in John," Cella said, smiling from the side at her sister, and linking their arms together again. "She got what we didn't, and there's nothing wrong with being happy for her, you know what I mean? And maybe for him, too."

"What's that mean—for him?"

"I don't think it's easy on John to be kind of distanced from us, either, but have you ever noticed how he doesn't push us for more than what we give? Yeah, he knows how we feel, and respects it, I think. And that's important, too."

"Never thought of it like that."

"Yeah, well …"

Cella trailed off, and left the rest of her statement unsaid. Liliana didn't mind. This had been more than enough for her to take another look at her previous feelings, and reevaluate them when it came to her brother, and what she thought was *his* imposed distance.

"So, *hey*," Cella drawled suddenly.

At just the sly tone her sister took on, Liliana knew Cella was about to get up to something. Whether or not Liliana would like it was a whole other story. Sometimes, it was a toss-up with Cella.

"What?"

"Last week at dinner—you know, the one with Mr. Built-Like-A-Brick-Shithouse."

Liliana blinked.

What?

Cella laughed hard, and pointed at her sister. "Oh, my God, the *look* you just had—*deceased*. I am dead."

"What are you talking about, Cella?"

"At dinner last week. You know, the mansion. Joe Rossi."

Oh.

Oh.

No doubt, Cella had not missed the passing glances, or the way the conversation between Liliana and Joe at the dinner had felt laced with something else entirely. Friendly, sure, but a little bit more, too. Not to mention, Joe hadn't bothered to pay any other woman sitting at that table any bit of attention but for *her*.

She adored that, too.

Liliana tried to school her features when she asked, "What about it?"

"Did I miss that there might be something there—or *could* be?" Cella asked.

"I mean, he's cute—"

"More than, actually."

A hot spike of jealousy flared in Liliana's gut at nothing more than the idea of Cella finding Joe attractive. Before she could think better of it, she said, "Don't look as much, and you won't notice, Cella."

"Wow, okay." Her sister nodded. "Definitely something there. Tell me *everything.*"

Shit.

Now, her sister wouldn't let up until—

Liliana's thought process shut off entirely at the sight of a black stretch limo passing by them on the street. There were probably thousands of limos in the city. One on every block, if someone wanted to look for them.

It wasn't so much the limo itself as it was the small flags on the front and back end of the vehicle. A signal to those outside of who might be *inside.*

And suddenly, Liliana shut down.

Or rather, broke down.

A full-blown panic attack right there in the middle of Fifth Avenue. Her heart raced to the point it felt like she was going to have a heart attack, and the only thing she could really hear was her blood rushing in her ears. No matter how hard she inhaled, it felt like she couldn't get enough air with every breath. So, her breaths just came faster and faster while her palms clenched into tight fists. Tight enough for her fingernails to break the skin of her palms, and likely leave crescent-shaped bruises behind.

None of it registered, though.

Even after the limo was gone.

Even through her sister trying to help.

None of it registered.

Faintly, Liliana heard Cella saying, "It's okay, breathe. In and out, slowly. Look at *me*, Liliana. *Me.*"

She couldn't.

She couldn't find her sister in the swarm of dizziness that had somehow become her mind, never mind the horror that was her anxiety.

A mess.

She felt like a total mess.

And then …

"I don't know what happened, she was just—"

"It's all right," said a soothingly dark, familiar voice. "Liliana, sweetheart … have you ever heard of grounding?"

She didn't reply verbally.

She *might* have shook her head.

"Okay," Joe's voice echoed back to her, "let's find five things to see."

The street. Pavement under my feet. A sky so pretty, and blue. Cella trying to smile. Joe with eyes on only her.

"Why are you here?" Liliana managed to ask.

Joe gave her a crooked smile. "And five things you can hear."

Liliana listened for sounds even as Joe explained why he was on Fifth Avenue.

"Thought I might do some sightseeing since I am staying in the city for a while," he said, and I happened to see both of you from across the road. I wasn't going to come say hi, but this seemed more important. And five things you can feel, and then we'll see how you're doing."

Liliana thought about how she could feel the thumping in her aching feet even through the soft compression wraps, and the cashmere dress she had thrown on to look presentable before coming out to meet Cella. She could feel the nice breeze, too, and the heat of the sun's rays on her skin.

But mostly important?

"You," Liliana murmured. "I feel you."

Joe grinned, and his hand on her wrist tightened just enough to make her smile, too. "Yeah, I suppose that's one thing."

Settled.

Calm.

Present.

The anxiety was there, sure, but not nearly as bad. Her breathing had returned to normal, and all was well again.

At least for the moment.

Liliana was lost in the daze Joe provided her when their gazes locked on one another. She didn't have to think about anything else, or why she had been thrown into her first anxiety attack in almost a year.

"You okay?" Cella asked.

And the daze was gone.

Liliana nodded quickly, and tried to offer her sister a smile. She didn't know if it came off as true, or not. "Yeah, I'm good."

"What happened?"

"Not important," Joe said before Liliana could try to deflect. "We don't need anyone going into another panic attack like that by triggering themselves when they explain details."

"Good point," Cella muttered. She gave Liliana a look, mouthing, "I like him."

Joe didn't notice.

He was still looking at Liliana.

"If you're good, then I'll let you two get back to whatever you were—
"

"No," Liliana said before she could stop herself.

Two sets of eyes fell on her again.

She felt that fucking blush coming on again.

Jesus.

Joe raised a brow. "No?"

"I just meant … well, I might feel a little better if you talked to me some more, or … we went for a walk. Maybe?"

Why was she dancing around asking him out like a lovesick *girl?*

Thankfully, Cella seemed to catch onto Liliana's nonsense, and out of the corner of her eye, she saw her sister nod.

"Um, I am going to head down the road to my appointment," Cella said. "Liliana, call me as soon as you are up to chatting."

Okay, so maybe she loved her sister.

A lot.

Joe passed a look between the two. "You're not doing something together? It kind of looked like it. I don't want to ruin whatever plans you two had for the day. I was just going to head back to my place—or, where I'm staying."

"We're not doing anything. Not now," Liliana said.

"And that is totally fine," Cella added. "Later."

They'd walked a bit, but not very far before Joe directed Liliana into a parking garage, and then into a black Mercedes. She hadn't thought to ask where he got the car from—a rental, probably. Apparently, what Joe meant by *where he was staying,* was the Waldorf Astoria hotel in Manhattan.

She figured it didn't matter.

"This suite is …"

"Something else, huh?" Joe asked, grinning from the wet bar. "Drink?"

Liliana made a face. "You know, I probably shouldn't."

"Ah, *dancer.*"

She shrugged. "Everything needs to be exactly as they want it."

"As long as one of the things they want isn't for you to starve yourself, or work yourself dead then … whatever makes you happy, *Tesoro.*"

"Some girls do."

"Hmm?"

"Starve themselves down to nothing but sticks in the hopes of being noticed, or whatever the case may be. Their brains and mind get so sick from it all that they don't even realize how much they need help. It's sad, really. Scary. Once, I might have been one of those girls, too. Not so much anymore."

Joe glanced down at the glass of whiskey he had poured, and twirled it a bit making the ice inside click against crystal. "Can't say that's a bad thing, though."

"No, growth is … good."

"It can be."

Joe kept his gaze on the whiskey, and Liliana suddenly decided to be a little bold. They weren't outside where anyone could see, or where her sister was right there to watch and make her feel nervous. There was no stumbling over her words, or feeling skittish.

Really, Joe didn't make her anything but comfortable.

And a little hot sometimes.

Crossing the distance between them, Liliana came to stand right in front of Joe. It was only then that he finally glanced up from the glass in his hands to give her one of his slow, easy grins. The kind that made her stomach do that weird clenching thing—like butterflies for big girls.

"Hey," she whispered.

Joe tipped his head to the side a bit. "Hey."

"Thanks for helping me today."

"Don't mention it."

"Lucky you were there to help me, really."

Joe quirked a brow high. "Yeah, *lucky*."

Before Liliana could over think her next move, and while she was still feeling that bit of boldness in her heart, she stood on her tiptoes, and kissed Joe. It was a fast kiss—nothing too spectacular, and certainly not lingering. Just a sweet press of her lips against his, and then she was pulling away again.

As fast as it had happened, it was over.

Then, she waited.

For him, that was.

Joe's gaze darted to hers, and she swore she saw a flash of heat behind his eyes. Without ever looking away from her, he set that glass of whiskey to the wet bar, grabbed her waist with a firm grip, and brought her even closer. She didn't even get the chance to take a breath before *he* kissed her.

His kiss was not like hers.

Deeper, harder, and hungrier. A teasing stroke of his tongue against the seam of her lips, demanding she open up to him, and let him in. She couldn't even help herself but to part her lips, and taste him.

Joe pulled her closer still until her chest was molded against his, and she found it hard to take in a decent breath. And only then did he pull away. His hand came up to cup her cheek, and his thumb stroked her cheekbone with a soft touch.

"I mean, if you're going to kiss me," he murmured as he pulled away, "then at least really *kiss me*, Liliana."

She laughed breathlessly. "I wanted to see ..."

"What?"

"I don't know."

"Did you see whatever it was?" he asked.

Liliana grinned widely. "I did."

"And?"

"Would you like to go out with me sometime, Joe?"

She expected an immediate response, but not the sudden silence that answered her back. And certainly not the slight stiffening in his body against hers. His mouth didn't even open to speak, but she didn't really need him to at that point, either.

She felt his refusal before he could even say it.

Rejection swept hard against the current of her lust.

Liliana blinked, and then took a step back. "Sorry, I guess I thought—"

"Hey, don't do that," Joe said, coming closer again.

"No, it's fine. I suppose *this* was fine, but anything else probably isn't your style, huh?"

Joe frowned. "You don't know that."

She knew enough about men like him to make an accurate assumption, as far as that went. And really, if he was going to reject her, she would much rather save some of her pride in the process.

Liliana waved a hand, and took another step back. Grabbing her bag from the spot where she'd set it down on the couch when she first entered, she slung it over her shoulder. "No, it's fine, Joe. I should really get back to my sister. Thanks for helping me today—I appreciate it."

"Liliana, just wait a damn—"

"See you around, Joe," she said at the door, not bothering to even give him the chance to say more, or make some lame excuse for all of this, "or maybe not."

FIVE

JOE STUFFED HIS hands in his pockets, and kept his head down as he walked on the Upper Manhattan sidewalk. In his leather jacket, and dark-wash jeans, he could have been any damn New Yorker taking a stroll. The baseball cap added in keeping his face covered, though he probably didn't need it.

He was being precautious today. Probably a little extra, really. He figured it was better to be extra safe than ruin the Marcellos plans before they could properly get started—even if he didn't know what those damn plans were for the time being. His entire job in New York was to stay out of sight, and live up to his namesake as the Shadow.

Joe could do that.

It was what he did best.

Joe had gotten a call earlier that Liliana would be staying late at the ballet company, and then heading to a dinner later to celebrate the upcoming show she had a major part in. Given her sister and cousin were going to be attending the dinner along with their mothers, there would be more than enough enforcers watching over them that Joe wouldn't be needed.

Which was fine.

Sort of.

After the week before in his hotel room, Joe was still trying to figure out a way to step in on Liliana without her realizing he was the one watching her, and also apologize. He hadn't meant to act like an ass, or offend her.

There were just things about them that was out of his control. Like the fact he was hired to do a job—one she didn't know about, and then on top of that, had gotten guarding her added on top of the list.

Joe suspected that despite being the daughter of a Cosa Nostra underboss, Liliana probably was not all too familiar with the underlying rules that suffocated and surrounded the made men in the life. Things like women and daughters and *dating* were not something a man like Joe could just jump in to without some sort of preparation.

But *Christ* ...

He wanted to.

More than anything, he found that he had wanted to say yes to her. To figure out some way to give her the date she asked for without showing them off to the public, so he could keep his cover like he had been told to do.

Surely, he could make it work.

Except he couldn't …

He hadn't said yes because respect came first in this life—it was the very first and last thing he had been taught before he was made. Sure, he liked to push the boundaries occasionally, but not so much that it might cause more tensions between the Marcello family and the Chicago Outfit.

Joe wasn't that stupid.

He couldn't explain all of that to Liliana, though. If she didn't already know, then maybe someone hadn't meant for her to. It did seem like her family gave her a little more leeway and freedom than most *principessas*.

That wasn't a bad thing, either.

Slipping down a shadowed alley beside a rather popular Manhattan restaurant, Joe came up to the exit door at the back of the business. A light flickered over head in red, probably signaling that the door was locked.

A bit of time in New York had taught Joe a few things when it came to the Marcello brothers, and how they worked. The men might have seemed like they roamed freely without any kind of protection, but that was far from the truth. They always had at least two—but sometimes three— enforcers nearby.

Usually within shouting distance.

At least.

He suspected if the enforcers were anything like the ones doing business for the Chicago Outfit, then they kept their posts at businesses and such to make sure their bosses were protected. Something he knew well.

Putting his theory to the test, Joe knocked on the exit door with two knuckles. He waited five seconds, and then knocked again. Not a breath later, the door was pulled open, and Joe was greeted by a man just about the same size as him in width and height.

"What?" the man barked.

"Joe Rossi."

The enforcer cocked a brow. "*And?*"

Apparently, not everyone knew he was working for the Marcellos in their *famiglia*. Joe wasn't going to dwell on it; he had other shit to do.

"Lucian Marcello owns this place, right? Spends most of his working hours here in the private dining room."

The enforcer's face hardened. "What are you asking about—"

"Let him know Joe Rossi would like to speak to him."

"You couldn't come in through the front door, or what?"

Joe looked down at his attire. "Not dressed for a place like this, for one."

"And for two?"

"You don't know about me—that's enough of an answer for you, man."

"What?"

"Just go tell Lucian what I said."

The enforcer didn't look entirely fucking pleased at being ordered around by a stranger. He all but gave Joe a look that threatened violence if he breathed the wrong way. Still, the guy closed the door, and Joe was stuck waiting in the alleyway.

It was another two minutes before the door was opened again. And this time, it wasn't the enforcer waiting. Lucian Marcello slipped out the back door, and gave the enforcer a nod over his shoulder before the door closed—a silent demand for the man to stay inside, and wait.

"You asked for me?" Lucian asked. "I figured with my daughter taken care of today, you might have … I don't know, taken a day off."

Joe shrugged. "I don't take days off."

"Interesting. What can I do for you, Joe? Oh, and thanks for being mindful about how you approached me."

"Yeah, well … I have something coming up soon, and I'm going to need to take care of it. I assumed coming here would be a quick job for me, and then I could be on my way."

"Us, too. Things came up."

Joe nodded. "That's fine, but regardless; I have other business, too."

"Chicago, I imagine."

"You would be correct."

"And what's going on in Chicago?" Lucian asked.

"A bar opening with my brother, actually."

Lucian gave Joe an amused look. "Isn't Cory a little young to be owning a bar?"

"That's why *I* have to be there for the … details," Joe said. "It's a joint effort—his idea. I placate him."

A half-smile edged at the corners of Lucian's mouth. "I have one of those, too."

"Hmm?"

"A brother you have to constantly indulge to keep him out of trouble."

"That's …"

"*Si?*"

"Very appropriate for my brother," Joe said dryly.

Lucian nodded once, saying, "It gets easier as they get older. The younger ones are always a little wild—being the baby gives them more legroom to run. They're always trying to catch up, you know."

Well, as fun as this conversation is …

"It'll help your cause, too, for me to go," Joe added.

Lucian cocked a brow. "How so?"

"I may not be well-known here, or have someone following me around to take pictures, and plaster them on some agent's corkboard, but I do in Chicago. His name is Gary, by the way, but he likes it when I call him *Agent* Gary."

"Do you—use the agent title, I mean?"

Joe barked out a laugh. "Never."

"They get so pissy—poor little feds."

"Truth." Joe shifted on his feet, and shoved his hands in his pockets. "Gary is used to me dropping off the radar for a bit of time, but he probably knows I have this thing coming up. Anyway, my face will be seen, it'll be said I am still in Chicago. And when all of the shit does finally go down here, nobody will even be thinking about attaching my name to it all."

"Smart," Lucian murmured.

"I try to keep business clean."

"Your father was like that, too."

Joe cleared his throat. "Yeah, well, we all learn from somewhere."

"Take your trip—just give us time to settle something out for Liliana. And speaking of her, she has a show this weekend. I won't be able to attend, but it's a small thing, anyway. She likes us there for the bigger ones. Do make sure you are close enough during that show to keep eyes on her."

Like he even needed to be told.

"Already have tickets, actually," Joe said.

"Oh?"

The curiosity lacing the man's tone couldn't be missed, but Joe simply opted to pretend like he hadn't heard it at all.

"And on the Liliana topic," Joe added.

Now or never.

"What about her?"

"I would like to take her out—call it a date, if you want. But out somewhere. Safe, and private, of course."

Lucian stayed quiet.

Joe waited the man out.

He didn't think mentioning the hotel would be all that appropriate, or good for his cause, so he just opted to leave those details out.

"Why?" Lucian finally asked.

"I think it would be good for her. Should I need to step in, maybe then she would trust me a little more, and it'll let me get to know her. And her for me, too."

Lucian quieted again, and folded his arms over his chest. A silent Lucian, Joe found, was rather intimidating. He didn't show that was how the man made him feel, though.

"Is there more to it?" Lucian asked.

Joe smiled at that question. "I don't know—can there be?"

"Well, that's not up to me, Joe. Have a good day."

As quickly as he had come out in the alleyway, Lucian knocked on the door, it was opened, and he was gone.

Joe hadn't gotten a yes.

But he also hadn't gotten a *no*.

That worked for him.

Row five, seat three wasn't the *perfect* spot to watch the ballet, but it was damn close. And for last minute tickets, Joe wasn't going to complain. He wasn't much for ballet, or something like the opera. It had just never been his style.

And yet, he had found it hard to look away during the showing of *The Sleeping Beauty*.

It might have been because the sleeping beauty in question was Liliana Marcello. He was known for his changing demeanor and masks whenever the right time called for it. Some people liked to say he turned into someone else entirely when business was at play, and Joe had never once denied that statement.

But *her*?

Liliana turned into someone else, too, when she danced. Some kind of human-angel hybrid moving across the stage with the kind of grace and beauty he hadn't quite seen before. The emotions and focus on her face as she moved from one step to the next was enthralling, and addictive. She played her character beyond just the dancing, and perhaps even, took the persona on for the moments she was on stage.

It was amazing.

She was beautiful.

He thought, at first sight, she had kind of captivated him. And seeing her like this only added to that strange enchantment, really.

The red corset top of her costume contrasted brightly against the white flowy tutu of the skirt. Her hair had been pulled back into a high, tight bun, and her face painted with a dramatic mix of white makeup, with the reddest lips.

On the very tips of her toes, with her legs perfectly straight, and her arms bent in front of her, she ended the slow with a final bow. Then, she tipped her head up, and stared straight into the crowd, and smiled when the applause started.

Joe clapped, too.

At the same time, he was already getting out of his seat, and starting to move to the area backstage. He was pretty sure he knew the custom of shows after the final act, and the stars came out to do their final bow. While he didn't want to interrupt Liliana during her celebratory moments backstage, he did want to make sure he could keep an eye on her.

That was his job, after all.

The small VIP stamp on the corner of his ticket allowed him to easily move past the man standing guard at the backstage entrance when Joe flashed it at him. Loosening his tie—fuck, he hated wearing a suit most of the time—he slipped into the shadows near the red curtain as the clapping continued just beyond the stage.

He watched as the man who he believed to be the owner of the ballet company waved for the dancers to go.

"*Move, move—and smile, everyone! Big smiles!*"

Jesus.

The guy couldn't get any fucking louder.

It took all of thirty seconds for every dancer to get out on the stage, do their final bow, and for the thundering applause to get even louder. A man and woman carrying several bushels of red and white roses passed Joe by without even noticing he was standing right there.

Each dancer was presented with one of each rose—a gift from the company, it seemed, and not from the guests. At least, if the director's words were to be trusted.

Liliana was one of the very last to leave the stage. This close—although she still couldn't see Joe or rather, hadn't noticed him—he was able to admire the way her skin-toned tights all but molded to her legs in the best way, and how her makeup had been overdone just enough to highlight her most beautiful features.

She was quite a sight.

"Liliana, you were *wonderful.*"

Liliana beamed at the man who had been directing the dancers earlier, and took the hug he offered. "Thank you, Gordo."

"Oh, they *loved* you."

"I hope so."

She had no idea, Joe thought. Not a single idea about how mesmerizing she was on the stage in her costume, and playing her character. She just wanted to dance, and dance *well*, but she did far more than just that. And that, he knew, was the reason why the crowd adored her when she was on stage preforming.

"You're looking well to get that spot in the next show," Gordo told her.

Liliana's face brightened all over again. "I look forward to it."

"Lilibet, look at *you*."

Lilibet?

What the fuck kind of name was that?

Liliana stiffened, and turned with the sort of slow grace he thought only a dancer could probably have. The man standing just a few feet to her left was dressed up in a suit that likely cost more than most people's monthly salaries, and shoes that shined against the hardwood floor. In his hand, he held a bouquet of flowers—blue roses.

How fucking *unique*.

Who the hell was this guy?

He looked familiar, but Joe didn't have time to think on it for long. He was a little too focused on the fact the guy had gotten backstage without Joe noticing at all. Likely because Joe had been too distracted watching Liliana to care.

Mistake number one.

He wasn't about to allow a second mistake to bite him in the ass, too. Once bitten, twice shy and all that good shit.

Joe opted to stay in the shadows and watch the exchange between Liliana, and the man. Only because for the moment, it didn't exactly look like she needed him to step in, and there were plenty of people around, anyway.

However, there was a lot Joe didn't miss.

The way her hands clenched.

How her gaze narrowed.

The bobbing of her throat.

Quick breaths.

Fear, Joe knew.

It all screamed fear.

Yet, Liliana did her very best not to show it other than those small, instinctive reactions. She practically forced herself to stay rooted in place as the man took a step closer to her, but Joe could tell that a part of her was screaming to step the hell back.

"What are you doing here?" Liliana asked the man.

"I came to see the show."

"I don't remember inviting you."

"With a ticket, I don't need an invitation, Lilibet."

"Don't call me that."

In the back of his mind, Joe was still trying to remember where in the fuck he recognized the guy from. Nothing was coming to the forefront to even give him a damn hint. Sometimes, memories were a bitch like that. Playing Hide and Seek like he had time for that kind of nonsense, when he clearly did *not*.

"I just thought I should check in," the man said.

Liliana's jaw hardened. "Well, *don't*."

The guy didn't even look fazed, and instead, offered the flowers to her. "Here, I brought them for you. And you were amazing, as I knew you would be."

She didn't even look at the flowers. She never reached for them. She only stared at the man with a dead gaze that reflected nothingness—a black, blank slate that gave nothing away.

"Have a good evening," Liliana told him.

Another dancer saved the day by pulling Liliana away to greet another three-piece, and the man's overly plastic wife.

The strange, unknown man still didn't look fazed. He did leave, though. Joe made sure to follow him out …

Just in case.

Then, Joe made a few calls.

"Joe."

The quiet way Liliana said his name made Joe smile. She opened the door of her Brooklyn studio apartment a little wider, but didn't move to silently invite him in.

"How did you know where I lived?" she asked.

Joe shrugged. "Someone let me know when I asked."

"And how did you get into the building?"

"I have my ways."

Like an extra key to get in … just in case, or so he had been told. He chose not to tell Liliana that, anyway. She was a part of his job, but he didn't want her thinking that's all this was for him.

Besides, he had shit to make up for.

"Big night for you, huh?" he asked.

Liliana blinked. "Pardon?"

"You were a feature in a show tonight, weren't you?"

Liliana laughed a little, and glanced to the side. "Something else someone told you?"

"Something like that."

"It was a good night. I wouldn't say big."

"Celebratory worthy?" he dared to ask.

Her gaze widened a bit. "Excuse me?"

Joe held up the items he had been holding at his back. A movie, a bag of takeout from a place he knew she frequented, and a bottle of red wine. "I thought—since someone let me know you would be here, and not out somewhere—that you might want to celebrate your night a little quieter than say, going out and doing something."

Liliana hesitated. "Joe—"

"You didn't give me time to explain at the hotel, you know," he quickly interjected before she could turn him down. "You didn't even let me *talk*, Liliana."

"You didn't need to. What you didn't say was enough."

"What I didn't say was that no, it's not okay to just go around asking daughters of made men on dates when some men would consider that to be a great disrespect to them. You don't know a lot about me, and I get that, but that wasn't how I was raised. I don't disrespect men better than me, or any man like me, either. I'm not that kind of man, but don't for one fucking second more, think that I'm not interested in you, Liliana. Because I am— *entirely*."

She blinked.

Smiled.

"Interested, huh?"

He liked the curling sweetness in her voice.

The way her gaze looked him over.

All of her, really.

Following this woman around day in and day out was nothing like actually being close to her, and interacting with her. A lot of the defenses that Joe kept built up around himself to stay safe in this life that he had chosen all seemed to fall down around him whenever Liliana came into play.

He didn't want to pretend for her. He wanted to be—and could be— exactly who he was, with no pretenses, and no worries.

Other than his closest family, he'd never really met someone before who allowed him that kind of comfort. And frankly, he really didn't even know this girl, and she still let him feel that way. How was he supposed to just ignore that?

He couldn't.

Liliana was still quiet.

Joe stayed right where he was, and waited her out. Waving the items again, he added, "And technically, if you want, we could call this a date."

Liliana wet her bottom lip, and grinned. "Oh, so does that mean you've got the *okay* now, or something?"

"Or something," he hedged.

"You just showed up here thinking I was going to let you in?"

"I think you want to save your pride, but it's okay to admit you might have been wrong at the hotel, and I am willing to never mention it again."

"Oh, really?"

Her amused tone made him smirk.

"Think of it like a restart," Joe offered. "This is our do-over."

She hummed a bit.

Joe still waited.

"Well, you must have made quite the effort to get information about where you could find me, and when to do all of this, right?" Liliana asked.

"You could say that."

He wouldn't.

She could.

"I do like *effort*," she said.

Joe smirked again. "I bet there's lots more you'll like about me if you let me in, Liliana."

Her grin matched his, and she stepped back from the door. "Kind of hard to say no to that, isn't it?"

"I've not been proved a liar yet."

SIX

"GOT A SCREW?"

Liliana's hands froze on the food she was unpacking from the takeout bag, only having heard *screw* in all he said. "What?"

Across the island, Joe glanced up from the wine bottle in his hands. "A corkscrew, Liliana."

Her cheeks reddened as she waved at a drawer behind her. "Somewhere in there."

"Great." With the kind of confident grace only a predator could have, Joe slid around the island and slipped in next to Liliana. She tried to focus on unpacking the food he had brought along, and not the way her body felt tucked in beside his. "Don't drink much?"

"What makes you think that?"

"Most wine lovers know exactly where their corkscrew is."

True.

"I drink a little to celebrate, and on special occasions, but other than that, no."

"Not a bad thing," Joe said.

He produced the corkscrew from the drawer with a triumphant grin, and then made quick work freeing the cork from the wine bottle.

"Glasses are on the top shelf in the far cupboard," she said.

Joe moved around her for that, too, and she got another whiff of whatever woodsy scent he seemed to prefer. A heady, rich scent that gave off an entirely masculine impression, and soaked into her lungs with every single breath she took.

Should she have let him in after he randomly showed up with some half-ass story, and a decent explanation-slash-apology?

That was debatable.

Truth was, Liliana had never been very good at denying herself things she wanted. It seemed there was some crazy part of her that *really* wanted something from Joe Rossi. She wasn't entirely sure what it was she wanted, but it was something.

And it would probably be fun.

Joe slid a glass of red wine down the island for Liliana to take, and kept his own sitting in front of him, untouched. "I didn't know what to grab for food—so I just got a spread."

Liliana looked over the burgers, fries, onion rings, and *more*. It was a small buffet, really, but she had little doubt it would be gone by morning. What she probably couldn't eat, Joe would likely handle.

"Did you put anything on the burgers?" she asked.

Joe shook his head. "Nope."

"Good—I have my own sauce."

His gaze darted to hers, and a genuine smile formed. "Your *own* sauce, huh?"

Liliana shrugged. "Yep."

"Made from scratch?"

"How else would I make it, Joe?"

"And is the recipe *super, secret*, too?"

"Are you mocking me?"

Joe let out a hard laugh, and straightened to his full, towering six-foot-five inches. "No, not at all."

Liliana side-eyed him. "Are you sure? Because it kind of sounded like you were getting there."

"I was just thinking …"

"What?"

"My mother would love you, that's all," Joe murmured.

Liliana froze all over, and glanced up to find Joe was still staring at her in that intense way of his. He could make her heart skip beats with that look, or get her stomach rumbling as it tied up in knots. That look invoked too many emotions for her to handle—shyness, lust, amusement, and curiosity.

Did he even know he did that to her?

"Why's that?" Liliana asked.

"I swear my mother has a secret sauce for everything," Joe said, shaking his head a little. He tipped his wine up for a drink before setting it back down, and adding, "And if you think I am kidding, I'm not. My dad even made her this special locked cupboard where she can keep all those super, secret recipes."

Joe's grin turned sly when he said, "We learned Dad put an alarm on the cupboard—because our mother gets a little crazy about the sauces— when my younger brother Cory accidentally put his head through the door."

"How in the hell did he—"

Joe cleared his throat. "He might have had a little help—you know, when I kicked him. We were rowdy teenagers, that's all."

Liliana guffawed. "Are you serious?"

"About the sauce thing, or the brother thing?"

"*Joe.*"

His teasing expression came back in a blink. "We're still a little ... rowdy. Is what it is when it comes to me and Cory."

"You must drive your mother nuts."

"My father is quick to say it's how we show our affection for one another. I can't say he's wrong, but a lot of the time, affection is the last thing on my mind when Cory and I go through one of our rounds together."

Liliana grinned. "He sounds awesome."

"Who, my dad?"

She nodded.

Joe shrugged one shoulder. "He certainly loves my mom, even when she's in one of her moods, and gets a little over the top."

"And you, too, clearly," Liliana returned.

"Me, what?"

"You love your mom. I can hear it in your voice."

Joe smiled. "All good Italian boys should."

Liliana laughed at that. "Truth."

Silently, Joe set his wine glass aside, and moved around the island to come close to Liliana again. So close this time, in fact, that he all but crowded her personal space. She didn't even mind a bit. His finger grazed under her chin, and with a little pressure, she found herself staring up at him.

"Thanks for letting me in," he said.

Liliana winked. "I mean, you *did* bring food and wine."

"Is that the only reason, though?"

Her boldness decided to make itself known again. "Not in the slightest, Joe."

"Thought so."

"And thank you, by the way."

Joe cocked a brow. "For what?"

"Telling me about your family. You seem so ... closed off, I guess. Not with me, though."

"Noticed that, did you?"

"A little," Liliana teased. "And you know, I can't think of any other way I would want to celebrate a successful show than just like this."

"Calling that *just* successful is kind of ... downplaying it, Liliana."

She stiffened a bit. "Pardon?"

Joe inched closer still, closing any and all distance between them. "That show was much more than just successful. *You*, in particular, were amazing."

"You saw my show?"

"I wanted to see you dance, *ballerina*."

Liliana wet her lips, and did her very best to ignore the way his words whispered over her skin. She could deal with that, and the throbbing heat between her thighs, in a minute. She was *trying* to focus on Joe right now.

His hand moved from her chin to her throat, and his fingers curved around the delicate column with a soft touch. He didn't squeeze, but she bet every drop of blood in her body he could feel the way her treacherous heart was racing from just his touch alone. His fingertips rested at her pulse point, and then his hand skimmed up to cup her jaw and cheek. And when his thumb stroked her cheekbone like it was the delicate, soft petal of a flower?

She *shivered*.

"And did you like it?" she asked.

"Seeing you dance?"

"Mmhmm."

"*Loved* it, Liliana."

There was something about the idea of him watching her dance from the crowd that she found to be incredibly fucking hot. Especially *because* it seemed like he had only really been there for her, and that meant all of his attention had to have been on her entirely.

She just had to check, though …

"Did you catch my missed eighth pirouette *en pointe* after I stepped out of turn too soon on the seventh at the end of the first—"

"Seven and a half, actually, but nobody noticed," Joe countered. "How could they when you were probably spinning too fast for them to count?"

"Somebody noticed—*you*."

"Missing things is dangerous in my business. I tend to take notice of everything."

His thumb stroked her cheek again.

Liliana could have melted right then and there.

"For the record," Joe said, "if you kiss me again, I would prefer it if you didn't run off like the last time."

She pressed her lips together. "Is that all?"

"Not even close."

"What else?"

"I didn't come over here with the intention to do anything else *but* celebrate your night with you."

"Does that mean you don't want to do something else with me, Joe? Because I am up for that, and the food can wait. It's always better when you nuke it, anyway."

"Killing me, woman," he said in a rumble of dark words.

Words that *promised*.

Sin, likely.

It promised sin.

It had been far longer than Liliana wanted to admit since she had indulged in that kind of sin with a man. There wasn't even one single ounce of her that wanted to back out right now with Joe.

"What do you want, Joe?"

His answer was a kiss that crashed down on her lax lips with bruising force. A hungry kiss that burned her from the inside out with every stroke of his lips, and every flick of his tongue against hers. His hands came up to grab her face, and drag her closer until she was pressed against him entirely. She could drown in his kiss—*happily*.

Joe's lips traveled a hot path over Liliana's cheek, and then down her throat. When she sucked in a ragged breath as his teeth pressed into her pulse point, she breathed out, "The bedroom is down the hallway—last door on the left."

"Too far," he grunted out.

Her laugh came out breathless and high, but was quickly swept away by Joe's mouth seeking hers again. She lost absolutely all train of thought when he easily lifted her from the floor with nothing more than his hands grabbing the backs of her thighs. Liliana's hands landed on his shoulders as her legs wrapped tightly around his waist.

There was no hiding the hard ridge of his erection rubbing against her center in the very best way with every step Joe took. Liliana barely blinked, and he dropped her from his hold. Her back hit the couch softly, and her hair created a curtain over her face, hiding Joe from view.

Liliana swept her hair back with one hand, and for a split second, lost her ability to breathe when Joe tossed off his jacket, and then yanked his skin-tight white T-shirt up over his head. She had gotten glimpses of some of the colorful ink littering his wrist, and the hint of one on his chest when the collar of his shirt dipped low. Those peeks had not been nearly enough. Colorful art colored up one entire arm in a sleeve—the mother Mary on his other.

And as quickly as her attention was tuned into the tattoos coloring up his skin, it was just as quickly distracted by *him*.

His body.

All of his hard lines, and defined ridges. The way the muscles in his arms bulged with every movement, and how he toted a fucking *eight*-pack leading straight down to a dark dusting of hair below his navel.

The man was fit.

Beyond, really.

Godly felt like an appropriate term.

Broad shoulders, strong hands, muscular chest, and artwork for *days*.

Yeah.

Liliana was *strung*.

Spun.

High, even.

"Find something you like?" Joe asked.

Liliana's gaze darted up to his, and then down to where his hands worked to undo the button on his jeans, and yank down the fly. A quick shift of his hips, and a pull of his hands, and those jeans were falling down.

Commando.

She never would have guessed.

The deep-cut V of his groin was sexy enough to make her wet between her thighs without him even needing to touch her. She was probably already soaked, anyway. But really, it was the thick length of his erection that make her pussy clench when it jutted out from his lowering jeans.

She was stuck silent until he kicked his jeans away—but not before he pulled a foil packet from the pocket, and tossed it on the coffee table—and she was finally able to see *all* of him.

"More than like it," Liliana admitted.

"I do aim to please," Joe returned. "And as long as you can *listen,* I think you'll end up very pleased by the time I'm done, Liliana."

Her gaze darted up to his again. "You're terribly cocky, aren't you?"

"I mean ..." He gestured at his cock—every beautiful nine, thick inches of it. "Got a reason to be, don't I?"

"Oh, my *God.*"

"Yeah, you'll be saying that, too."

Liliana didn't even have time to come up with a quick-witted retort for that one because Joe leaned over the arm of the couch, hovered above her, and dropped a hot kiss to her mouth. Then, he asked, "Can you?"

Her tongue felt numb.

Her lips tingled.

"Can I, what?"

"Listen," he murmured, a breath away from her lips. "Can you?"

She watched him through her lowered lashes. "Guess we're going to see."

"Lift up," he demanded.

His tone offered no other option, so Liliana did exactly what he said. His hands fisted the waistband of her sweats, and dragged them down over her legs along with the simple, black cotton panties she had on, too. Then, his hands came to the compression wraps around her feet. They hid the bandages, helped with swelling, and whatever other hell her feet were going through for the week.

"Leave those, if you wouldn't mind," she said quietly.

Joe glanced up at her. "You sure?"

Her feet were just about the least sexiest thing on her body, and she did not want to have that conversation tonight. "Yeah, I'm sure."

"Your choice, sweetheart."

Discarding her pants and panties, he kissed a slow path from where her cropped top stopped above her navel, down to her bare mound. He stopped just above her clit, and blew a slow, steady stream of warm air against her pussy.

"Rules go like this," Joe said, "you listen, you never hide your cunt from me when I want to see it, and you speak up if something isn't right. Got it?"

Liliana swallowed hard, and nodded.

Joe cocked a brow, and glanced up at her from between her spread legs. "*Speak up*, Liliana. I need you to use words, sweetheart. It's the most important part."

"I got it," she whispered.

"Now, *this*," he said, his words a thick murmur that heated her skin as his thumb suddenly dragged through the lips of her pussy, "this is beautiful, my girl. And it needs to be loved like it is, too. Sucked, and licked, and petted, and fucked until it's sedated and *pleased*."

Liliana tipped her head back, and couldn't even try to hide the moan that escaped. "Jesus."

"And what does it like the most, huh?"

"All of it. All of that sounds—"

"Good enough."

His words were the only warning she got before his mouth was on her sex. First, his tongue was tunneling into her pussy, and it was his rumbling groan when he first got a taste of her that damn near made her come just like that. It was shocking to Liliana how nothing more than a touch from this man put her on edge *just like that*. His thumb toyed teasing circles around the hood of her clit, making her thighs shake, as she grinded her pussy into Joe's mouth to get more of his mouth on her.

"Oh, my God," she gasped.

One of her hands fisted into his hair, and the other grabbed hard to the cushion behind her. She needed *something*—anything—to stabilize herself from the onslaught of sensations coursing through her system.

Without a word, he switched his target. His tongue started assaulting her clit in the best way while his thumb slipped into her pussy. Nothing more than just his thumb massaging her G-spot like he had no problem at all finding it, and his tongue flicking a hard, fast beat against her clit.

The orgasm came on swift.

So fast.

Wrecking her.

She felt the loss of him between her thighs, but the orgasm was still overtaking her senses enough that by the time she could see properly again, Joe had wrapped his cock in latex, and was reaching for her. His hands locked around her wrists, and he yanked her up from the couch.

"Trust me?" he asked.

She nodded when he bent her over the arm of the couch, and put her ass high. A hand snapped against her backside, leaving a beautiful sting behind that shot straight to her pussy. She knew her mistake instantly.

Listen.

And speak.

"Yes," Liliana said, glancing over her shoulder at him, "I trust you."

"Good—it's always better when you take something away."

"What?"

"A sense, say. Take one away, and everything focuses in to make up for what you lost. There's only so much I can remove—how about your sight?"

Liliana blinked.

Her throat tightened.

Joe waited her out, and his hand smoothed gentle, repeated circles with his palm against her ass. He was asking for a lot—asking to remove some form of control from her in a situation that could end badly, and she would have no say at all.

Still, she did trust him.

Some part of her did, anyway.

"Sight it is," Liliana whispered.

Joe grinned. "There she is."

"Who is this *she*, Joe?"

"Someone I'm still trying to learn, Liliana. Don't panic when you can't see, okay?"

"I'll try."

And that was *honest*, too.

He used that shirt of his he'd discarded earlier as a makeshift blindfold. He rolled it into a rope of sorts, and lowered it down over her eyes. She felt the way he twisted it around his fist at the back of her head, and then tugged hard. It pulled her head back, and made her suck in a sharp breath.

His hand skimmed her spine. "Breathe."

"I'm good."

And she was.

Joe had been right, too. She couldn't see a damn thing, but the rest of her senses kicked into overdrive to make up for it. She swore the scent of him was even more heady with blackness saturating her vision. His fingertips tracing her spine, and his lips ghosting over the swell of her ass was intoxicating. She heard the shudder of his exhale, and the shift of his body before she even felt him press into her from behind.

One simple, smooth flex of his hips.

Hard and oh, so *deep*.

He filled her full, and stretched her open all at once. He slid through her wet, clenching sex easily, and yet it still took her a few breaths to adjust to his size.

Liliana all but fell forward, dropping her lower half to the couch with a broken cry when Joe pulled out just as fast as he had first taken her, and then slammed right back in again. His hand came up to press against her back, and keep her firmly down on the couch.

All she could do was fist the couch, and let him fuck her like that, but *Christ* …

She loved it.

His thrusts came on unrestrained, and wild. A little brutal—a deep ache settled in her pussy with every hard flex of his hips. He grabbed her waist, and pulled her body into every thrust, only adding to the sensations taking over her body.

"*Please, please, please.*"

Liliana heard her voice.

Heard her own words.

Heard her cries.

And yet, it didn't sound like her at all.

"Fucking give it to me," she heard Joe say. "Give me that come, sweet girl."

Yep.

He was going to kill her.

But in the *best* of ways.

Liliana smiled at the warm kisses teasing the back of her neck as sunlight painted across her skin, waking her up further. "Good morning."

"Morning," Joe murmured from behind her. "I ordered breakfast in from the place down the road. It'll be here in a few, if you want to get up."

She hummed indecisively. "I don't know."

"What, you want to cook?"

Her laughter came out breathless and high until Joe suddenly flipped her over, and was hovering above her naked body on the bed.

"Laughing in bed with me is probably not a good idea," he said with an arched brow. "I take it as a *challenge*."

"Is that so?" she dared to ask.

"Very much so, yeah."

"Maybe that's why I didn't know if I wanted to get out of bed to eat or not, Joe."

He cocked his head to the side, considering her words. "Fair enough. Are you getting up, or what?"

"How long until the food gets here?"

"About twenty, now."

Liliana nodded. "Lots of time."

"For what?"

"Stretches," she told him. "Preps me for the day, and gets me loosened up before I go into the studio. It's like a fucking warm up for *their* warm up."

Joe scowled.

"What is that for?" she asked, pressing her thumb into the furrow between his brows.

"You don't even get a break after a show, huh?"

Liliana shrugged. "That show is one of three this week for that ballet. All sold out, too."

"Huh."

"I like it, though."

"Stretches, then?" he asked.

Liliana nodded, and let him pull her out of the bed. "Stretches."

Shame, though, as it seemed he had gotten up long enough to pull on his pants, and shirt. She was still naked, and felt that was incredibly unfair.

Although, the way Joe watched her as she passed him by was enough to make her grin at him. "Now who's found something they like?"

His laughter followed her out of the bedroom as she snagged a pair of leggings, and a sports bra on the chair next to the door. After freshening up and dressing in the bathroom, Liliana moved to the living room to the *barre* she had gotten installed in the studio apartment along the floor to ceiling windows overlooking the street down below. She could have put on her pointe shoes, which she sometimes did, but she just needed to wake up her muscles. Not get *en pointe* for the whole time.

Peering out the window, Liliana lost time as she did a quick fifteen minute warmup that included basic stretches, and some moves that were meant to test her flexibility after a hard day like yesterday. One included having her right leg resting along the *barre*, and then letting her back and left arm fall as far backwards as it could go before she quickly came back up. She could just about fold her body entirely in half doing that move.

"Jesus fucking *Christ*," she heard.

Liliana dropped her leg, and found Joe staring at her from the kitchen island. The ease of his body leaning against the counter belied the intensity in his gaze as he watched her. "What?"

"You just bent in half. *Backwards*."

"And?"

Joe swallowed thickly as he pulled out a phone that buzzed in his hand from his pocket. "You know what—nothing, babe. Just know I'm going to remember that you are limber enough to bend in half."

She only laughed at him, but quickly went back to her exercises. Although, a part of her was listening to his conversation on the phone, too.

"Rossi here," she heard him say.

Liliana switched to another move that allowed her to face him, but she only watched Joe from the corner of her eye as she began the set of stretches. With nothing more than a reply to his name, she watched Joe's entirely demeanor change.

Like when made men were around.

Like when he was at the dinner.

Cold.

Black.

Hard.

Nothingness.

Liliana blinked, and stopped her stretches when Joe said, "No, I need you to look into that for me—yeah, business reasons. Find out who the fuck it is. Later."

He ended the conversation.

She didn't move a muscle.

"Joe?"

"Hmm?"

Instantly, the coldness was gone. He was *Joe* again, looking at her in that beautiful way of his.

"Why are you still in New York?" she asked.

One of many questions she had.

Joe shrugged his shoulders. "Business."

"That's all you want to say?"

"That's all I can say."

"You kind of give me whiplash, Joe."

He, too, stayed still as stone. "Why's that?"

"Sometimes, it's like you're someone else entirely. You go back and forth between this person I get to see, and someone else you let the people around you see. And I'm not sure how I feel about the other Joe when he comes out to play."

"I beg your pardon?"

"He's cold—blank, I guess. It almost makes me wonder if you feel anything when you look like that, you know?"

"And what else?" he asked.

Liliana glanced down at the floor. "I just … what do you really do in the business, Joe?"

"I'm the shadow people need when something needs to go, and nobody needs to know about it."

That … told her nothing. Or, maybe she just didn't want to think too hard about what that meant. She was not dumb—she knew the men in her life weren't entirely good people. They were criminals, and yet, she still loved those men. They were good to *her*. And that's what counted the most.

"So, what does that make you, then? A good, or a bad man?"

And what was she supposed to do with it?

Joe's expression gave nothing away when he said, "The only man I know how to be, Liliana."

"I fucked him."

Cella's head popped up from staring down at her phone, her eyes became impossibly wide, and she choked on the latte she had been sipping on just seconds before. So, maybe that hadn't been the right time to blurt that information out to her sister.

It took another few seconds, a long drink of the latte, and only then was Cella seemingly ready to digest what Liliana had said.

"Who, Joe?" her sister asked.

Liliana shrugged. "Who the hell else would I be messing with right now?"

"Well, I don't know. You're busy, so I only get bits and pieces lately."

"You *know* I haven't been in a relationship—sexual or otherwise— since fuck-head, Cella."

"Yeah, but still."

Liliana rolled her eyes. "Yes, *Joe*."

Cella wet her lips, and leaned back in the café chair. "And when did that happen?"

"Three days ago. The night of my show."

"Opening night—'cause I came to the second one, and he wasn't there."

"Opening night, yeah."

Cella nodded, and then grinned slyly. "How was it?"

Jesus.

Liliana couldn't help herself, though. She grinned, too. "Fantastic."

"Then, what's the problem?"

"Not sure."

Cella raised a brow. "That's not a good answer. You get a great lay, and you should be ecstatic about it. Plus, I mean ... *look* at the guy, Liliana."

"I did—too much, probably."

Her sister laughed.

Liliana shrugged.

What could she say?

"At least you can say his skills in bed match his looks," Cella offered. "Just because a guy looks decent means nothing. It's always the good-looking ones who can't seem to find a fucking clit."

Just the level of her sister's voice drew the attention of people sitting nearby. Liliana would have shrunk into the chair if she could. Instead, she just settled on giving her sister a look she hoped shut her up.

Not Cella.

Never.

"What?" her sister asked.

"You're terrible."

"I know."

Cella seemed all too happy about that.

"I haven't seen him since, though," Liliana added.

"Yikes."

"I mean, he texts me, or whatever."

"That's *something*," Cella pointed out.

"I think maybe he's trying to let me figure some shit out."

Cella's brow dipped. "Figure *what* out?"

"Him, I guess."

"I need more to go on."

"Just ... him," Liliana said lamely. "Sometimes, I don't think he is who he says he is. I know he's not entirely on the right side of life, just considering his last name and where he comes from."

Cella glanced upward. "Uh, neither are we, technically. Or our father ... uncles, grandfather, cousins, and—"

"I get it, Cella."

"Listen, we're not new to men like him, Liliana. We've grown up around them. This shouldn't be ... a *thing* for you. Why is it a thing?"

"Because he's not telling me, maybe? I mean, maybe if he told me, then I wouldn't feel like there are two different men I'm trying to figure out right now."

"Maybe you're not in deep enough for him to need to tell you shit. Ever consider that? You're stuck in your head and feelings with the idea he owes you something that we *both* know men in this life keep carefully guarded, Liliana. And right now, at this stage, he doesn't owe you anything about that part of his business. Think about it."

Liliana blinked at that statement.

"You never even considered that, did you?" her sister pressed.

"No, I suppose not."

Cella nodded. "Yeah, I figured."

Huh.

"Funny," Liliana mumbled.

"What is?"

"Aren't you the one who always said you wouldn't marry into the mob? How the fuck did you get this in-depth understanding of men like Joe Rossi, huh?"

Cella *meh'd* under her breath. "Just because I don't want to love a made man doesn't mean I don't know this life, Liliana, and the men inside it. I know. Inside, you do, too."

SEVEN

A BLACK TOWN car pulled into the alley, and honked once. Joe quickly rounded the side of the car, and came up to the driver's side window just as it rolled down enough to show the man waiting inside.

"You called?" Johnathan Marcello asked.

"Where's your boss today?"

John chuckled dryly. "Which boss—seems like everybody rides my ass enough to wear the title, so be specific."

Joe would have sighed had he even had the patience for that today, but he didn't. "Dante. Or shit, even Lucian would probably do, if the boss is busy. I have questions, and they need to be answered."

"Because *that's* going to get you everywhere with them," John muttered.

Shrugging, Joe said, "Yeah, well."

"Dante is out of town for the weekend. My father is picking up the slack."

"Makes sense why Dante isn't answering my calls, then."

"Yeah, whatever." John drummed his fingers on the leather-wrapped steering wheel before adding, "You want a meet with my father, or what?"

"Today, preferably."

"All right, get in."

Joe chose not to question John. He jogged around the side of the car, and slipped in the passenger seat. It took ten minutes, and three phone calls for John to finally get a hold of his father, and request the meet.

Shit, Joe would have just *showed up* again on Lucian like he did the first time had he simply known where the man was. Well, as long as he had time.

Joe checked the digital clock on the dashboard of the Mercedes. Seemed like he was kind of running short on time, actually. He only had another two hours, at the most, and he was going to need to get back to watching Liliana until she was safe at her studio apartment.

"So," John drawled from the driver's seat.

"What?"

"I hear you're looking after my sister."

Joe cocked a brow. "Someone thought it was a good idea."

John smirked. "Yeah, they always have the brightest fucking ideas."

"Mmm."

"Be nice to her, huh?"

Joe eyed John from the side. "I beg your pardon?"

"My sister, I mean. Be nice to her. She took enough shit from me growing up, and whatnot. She just … doesn't deserve anything less than kind people treating her with respect."

"What kind of shit did she take from you, exactly?"

John glanced over at Joe.

Fuck.

He could tell he hadn't been successful in hiding the warning of violence flashing in his tone when he spoke. Just the idea of someone being terrible to Liliana was enough to make Joe want to spill blood, and hear screams echo.

For a long while, John's gaze continued to drift between Joe, and back to the slow-moving Manhattan traffic. "What's that about, man?"

Joe cleared his throat. "I don't know what you're—"

"Cut the bullshit. I don't care. I'm not the one you have to worry about spilling your business. Just tell me what it's fucking about."

"This isn't the inquisition, John. Don't be a prying fucker."

"Fine," John said heavily, glancing back out the window. "I'm bipolar. Diagnosed when I was seventeen—closer to eighteen, but still seventeen. I went the majority of my teen years in a constant up and down spiral of mania, and depression. My sisters—more the two older ones—were always right there in the line of fire given we lived in the same fucking house."

Joe's head jerked to the side again, and he found John was watching him, too.

"So yeah, that's the kind of shit my sister took from me," John said, "and if anyone in this business ever learns I'm bipolar because you told them, all that's going to be left of you will be a fucking *shadow*. Got it?"

Well, *damn.*

Joe didn't feel the need to question John's threat because he felt it well enough in the way the man's words stabbed at him.

"I like her," Joe admitted. "Liliana, I mean."

John drummed his fingers again. "Oh?"

"Complicated, at the moment."

"I guess it would be considering you're hired to do a job for our family, and they added her into the mix. Although, that's not *really* complicated."

"It is when I haven't told her she's part of the job. And for that matter, explaining that bit would mean also telling her what my work is. I don't like to talk about that with anybody, if you get my drift."

John made a sound in the back of his throat. "Yeah, edging toward issues there a little bit."

"Don't need the reminder."

"What can you do?"

Without saying another word, John pulled the Mercedes to the side of the road. He put the car in park in front of what looked like a restaurant that was currently undergoing serious renovations given the blacked out windows, and building permits.

"He's here?" Joe asked.

John shrugged. "He had some unpleasant meetings today, I think."

"Won't the workers coming in to work on the place be pissed to find a mess?"

"Oh, they just keep this place for this sort of shit. It's never actually undergoing anything but a mop of the floor to clean up the blood."

Huh.

Good to know.

"Thanks, John," Joe said, climbing out of the car.

John's voice stopped Joe from closing the door when he replied, "No problem, man. And like I said ... be kind to her."

Joe nodded, but didn't reply.

He figured he didn't have to.

"Leave him," came the order from the far end of the restaurant.

Joe had barely managed to walk in through the front door before he was faced with two surly looking enforcers that often trailed close behind wherever Lucian Marcello went. One was the enforcer from the restaurant, but it didn't seem like the man cared if he recognized Joe or not at the moment.

However, at their boss's order, the two men took a few steps back from Joe. They quickly went back to their posts at the wall.

Joe didn't miss how one of the enforcer's knuckles were a reddened, swollen mess. Like he had the time of his life punching the daylights out of someone that day.

It was possible.

Now that he had a bit of breathing room, Joe took the chance to look around while he could. There wasn't very fucking much to see inside the place, actually.

It certainly *looked* like the business was undergoing some kind of renovations, but that was probably all to keep the act up, and the building permits still legal. Wires hung from the exposed ceiling, the floor was torn up to showcase stained cement beneath it, and old tables and chairs were scattered in every direction. Some were covered by dusty, old sheets, and others were overturned or cleaned off to sit.

Lucian pushed off the corner of a table at the far end of the rundown restaurant. "Aren't you supposed to be *watching* someone today?"

"Do you think I left her unprotected?"

"I think I asked a question, actually."

Joe sighed. "She's with her mother and sister, as you probably already know. Dinner, and a movie. I suspect it's a girls' day out, but who knows? The other two have enforcers, and they're in well-known, public areas. I chatted with their enforcers for a minute to let them know I had to step away."

He then flashed his phone in the air, saying, "I get a text every time they move to a new spot, and I know exactly where she is at all times. She's fine."

"I know she is," Lucian murmured.

Joe swore the man *almost* fucking smiled, too.

"I hate it when people doubt me," Joe said.

Lucian shrugged. "Not my problem. What can I do for you?"

Yes, that.

The whole fucking reason why Joe was here to begin with.

"Rich *Earl*," Joe said, trying to keep his tone as level as he could. He also failed like a fucker because he knew something was fucking up, now. "Son of George Earl—you know, the politician you want me to kill."

Lucian folded his arms over his chest, but otherwise, kept his face impassive and unreadable. "What about him? Most men George's age have families, Joe. I'm not sure why you're looking into the personal details and lives of your mark. That's not typical, is it?"

"What I do for my job is none of *your* business," Joe said, tossing the man's words back at him.

"On the contrary—I'm the one paying you."

"Dante, actually," Joe countered.

Lucian smirked. "On the surface, maybe."

What?

Joe decided Lucian's word games weren't all that important right then. He had something else he needed to deal with. "I want to know why one of the sons of my mark approached Liliana on opening night of *The Sleeping Beauty*?"

That was what did it.

That was what made Lucian's calm façade crack.

"Excuse me?"

82

Lucian moved a step forward—a calculating step if Joe ever saw one. It was like suddenly the man's body was a coiling snake readying to strike, and Joe very well might be the target it came to kill.

"Rich Earl—approached Liliana during opening night of the show. I saw from the background, and didn't step in because even though she seemed uncomfortable with him around, she had it under control. Also, I didn't want to expose myself being there. She didn't know. I didn't want to freak her out or anything."

"And you know who he is *how*, exactly?" Lucian asked, reverting back to the calm tone.

"I thought he looked familiar."

"That tells me nothing."

"I made some calls, and had some information pulled."

"And what did you find?"

Joe's gaze narrowed. "Why are you questioning me?"

"Because I can!"

Jesus.

"I found what I wanted to know—who he was, and because of that, how he's related to this job considering he's Earl's son. Now, could you answer some fucking questions of mine, Lucian, or no?"

"He *approached* her?" Lucian asked.

"I've said that two or three times now."

Glancing to the side, Lucian said nothing for a spell. Joe thought the man might have been considering his words, but it was possible that it was something else entirely. Like maybe Lucian was trying to check his rage.

But *why*?

What was Joe missing?

He was missing something, *clearly*.

"No," Lucian finally said, "I am not going to answer your questions."

Joe stared hard at the man.

Lucian stared back, unflinchingly.

"This is Marcello family business," the man continued, "and you were hired to do a job for us, nothing else. Do your job, Joe, or someone else will."

Joe's jaw clenched. "All I am asking—"

"Is for something I won't give you. Why haven't you hit the marks yet, anyway?" Lucian cocked his head to the side, and his gaze narrowed in on Joe. "I do believe Dante gave you the okay last week to go ahead with the hits."

Yes.

The day after Liliana's show.

Joe hadn't gone forward.

Yet.

"And why haven't you *done your job?*" Lucian demanded.

"Because."

Lucian sneered. "Because you were digging through information, and waited to see what you could find, hmm? Didn't want to jump ahead of the gun lest it shoot you in the ass."

Joe stuffed his hands in his pockets. "I said from the jump that these are high profile people, Lucian. I want to know why I'm supposed to kill them."

"Just do your fucking job, Joe." Lucian eased out of his defensive posture, but the hard, coldness in his gaze remained. "You're heading to Chicago in a couple of days for that ... business opening, correct?"

"Yes, the bar with my brother."

"Do make sure you're ready—or damn close—to finishing what we hired you for by the time you get back. Understood?"

How was he supposed to respond?

No?

"I'll see what I can do," Joe settled on saying.

Being back in Chicago was like crawling back in your comfortable bed after being away from it for far, *far* too long. Joe stepped off the private jet onto his home soil, and instantly felt like he might be able to let his guard down a little bit. It helped to see his father and brother waiting just across the tarmac.

And yet, something was still holding him back from being entirely happy that he was home a day later. Probably, the text messages coming into his phone, and the beautiful woman he'd left back in New York.

But who knew for sure?

You free tonight?

That had been Liliana's last text.

Joe was still struggling to answer her back. Likely because he didn't want to tell her no, or make it seem like he was rejecting her again. The very last thing he wanted Liliana to feel was as though he had just fucked her and run like a coward after. Because really, he hadn't gotten to see her again since that night. At least, not while she knew.

Most of his days were spent following her around, and making sure she was safe, now. But that left him with very little time to do anything else, and the girl was a damn social butterfly. Always out and about, and it wasn't like he could step in public and make himself known.

Not in the job description, unfortunately.

There was nothing more he wanted than to climb back on a plane, and head to New York to spend an evening with her instead of this goddamn bar opening.

And he *hated* flying.

Shit, that alone should have told Joe something.

Finally, he answered Liliana's text back with a simple, *How about Monday? Something came up.*

Monday is good—I am free anytime after four.

Joe grinned down at his phone, pleased that had worked in his favor. *Monday it is, sweetheart.*

He stuffed his phone back into his pocket just as Cory rounded the bar with one of his usual cocky grins. "What are you behind here smiling like a fucking boy for?"

Joe gave his brother a look. "I am not. I'm … enjoying a good opening."

He mentally patted himself on the back for coming up with that lie. Although, he should have known better because if there was anyone in his life who knew him well, it was Cory. He couldn't hide shit from his brother.

"Nah, you were checking out your phone," Cory said, resting an elbow to the bar. "And I know how much you hate these openings—you only like owning businesses because *money*. Cut the shit, and tell me what's up."

Yep.

"Just drop it," Joe muttered.

"Met someone in New York?"

Joe stared hard at Cory, and silently willed his brother to go away. And of course, when he didn't, all Joe could do was shake his head. "How do you even guess shit like that?"

"So, I'm right, then."

Cory grinned in that way of his again.

Joe kind of wanted to punch him in the mouth.

"*Maybe* I met someone," Joe finally settled on saying. He knew how his brother worked, and if he didn't give Cory something to chew on for a while, then his brother would never shut up until he did get what he wanted. "And maybe it's a little complicated because of circumstances and the job I'm supposed to be doing."

"Who is she?"

"You don't care, Cory."

"Hey."

The hurt in his brother's tone actually made Joe turn to face his brother full on. Cory cocked a brow in challenge, and his posture matched with arms crossed over his broad chest. Both Rossi brothers were tall, wide, and built like brick shithouses. Something they took from their father, he supposed.

"I get you're not like me, Joe," Cory said.

"What the fuck does that mean?"

"*Women*, dumbass. You're not like me with women."

"To say the least," Joe muttered.

Women were like tissues to Cory. Fun and easy to use, and then quickly disposed of once he had gotten what he wanted from them. Joe didn't have serious relationships, but he wasn't interested in just busting a nut and moving on, either.

That wasn't his style.

"Yeah," Cory continued, "so when you say *maybe* you met a woman, I'm gonna stop and ask about her, fucker. Because I know that means something to you just based on the way you are with females. So, what's her name, and don't try that ignorant shit with me again or I'll bust your mouth."

Had it been any other man ...

Any other time ...

Joe likely would have stood up for that challenge, and dared his brother—or whoever—to go ahead and fucking *try it*. He got his kicks out of that kind of shit, but especially with Cory considering the two had grown up beating the hell out of each other every chance they could.

But tonight, it just amused him.

Because it meant Cory gave a fuck.

"Liliana Marcello," Joe said.

As soon as he said it, he plucked up the drink he hadn't touched all night—three fingers of whiskey—and downed it in one single go. Because yeah, he needed a drink after admitting that.

Cory whistled low. "*Damn.* If that ain't playing with some kind of fucking fire, I don't know what is."

Joe shrugged. "She's ..."

"Are you gonna give me some sappy shit, or ...?"

Not even thinking about it, Joe struck out with his fist, and punched Cory right in the gut. His brother doubled over with a half-laugh, and half-moan. The commotion gained the attention of several patrons in the opening bar, but since it was mob-owned, and Joe recognized most of the faces, he just grinned and waved a hand.

These people knew how the Rossi brothers were.

"You are a *fucker*," Cory said in a sneer as he stood straight again.

"Says the fucker who probably helped make me this way," Joe countered.

Cory considered that before admitting, "Truth."

Joe gave his brother another look. "No, I wasn't going to be *sappy*. I haven't grown a cunt in my absence, you shithead."

"What, then?"

The two leaned against the bar, and watched the bartender down the way serve drinks with a fun flair to the people on the other side. Silent for the moment, it gave Joe the chance to think over his words before he just blurted something stupid out.

Plus, he didn't exactly know *how* to describe Liliana, or what he thought and felt about her. It was complicated, and difficult. She was also different, and wonderful. Beautiful like nobody else. A fucking star in his eyes—captivating him with nothing more than a smile and a twirl.

"Ma would love her," Joe said.

Cory stiffened beside him. "Oh?"

"She's that kind of woman, you know."

"Huh."

"That's all you've got to say?"

Cory's gaze met Joe's and he replied, "That's all I need to say."

"There's strange shit going on down in New York, though, and I can't really say I like it."

"That sounds bad."

"A little."

"I could come to—"

"No, you can't come to New York with me," Joe interjected.

Cory scowled. "Why do you have to ruin all my fun?"

"Because you don't know how to stay under the radar, Cory."

"Fine—that's fair. What's the problem?"

Joe wondered how much he should tell his brother, but it really wasn't all that much of a question for him. Out of everyone in his life, he trusted his brother the very most. Maybe it was their raising, or the fact they were so close in age and only really had each other to fall back on a lot of the time in this life. Nonetheless, he would *give* his life for Cory, and knew his brother would give his in return, too.

"All right, it's like this," Joe started.

It took a good ten minutes for him to get through the job the Marcellos asked him to do, and then all the weird shit that came up after. He didn't leave out the fact he thought the two hits were too high profile to be doing close together, not to mention that he all but knew the Marcellos had to have a good reason for doing it, and it was likely going to draw attention to them. He added on the son of the politician approaching Liliana at her show, and then the meeting Joe had with Lucian just before he came.

"They keep telling me to mind my fucking business," Joe said, "but I feel like there's a lot of shit going on under the surface, and I need to know why this job was put in my hands to begin with."

"The Outfit's spoiled you, man," Cory said.

Joe's brow dipped. "What?"

"You're a hired *gun*. A hitman, at the most. And you were hired to do a hit for them—nothing more, Joe. You're used to Tommas or Dad giving you every reason why someone has to die, so you can do your strange guilt shit when you have to justify it to God."

"First of all—"

"Shut up. Point being, they don't owe you that information. You took the job, so that means you do it."

"No, I took it because Dad asked me to," Joe replied.

"You didn't mention that."

Joe shrugged. "Yeah, basically said because *he's* asking me to do it, so I did. And even now when I try to raise my concerns about all of this, he brushes me off."

Cory frowned. "That's not like Dad, either."

"See," Joe said pointedly, "something is fucking up, man. I'm not crazy."

"You think it maybe has something to do with Liliana? You said Lucian told you on the *surface* it may look like Dante was paying you, right?"

"Kind of suggested it was Lucian who was getting me to do the job, yeah."

Cory nodded. "All right, now add on the fact the son of a senator you're meant to kill was acting kind of friendly with Lucian Marcello's daughter—"

"She has a goddamn name, Cory."

"First, I realize she has a name, Joe. Step out of your feelings for five seconds, and think about this whole thing objectively. That's probably half of your damn problem. You haven't been able to really get your eyes away from the prize long enough to properly think about all of this."

"The prize—what?"

"Liliana's pus—"

Joe punched his brother again, but this time, in the shoulder. "Watch your fucking mouth."

Cory rubbed the spot, and scowled deeper. "Keep hitting me, and I'm not going to help you at all."

"You're not helping very much right now."

"You said *she* looked uncomfortable, and this ... Rich Earl, the senator's son, acted familiar with her. Maybe a previous relationship or something?"

Jealousy surged through Joe.

Hot.

Heavy.

Dangerous.

He swallowed the bitter taste it left behind, and tried to keep it from showing in his tone when he said, "That's fair to say, sure."

"How about I look there, then," Cory suggested.

"What—at Liliana and Rich? She's not seeing him."

"But she might have been."

Fuck.

True.

And that might give Joe some of his answers, too.

"I know some people," Cory added under his breath. "I could have the info to you relatively soon."

"How soon?"

"Depends on how much digging I have to do. I mean, if it were easy to find, you would know already. There would have been news about the Marcellos and these high-profile men they want you to hit, but you said there's no direct connection that you've found. None that are obvious between the marks of yours, and the main men of the Marcello organization, anyway. That means, it has to be something deeper in their family. Something—or some*one*—behind these men that they're protecting."

Someone like Liliana.

Joe swallowed hard, not liking how this was starting to look. "All right, then. Don't tell Dad you're looking into shit. He's already being a prick about this when I try to ask."

Cory nodded. "You got it."

EIGHT

"*RETIRÉ DEVANT!* I said *retiré devant*, Anabel. Jesus Christ."

"I *did.*"

"Then why was your leg still on the floor, girl?"

The argument continued on between the director and a dancer, but as long as it wasn't her who was fighting with him, she found it easy to tune the man out.

Liliana fell from her position, thankful that at the moment, Gordo's anger wasn't on her. She felt bad for Anabel, though, because the girl had been in the correct move, and position. It didn't matter—they were working on seven hours, and at the six-hour mark was about the time when Gordo's patience ran thin when it came to training and rehearsals.

He couldn't possibly have his eyes on twenty dancers at once, but he certainly thought he could. And thus, when his frustration or irritation with anything spilled over, he liked to take it out on the dancers.

Regardless if this was just another one of Gordo's outbursts, or if the girl was actually missing her moves, Liliana was grateful for the break. It allowed her the chance to catch her breath, grab the towel hanging over the *barre* along the wall of mirrors, and wipe her face, neck, and shoulders down.

She was taking in her tired reflection when a familiar man stepped into the entrance of the studio. Her father was formidable on his good days— tall, dark, and brooding. Her mother liked to say Lucian could silence someone with nothing more than a glance in their direction, and a smart person could guess his mood just based on how dark the hazel of his eyes were on any given day.

Liliana knew it was all true.

She also knew that he was her dad. Lucian never scared her, and he certainly didn't intimidate her, either. How could he when he was the same man who used to sing her a special bedtime song he made up just for her, or all the tea parties he joined in on when she was a little girl?

He was her *dad.*

That's all she saw.

"Excuse me, but you can't be in here," Gordo said.

Lucian didn't even grace the director with his attention as his gaze finally landed on Liliana across the studio. He pointed a single finger at her, and then hooked it as if to silently demand she, *move.*

Liliana didn't know what was up, but a spike of dread settled hard and fast in her gut. Her father never showed up to her dance studio because, in a way, this was where she worked. She was here for that, and not for anything else. He didn't get in the way of that kind of thing.

"I'll be just a sec," Liliana told Gordo.

As she was passing the director by, the man replied, "Tell your guest, he is *not* welcomed in my studio again! I won't have these sorts of distractions for my dancers, Liliana!"

"Oh, would you shut up already?" Lucian barked from the doorway. "Jesus Christ, man, everybody can hear you yelling from the goddamn street. They *dance* for you, but they're not your property. Treat them like humans, huh?"

"Dad," Liliana hissed.

She pushed Lucian out of the doorway—although really, she just had to press her hands against his chest to make him move out of the way. It wasn't like he put up any big fight to move, or anything.

Thank God.

"Don't do that," Liliana told her father.

"He sounds like a jackass."

Liliana almost rolled her eyes, but settled on nodding instead. "Yeah, he kind of is."

Behind her, she heard Gordo call out, "All right, take fifteen, but then get back to it. And Trent, I swear if I see you outside smoking again, I will cut your fucking lungs out."

Lucian scoffed. "Right. That man is definitely capable of cutting something out of someone else. I'm *sure.*"

"Did you need something—or did something happen?"

Liliana figured the quicker she got her father onto the topic of why he showed up at the studio, the quicker she could get back to work, and be done for the weekend. It was Sunday, and she was looking forward to the next week for more reasons than she cared to explain.

A charity dance, for one.

And Joe, for two.

Her phone had been silent for the day, but he promised he would do something on Monday. Well, she already had something in mind, but he wasn't exactly here yet to make the offer, so …

Lucian scowled at the dancers coming out of the studio. "Is there somewhere we could chat for a little bit—*privately?*"

Liliana gave her father a look. "Bathrooms, and locker rooms. A storage closet. Gordo's office—don't even ask, no one is allowed inside. And another studio. Take your pick."

"Studio."

Fine by her.

Liliana led the way, and her father followed close behind silently. Soon, they were in the studio at the end of the hall, but like with the other one, there was no door to close to give them privacy. It was just an illusion.

"Now, will you answer me?" Liliana asked. "Did something happen, or—"

"Why didn't you tell me that Rich Earl approached you a while back during opening night of *The Sleeping Beauty*?"

Liliana blinked.

Her throat tightened.

Her chest ached.

She felt the shake in her fingers, and the tremor that worked its way up her spine at just hearing the man's name spoken out loud. It made her sick to her stomach, and her head feel a little too light. A fear landed dangerously hard in her stomach—like a balling, tight knot there that she couldn't get out no matter how hard she tried.

Yeah …

That's what Rich's name invoked.

Liliana had taken great pains to teach herself not to react outwardly, though. Especially not when it came to Rich fucking Earl. The man did a lot of things, but she refused to let him terrify her for one more fucking minute.

What he had done once was *enough*.

No more.

"Sorry," Lucian murmured quickly. "I didn't mean—"

Shit.

"I thought I was getting better at it."

Her father cocked a brow. "Pardon?"

"Hiding how he … bothers me," she said dumbly.

Lucian shook his head, and wrapped an arm around her shoulder. In a blink, she found herself dragged close into her father's comforting, warm embrace. It was safe there—nothing ever hurt her there.

Just like she was a girl again.

Resting his chin on the top of her head, Lucian said, "You do hide it well, and that's admirable. But I'm also your father, Liliana, and I can see when things are affecting you in a bad way. Although, I'm sure it pissed him off like nothing else that he didn't get a reaction out of you when he approached you. We both know how men like him enjoy seeing the hell they cause."

Liliana swallowed the ball of emotions in her throat. "Maybe—I don't know. I just wanted him to get the fuck away."

"But *why* didn't you tell me?"

"There was nothing to tell. He hasn't approached me since, and Gordo was made aware that he shouldn't be allowed back into any showings. What else can I do, Daddy?"

"*Tell me.*"

The pain in her father's voice mixed heavily with his anger. Liliana knew the anger wasn't for her, but rather, at a man who had not yet gotten what he deserved for the things he did.

"And what would you do?" Liliana asked. "You tried to do something once, and it—"

"This time is not the same."

Liliana stiffened, and glanced up at her dad. "What does that mean—what are you doing now?"

Lucian shook his head. "It's not for you to worry about."

"I think maybe—"

"If he approaches you again, I *need* to know."

"How did you know this time?"

"Someone who saw what went down from afar, I suppose."

Liliana only struggled for a couple of seconds to put together who exactly that might be. There was, after all, only one person she knew who had been at the show that night. Only one person who would have contact with her father.

Joe.

But why would he be giving Lucian information?

And how much did he know about Rich?

"You have to tell me if this happens again—understood?" Lucian asked.

Liliana nodded. "Yeah, I got it."

Now, though, she had more questions than answers.

On her back staring up at the ceiling of her studio apartment, Liliana heard nothing but the lyrics of her favorite artist in her ears coming through the earbuds. A warm soak in Epsom salt kept her feet from aching too much, and the music let her relax enough not to care about the slight stinging in her toes.

Nobody said being a ballerina was easy.

Nobody said they didn't sacrifice for it.

Closing her eyes, Liliana mellowed out in the sounds of the artist belting out the final chords of a song about a woman missing out on a man she never even got to know. How strangely appropriate that felt for her.

In more ways than one …

Once the song was over, she tugged the earbuds out, and released a hard sigh. She moved her arm from where it had been resting over her eyes, and damn near screamed at the sight of the man standing right beside her.

The shout died in her throat.

But only because it was Joe.

Still, her fucking heart *pounded.*

"Jesus Christ, you can't make some noise?" Liliana demanded.

Amusement danced in Joe's gaze as he looked her over. "I came to see you earlier than I said I would, and you want to fault me for it?"

He looked so fucking smug.

She glared.

A little.

"How did you even get in here, Joe?"

"I knocked *several times.*"

"That's not what I asked," she pointed out, "and I was listening to music."

"You have a stereo system. Put it through the speakers."

Liliana shrugged as well as she could on the floor. "Sometimes, I need music delivered right to the brain, or as close as I can get to it."

Joe tipped his head to the side. "What are you doing down there, anyway?"

"Nice deflection on not telling me how you got inside my apartment."

"I picked the lock because I got worried. Now, what are you doing?"

"Relaxing."

"That doesn't look very relaxing."

"Something flat and hard against my stiff back, and a good soak for my feet?" Liliana sighed happily. "It's *perfect.*"

"I will take your word for it."

Liliana side-eyed Joe, and took in the suit and tie he wore. Usually, he was in a leather jacket, and jeans. This was new.

She liked it.

A lot.

"Why the attire?" she asked.

Joe dropped down on the floor beside her—gracefully, despite his large size. It was almost cute, but she didn't think he would appreciate her telling him that. "Came over here right after I finished something else. Didn't take the time to change."

Her heart stuttered.

She grinned.

"What, couldn't wait to see me, or something?"

Liliana was only half-teasing.

A part of her wanted him to say—

"Yes, exactly that," Joe murmured.

She abused her bottom lip with her teeth, trying to discern how all of this made her feel. A little light-headed, but not in a bad way. Overwhelmed, definitely.

"I'm not really sure what to do with you, Joe Rossi."

He flashed his teeth in a sinful smile. "Yeah, me either."

"So, where were you, anyway?"

"Out of town."

He offered nothing else.

Liliana chose not to push. "I should warn you, I don't plan on doing very damn much tonight. I was on my feet for nine hours in rehearsals, and I don't plan on being on them any more today."

Joe didn't bat an eye at her statement. "I didn't come over to do something. I came to see you, sweetheart."

"Oh ... well, okay."

"Are you nearly finished?"

"With what?"

Joe gestured at the extra-large plastic tub she was using to soak her feet in hot water, and Epsom salt. "This."

"Yeah, just let me dry off."

Liliana moved to sit up, and grab the small towel she had set aside for when she was done. Joe was a little quicker than her, and his large hand wrapped around her left ankle with a soft touch. He grabbed the towel with his other hand, and lifted her foot from the warm water.

Her immediate reaction when someone might touch her feet or see the abuse they suffered was to pull away, and hide them.

And yet, she just ... didn't.

Joe was silent as he dried her feet with careful pats of the towel, and grew still as his fingertips grazed over her bruised toes, split skin, and cracked toenails. The discoloration and swelling in her feet could be better or worse depending on how much dancing she had been doing, or other factors.

It wasn't a pretty sight.

"Everyone wants to be successful," Joe murmured, glancing back at her, "but no one truly understands what it takes, or what they have to sacrifice for it."

Truer words had never been spoken. Liliana was sure she wouldn't hear anything more honest than that for a long while.

"Hazard of the job," she replied, glancing at her feet.

Silently, he moved her feet into his lap with careful hands, and then he was reaching for her, too. His fingers locked tight around hers before he pulled her up from the prone position, so she could sit across from him.

"I think I might have missed you since the last time you were here," she admitted.

Joe laughed. "You *think*?"

"It's still up for debate."

"Oh, I think I could remind you of exactly why you missed me, *Tesoro*."

The suggestive dip in his tone couldn't be missed. Liliana was all too willing to indulge his suggestion, too.

"Maybe you should do that, then," she whispered.

Joe cocked a brow, and glanced up from her feet that he had been rubbing soft circles into. The blues of his eyes pierced into hers, and instantly, a shot of heat curled deliciously in her stomach. Oh, good things were about to come from this man.

She *knew* it.

He didn't disappoint, either.

Liliana found herself leaning back on her arms when Joe suddenly loomed over her in the blink of an eye. His gaze drifted over her face, and lingered on her lips just long enough to make her breath catch. Then, he kissed her. A hard, hot kiss that spoke of just how much he might have been missing her, too, without actually saying the words.

Not that she minded.

This was good, too.

So good.

Joe's fist clenched into Liliana's loose T-shirt, and he pulled her up higher, and then into his lap once they were both sitting. She heard something hit the tub of water, and the splash as liquid spilled to the hardwood floor. She really couldn't find it in herself to care that she was going to have a mess to clean.

All she really cared about in those moments were the way Joe had locked her legs around his waist in such a way that his erection dug into her core. With every shift of her hips, the length of his cock pressed against her a little more.

Teasing …

Promising …

One of his hands slipped up her shirt to palm her naked breast beneath, and tweak her hardened nipple with his fingertips. The other slid between her thighs, and snaked up the leg of her small, cotton sleep shorts. Almost right where she wanted him.

"These clothes are making things easy on me, so thanks," he muttered against her cheek.

Liliana laughed, but it quickly melted into a low moan when two of his fingers slipped between her folds. Instead of filling her pussy with his fingers, he stroked her slit, and then dragged the wetness he found there up to her clit. Pressing small, fast circles into her clit, he worked her body into a fast fever, and whispered dirty words to her all the while.

His lips moved against her throat, and then along her jaw. His words never stopped, not even when she started to shake, and got a little close to the cliff he was dragging her to. *Jesus.* She couldn't wait to jump off it.

"Aren't you going to come for me?"

"*Please.*"

Joe chuckled. "You like this, don't you? A little greedy, I think."

To say the least.

He pulled back enough to catch the way her mouth fell open as the orgasm started to creep in on her. And then he caught her bottom lip between his teeth, and nipped just hard enough to send her flying over the edge with a broken whine.

"*Joe.*"

"There it is," she heard him whisper. "Now fucking give me the rest, too."

She hadn't even finished catching her breath before he had pulled her shirt up over her head, and tossed it somewhere to the side. His jacket, tie, and shirt quickly followed the same path.

Liliana found herself picked up from the floor, but her legs still stayed tight around Joe's waist.

"And don't even try to tell me you don't have the balance," she heard him say.

What?

"Show me how well you can *stretch*, ballerina."

Liliana blinked when her bare feet were set back down on the floor. She realized then that he had brought her over to her *barre* against the windows. Without coverings, although her place was dark with the lights turned off, just about anyone could probably see at least her naked silhouette if they stared hard enough.

"Joe," she said in a whine, glancing back at him.

He shook his head, grinned, and took a step back. "Show me—and take off those shorts, too."

A heat climbed up Liliana's throat. She was sure her cheeks turned red with the color, too.

Joe didn't miss it. "Don't get shy on me, sweetheart."

Liliana swallowed hard, and glanced out the windows again. Just as quickly, her embarrassment washed away when she turned back to see Joe discarding the rest of his clothes. He snatched a condom from his pants, and made quick work of sliding the latex down his cock. Only he could make the sight of putting on a condom sexy.

Fucking hell.

Naked, with nothing but his black rosary hanging around his throat, and the backdrop of her wall of paintings behind him, he looked like every inch of sin.

Delicious.

Dangerous.

And *perfect.*

He would test the morals of a *nun.*

Fisting his length, he flashed his teeth in that teasing way, saying, "Stretch for me."

If that's what he wanted …

How could she say no?

Liliana was quick to drop those shorts of hers, and didn't miss the way Joe's gaze drifted down to her bare sex. She had to keep her eyes on just about anything but him in order to focus on at least doing what he told her to do.

She remembered what he said that first time.

Listen.

Listening got her everything from Joe.

Liliana went through the motions of stretching against the *barre*—her arms, core, and back. Nothing too strenuous. It was only once she lifted her left leg high to lay flat against the bar, and bent her entire body to the right, that a sound from Joe made her hesitate.

Or shit … *anticipate.*

A grunt, maybe.

Or it could have been a groan.

Either way, it was by far one of the sexiest sounds she had ever heard in her life. Like he hadn't even been able to contain it coming out of his mouth.

"Do you know how fucking good you look like that?"

Jesus.

Liliana twisted just enough to see Joe had come to stand right behind her, and he'd barely made a noise.

"I'm going to get you a bell to wear," she told him.

"Fuck the bell." Joe's gaze darkened, and his hand finally left his cock, then. He stroked the curve of her back, and down over her ass. His touch left her skin on fire, and shiver racing through her blood. "Keep hold of the bar, *Tesoro.*"

Liliana laughed. "And don't drop my leg?"

"Don't even fucking think about it."

He fitted his body in behind hers, and slid into her pussy with one long, deep thrust. The force was enough to send her flying up on her tiptoes with a gasp. The head of his cock hit something wonderful inside her cunt, and she wanted him to repeat it.

"Again," she demanded.

Joe chuckled darkly, and his hand pressed hard into her lower back. "Liked that, did you? Fuck, this is a nice sight. I've got the best view of your cunt swallowing my cock, babe. You're so damn wet—soaking me to my balls."

His filthy words were a drug.

She wanted more of them.

And more of him.

"Do it again, Joe."

Liliana barely got her demand out before he was pounding into her. A hard, brutal rhythm that sent her resting back over the *barre*, making her hold on for dear life. But damn, it was good, too. So fucking good.

He fucked her fast—relentlessly.

He fucked her wild   breathlessly.

She couldn't think beyond the sounds of her own moans, the way his fingers felt digging into her skin hard enough to leave marks behind, and the noise their bodies made every time they met.

And Joe …

God, Joe.

Take my cock, Liliana.

Give me that pussy, girl.

And her personal favorite … *Don't you want my cum, ballerina?*

She was a shaking, breathless mess against the *barre* after her third orgasm. And it was only then that Joe finally pulled out of her body, and yanked her leg down. She felt the loss of him instantly, but the deep pulsing between her legs only made her sigh.

Joe put her on her knees.

The condom was gone, then.

"Get my cum, ballerina," he told her, "and don't waste a fucking drop."

Yes, please.

She sucked him off, and smiled at the sight of him losing control above her. So, maybe nothing was hotter than *that*.

Except the sight of him coming.

And the taste of him sliding down her throat.

Yeah, that was pretty good, too.

Taking a deep breath, and trying to regain her bearings, Liliana leaned back on her heels, and used her hands to hold onto the *barre* as she stared up at Joe. "About tomorrow—you did say we could do something Monday, right?"

Joe cleared his throat, but a huskiness still remained when he replied, "Depends on what it is, really."

Liliana tried not to take that personally.

It was a little hard when his cock was still semi-hard, and this close to her face. It was even more difficult because she could still taste his cum on her tongue.

"There's a charity event—I was hoping you'd come with me," she whispered.

Joe glanced down at her.

Liliana knew his answer before he even said it.

It still fucking *sucked*.

"I can't, Liliana."

Not, *I would, but* ...

Not even, *It's not my scene, sorry.*

No.

Just an, *I can't.*

It shouldn't have felt like a rejection, but it still kind of did. Mostly because she didn't know what in the hell the deal was with this man, or what he was trying to do with her. But she didn't like the way this left her feeling a little too used.

No woman wanted to feel *used*.

"So, is this all we're doing, then?" she asked him. "We fuck, and meet up at night, or whatever. Nothing else, though?"

Joe's brow knotted together. "I didn't say—"

No, she got it.

"Thanks for letting me know, Joe."

NINE

JOE FELT LIKE a jackass, and that was probably the worst thing about this whole fucking night next to the scowl Liliana couldn't seem to drop. He had no doubt that he was the cause of her bad mood, and he wished he could fix it.

Shit.

More than anything, he wished he could fix it.

Even as he moved around the women dressed in ballgowns, and the men in their three-piece suits at the charity event, he knew this kind of thing wouldn't have been his scene to begin with. *But* ... Joe would have come for Liliana, and put a fucking smile on because he was there with her, and nothing else.

Except he couldn't do that at all.

This event was quite public. Media outside, and the whole fucking shebang. Being pictured and seen with Liliana would have defeated the whole purpose of staying under the radar in New York. And it most definitely would have defeated the purpose of being her bodyguard of sorts that no one was supposed to know about.

Problem was, Joe couldn't even explain all of *that* to Liliana. He gave his word that he wouldn't tell her—he was nothing if not a man of his word.

To everyone else but her, apparently.

Damn.

His thoughts were something else tonight. Punishing and cruel. They were giving him all kinds of hell for being such a fuck up, and frankly, he deserved it.

Slipping in behind a group of too-loud guests at the event, Joe found Liliana with her mother and father just a few steps away. Cella—one of Liliana's younger sisters—joined them soon after, too.

Joe was in just the right spot—slightly hidden by the group of people, and half in the shadows the cascades of lights created against the backdrop of silk draperies hanging from the walls and ceilings. He wasn't a huge fan of the way the organizers had decorated the place, but what did it matter about how he felt?

If anything, the way it was set up gave him ample room to move, and yet, stay out of sight at the same time. He knew—at the very least—Lucian had to know Joe was there, if only because the man was the entire reason why Joe knew about the event, and had the ticket to get in the door.

Although, Joe entered the less conspicuous way through the back entrance, and had his ticket snipped there.

The clang of silver against crystal echoed through the speakers strategically placed in the venue, and brought the attention of the very rich guests to the front of the ballroom. A woman standing on the raised platform at the front—where the band had been playing for a good majority of the night—set her glass aside so she had a better grip on the microphone in her hand while she spoke.

Joe wondered why she had to clink her fucking glass into the microphone instead of just speaking into it to begin with.

Who knew why people did what they did. Certainly not him, anyway. *What was this charity event for again?*

Women's shelters, and domestic violence awareness, he thought. Joe couldn't be sure, but he was pretty sure that's what all these people had gathered for. His part there wasn't really to do anything regarding the event, but just keep an eye on Liliana from afar—especially considering Lucian could only get a couple of men inside the place for the night.

Lucky Joe got one of the short sticks on the draw, apparently.

Here he was.

Joe's gaze drifted to Liliana as the woman at the front began to speak. He could have been *over there* ... with her. She probably wouldn't be feeling like a discarded piece of trash—yeah, he saw that look of shame and embarrassment she tried to hide the night before. And she certainly wouldn't be wearing a semi-permanent scowl, either.

"The silent auction in the connecting room will be open in five minutes!"

Shit.

Less people would be around for Joe to use to blend in and hide himself as the guests moved between the ballroom, and the next room for the auction. He didn't want to risk blowing his cover to Liliana. He didn't think she would appreciate seeing him there—even if he could excuse it with a lie—after refusing to come *with her*.

The universe was having a good laugh at his expense.

Or ... God.

One of the two.

The quiet conversation happening just a few feet away drew in Joe's attention for a moment. He had a couple of minutes before he had to find another way to make himself scarce, anyway, so he listened while he could.

Punishing himself more, clearly.

"Why are you in such a shitty mood tonight?" he heard Cella ask.

"Leave her be," the Marcello wife replied.

Jordyn, Joe knew. The woman's name was Jordyn. Lucian's wife, and Liliana's mother. Although, Joe had never gotten a proper face to face with the woman, or even had a conversation with her. It didn't matter—he could easily see where Liliana took the majority of her features from, the shape of her eyes, to the high cheekbones, and pretty bow-shaped lips. Those eyes were all her father, though.

"Oh, wait—is this about that guy?" Cella asked.

Joe stiffened.

So did Lucian.

"What guy?" Lucian asked.

Liliana gave her sister a look that silently screamed for her to shut up. Cella only shrugged. "My bad."

"What *guy*?" Lucian asked again.

"Joe Rossi," Liliana muttered, and then sharply to her sister, "And *no*, it's not about him, thank you very much."

"Oh-*kay*." Cella's brow lifted high. "Considering your tone right then, yes, it absolutely is."

Liliana sighed loudly.

Lucian was still staring at his daughter. "Care to tell me what's going on between you and Joe?"

"Not particularly, and nothing, now."

"What?"

"Lucian," Jordyn said, tugging on the arm of his jacket, "let's move into the auction room. They're opening the doors."

Joe could plainly see the man was not quite finished with his discussion, but his wife had spoken. Clearly, when the wife spoke, the man moved. Much like the men in Joe's family, too. It was almost comical how no matter where he went, that same thing never changed between husbands and wives.

He glanced at Liliana again …

She was pissed.

Sad.

Uncomfortable.

This was supposed to be a fun night for her, he imagined, and his refusal had ruined her mood and the whole thing.

So, yeah. Maybe Joe understood why when a man cared a great deal about a woman, he simply gave her whatever she wanted to always keep her pleased, smiling, and happy. He would do just about anything to make Liliana happy right then, but he couldn't.

Duty called.

People were moving.

Joe had to move, too.

Shit, where did she go?

Joe had moved toward the front of the venue when he heard Liliana mention she was leaving the event early, but here it was ten minutes later, and the girl *still* hadn't passed him by to exit the building.

Fucking hell.

He had no real reason to be concerned—Liliana might have gotten mixed up in a conversation with someone she knew, or maybe her sister or parents convinced her to stay for a little while longer. It wasn't necessarily a reason for him to be worried like he was.

Still, he did worry.

A lot.

Something just didn't sit right with him, and Joe wasn't the kind of man who ignored when his instincts started screaming at him. Men who had a death wish ignored when something felt off because that's all it did for them—brought *death*.

Moving back through the crowd, Joe quickly scanned the people. He searched for the one dress in the crowd—finding Liliana's wine-red gown would be easier, considering no one else had worn that color. Or at least, not that he had seen.

And then … *shit.*

There she was.

Tucked into the corner of the room with a man Joe didn't recognize. The two stood a little too close for his liking. Maybe only a foot apart. The man was smirking, and not in a very kind way. Although, when was smirking *ever* kind?

It didn't matter.

Joe could tell by the tension in Liliana's shoulders, and the way her fists were balled at her sides that she wasn't comfortable with the man—whoever in the hell he was. Moving closer, at least enough to hear their conversation, Joe was careful about not drawing their attention to him.

"What do you *want?*" Liliana asked.

"Don't be like that, Lilibet."

Joe stiffened on the spot.

She *hated* that name.

Rich had called her that name, too.

Before Liliana could even respond, the man went on to say, "Rich misses you, that's all. He knew I was going to be here tonight, and thought I could pass along a message."

"Or did he *send* you, Trevor?" Liliana asked, venom coating her every word. "This isn't exactly your scene, is it? You don't have deep enough pockets to be on the guest list."

"Ouch," Trevor murmured, "shoot me right in the heart."

"I might be more polite, except I'm not stupid. I know why you came."

"He'd like to see you."

"Nope," Liliana said.

Joe didn't miss the clenching of her jaw when she said that, or the way she swallowed hard, too. All signs of fear, even through her anger.

"You could—at the very least—see him for dinner, or something," Trevor offered.

"Okay, that's enough." Liliana picked up the skirt of her dress, and turned to walk away from the man. "The least I could have done for him, Trevor, I did. It's Rich who can't say the same for me. Considering what he did—"

Before Liliana could even walk away, Trevor grabbed her by the back of her arm. A hard enough grip that even from ten feet away, Joe could plainly see the way the man's fingers dug into her arm hard enough to redden her skin.

Joe's anger burned hotter.

His rage spilled over.

For a second, he forgot what his purpose was being here at this event. He forgot that he wasn't supposed to be noticed, or draw attention to himself.

He forgot … because the man put his hands on Liliana. Trevor *touched* her, and Joe blew his fucking top.

It certainly didn't help to soothe Joe's rage when Trevor yanked Liliana back, and caused her to stumble over her dress. It was her quiet cry of surprise that sent Joe ramming forward through the crowd.

It was amazing to him how easily—considering his size—that he could blend into a crowd. And then just as fast, how his size could fucking *part it*, too.

Liliana saw Joe coming first.

Widened eyes.

Confusion.

Concern.

All that stared back at him, but he wasn't really paying attention. His gaze was laser focused on the foolish fucker with his fingers still wrapped too tightly around Liliana's arm. He had exactly one-point-two seconds to let her go before Joe *made* him do it.

Trevor saw Joe, then, too. He didn't recognize him if the expression on his face was any indication. Joe was going to consider that a win for the whole staying-under-the-radar thing.

That one-point-two seconds was up.

Joe's fist reared back, and then slammed into the man's face. All at once, several things happened. Trevor bled from the busted mouth he now sported—he'd be lucky if Joe hadn't broken out his front teeth from the force of the punch—and Liliana fell from the man's hold as he dropped to the ground to clutch his broken face.

"Fucking stay down there like the dog you are," Joe spat at the man.

"Joe?"

He was still considering hitting the man again. All it took was looking at the idiot on the ground, and Joe's rage swelled all over again.

"Joe," Liliana said, forcefully the second time.

Joe's attention went back to her, and everyone else.

Shit.

He'd drawn attention. Gazes were on them. Large men in three-piece black suits with comms in their ears were coming his way.

So, maybe he didn't think this through.

"Why are you here?" Liliana asked.

Joe gave her a look, and then scanned the crowd.

He didn't have an answer.

Not a good one.

"Are you *following* me?" she demanded.

Joe's gaze darted back to hers. "You won't like the answer to that one, Liliana."

Disbelief, and disgust colored up her pretty features. He hated seeing that expression on her face, and hated even more that it was directed at *him*.

"What do you want, Joe?"

He pointed down at the man still on the floor. "What does *he* want, Liliana?"

Joe didn't get the chance to pull an answer out of her. Lucian slipped through the semi-circle of the gathering crowd, and his gaze met Joe's.

"Get out the back, and don't be photographed," Lucian demanded. "Be at the mansion—this will be handled."

Joe knew better than to argue.

Liliana still looked like she hated him.

Great.

Liliana didn't even see Joe standing beside the window when she was directed into the sitting room of the Marcello mansion. He kept his back to the wall, and his gaze on her as she moved to one of the plush leather couches, and fell into it.

"Are you still pissed at me?" he asked.

Liliana jumped, and her eyes widened when she found where he was standing. "Do you just … always do that?"

Joe's brow furrowed. "Do what?"

"Hide like that. Sneak up on people. Scare the hell out of them, Joe."

Joe didn't get the chance to answer, as Lucian strolled into the room and spoke for him. No one followed behind the man.

"That's kind of the point of Joe," Lucian said to his daughter. "He's called the Shadow for a reason—people aren't typically meant to see him."

Confusion lit up Liliana's features as she glanced between her father, and Joe. And then, as though it all came onto her at once, and understanding dawned in her eyes. She settled on looking at Joe when she spoke, and not her father.

"You're working for him," she said. "That's what you meant when you said I wouldn't like your answer about if you were following me or not."

Joe swallowed thickly. "Does it really matter?"

He could tell she was hurt. For what reason, he didn't quite know yet. It didn't really matter, either. Her hurt was enough to pain him, too.

"It matters," Liliana said. "Is that what it is, Daddy? He's working for you, or Uncle Dante?"

Lucian sighed. "Joe has been hired to … look after you, we'll say. We didn't want him letting you know that was the job. You have a lot on your plate, and I didn't want to worry you with anything that wasn't important details."

"Important *details?*"

Liliana scoffed.

Hard.

Lucian cleared his throat, and glanced at Joe before saying, "No, I didn't feel it was important. Just like you didn't know who I had acting as your enforcer *before* Joe. It's no different."

"It is different." Liliana's attention cut back to Joe, and her burning gaze felt like a sharp knife slicing through his skin. "And he knows exactly why it's different."

Shit, yeah.

He did know.

He knew exactly why she was hurting when she put it like that, and he was more than willing to take the blame for it, too.

Joe had gotten close to Liliana on a personal level, and that left her exposed. Maybe had he been honest with her upfront, she wouldn't be feeling like she did right now. Betrayed, and so confused.

He got it.

How could he fix it?

"I should have told you," Joe said.

"You think?" she asked.

"He was ordered not to," Lucian added.

His words made no difference.

Joe knew it before he even said it.

Interestingly enough, Joe didn't miss how Lucian offered information about how Liliana was the job, and not the other pieces of information that went along with it. Like how Joe had been first hired to kill two men—one of which was the father to a man Joe suspected she had been involved with in some way.

No, Lucian didn't mention that at all.

Liliana glanced back at Joe, and he swore he saw a line of water filling her hazel eyes. "So, that's what it is, then."

"I don't follow," Joe said.

"A job. I was a *job*."

Joe blinked. "Liliana—"

"No," she said, standing from the couch. "I get it, Joe."

There was a lot of things he wanted to say in that moment. A hell of a lot he thought Liliana needed her eyes opened to.

Like the fact that when something happened she didn't like, the first thing the girl did was get up, and run. For some, that might be seen as cowardly, but Joe saw it as a way Liliana protected herself from getting hurt.

He understood.

But it hurt him, too.

And she should know *that*.

And yet, the woman's father standing in the room kept Joe from blurting out some kind of personal shit that he didn't want people knowing. He especially didn't want other men in this life to know he'd found a weakness in himself.

Or rather, this woman brought out Joe's weakness.

Maybe that was Joe's flaw—Liliana ran, and Joe was too cold. She had her way of protecting herself, and he had his way of safeguarding his secrets, too. That didn't mean it was good, but humans were predictable that way.

"Yeah," Liliana said, giving Joe another look. "I fucking get it, Joe."

He knew what she was seeing; his blank expression, and stiff posture. A cold aura, and a dispassionate delivery to his words. It was the mask he kept firmly *on* when other men like him were present, and he was not going to drop it right then, either. She didn't know these things, but he had never offered an explanation, either.

Whose fault was it, then?

Liliana nodded. "I'm just a job."

"Liliana—"

"Call me a driver," she interrupted her father. "I need to go home."

"You could stay, and—"

"I'm going *home.*"

Lucian didn't bother to argue with her further, and instead, waved his hand at the door for her to leave. Liliana didn't even give Joe a look over her shoulder as she left in her floor-length, beautiful wine-red gown.

He didn't blame her, either.

Once her footsteps couldn't be heard anymore, Lucian turned to Joe again. He didn't want to talk—really wasn't in the mood for another lecture about how he hadn't followed through on his hits, yet, and the rest of that bullshit.

Joe was too busy being stuck in his own head, and trying to figure out how to *fix* what he fucked up on. He'd never had to fix something with a woman before, and he didn't like how much it hurt in his chest to know that he'd caused Liliana some kind of pain.

Or that he made her feel anything less than ... adored.

Because he did adore her.

"I know," Joe murmured, pushing away from the wall, "get the fucking job done. Save your breath, Lucian."

"Actually," Lucian said, clearing his throat, "I was going to say that should you finish this job out, I wouldn't mind giving you a second chance to correct whatever happened here tonight, Joe."

"I'm sorry?"

"My daughter, and all my children. I tend to ... stay out of their personal business. Something my wife and I chose a long time ago where our children were concerned. I didn't realize there was something going on between you and Liliana, and I realize I may have just made your situation worse. I apologize."

Huh.

"She's a good girl," Lucian added quieter. "And the thing about her is—well, she doesn't care who you are, or the things you do, Joe. If she loves you, then she overlooks the rest. I'm sure you know being in this business ... a woman like that is terribly hard to find, and the men who do have a woman like that are the luckiest of us all."

"You're right about one thing."

"Which one?"

"It was hard to find her; twenty-one years, actually."

Joe wasn't sure he would say *love*—not yet, anyway. He would say that if he had one person in the world, he thought it might be Liliana. There was something about her that kept drawing him in. She was spectacular; captivating. And she had done exactly that to him with nothing more than a sly smile, and a few quick words in a darkened hallway.

Captivated him.

And so maybe, he wanted to see where this might go with her. He wanted to have that chance, but the circumstances just weren't lining up for either of them at the end of the day. Things kept getting in the way.

Lucian nodded. "You *could* drop your walls down a bit with us—my family, I mean. Let her see something from you other than ... this person I'm looking at. We're not out to hurt you, Joe."

"Right again," Joe returned, heading for the entryway of the room, "I *could*, Lucian, but I probably won't. I am who I am."

Joe left the rest of his words unsaid.

He figured he didn't have to say them.

They can take me as I am, or not.

Liliana included.

"*Fuck*," Joe groaned.

He wasn't a drinker, but sometimes, a man needed a few shots—or a bottle, who was counting?—of whiskey to be able to close his damn eyes, and go to sleep. After the night before, he figured drinking was the very least he could do to feel better.

He was seriously regretting that choice now that he was trying to peel his eyes open, and the sunlight filtering in through the windows all but burned his eyelids.

Jesus Christ.

And what was the *noise?*

It made the throbbing in his temples pick up speed. Joe pressed his palms to his eyes to try and relieve some of the pressure, but it didn't work.

His phone.

Yeah, that's what the sound was.

His goddamn phone.

Blindly, Joe swung his arm out and felt for his phone on the nightstand. It kept ringing, vibrating, and beating like a damn drum inside his head. Finally, he found the stupid thing, and turned it on before dragging it to his head.

"What?" he snapped.

"Who shit in your Cornflakes?"

Oh, God.

Why did Cory have to be this cheerful in the morning?

It never ended.

"What do you *want?*"

"You don't sound good, man," Cory said.

"Cory, I don't even have a nerve left for you to work, all right. So, whatever it is, get it the fuck out."

"I mean, if you want to be a prick about it, then maybe I got nothing for you. If you want to perk your attitude up, and act pleasant like our mother taught you to, then maybe I have some information about your Rich Earl. Which do you want to choose, Joe?"

Damn.

"I'd prefer the bad mood," Joe grumbled.

"And yet ..."

"What do you have, Cory?"

He forced his tone to be pleasant.

It was the best Joe could do.

"Well, nothing concrete."

"Then why are you calling me? Because I am pretty sure you told me it was going to take a week or more to get any kind of useable info, so if you're just calling to fuck me around, then don't bother. I have better things to do, man."

Yeah.

There went his pleasantness.

"First, I *figured* it was going to take that long. Second, cut the attitude. New York is a twelve hour drive, but I know a guy with a jet on standby, so I can be there even quicker to beat your ass."

"You could try."

"Knock it off, Joe." Cory sighed. "It's not concrete because it's not on actual, official paper. But it's rumors, and we all know what people say about those."

"It all starts somewhere, and usually with a grain of truth."

"Exactly. But, uh ..."

"Spit it out."

"The rumors—the stories, or whatever—they're concerning."

Okay, now he had Joe's attention. Despite the way his head ached even more, he sat up on the bed, and kicked the comforter off his legs.

"Talk to me," Joe mumbled.

"Seriously, were you drinking last night?"

"A little."

"A little doesn't make you sound like vomit is on the back of your tongue, Joe."

"Yeah, well, are we talking about the info you found, or my hangover?"

"I'd like to talk about both."

"Well," Joe replied, "I'm only offering my conversation skills on one thing today. Sorry to burst your bubble."

"You're seriously an asshole."

"And you don't get to pick family, brother. You're stuck with me—shitty luck for you, I guess."

"Fine—the info," Cory grumbled. "Liliana was definitely involved with Rich Earl, although I can't say it was for very long."

A hot ball grew in Joe's gut.

Jealousy, likely.

Fuck.

Not the right time.

"What makes you think it wasn't for very long?"

"He's the son of a senator, and she's the daughter of a high ranking made man. They both come from elite New York families, Joe."

Cory offered all this like whatever he wasn't saying should be obvious. It probably was, but Joe was just too tired and hungover to put it together.

"Stop fucking with me today," Joe warned.

"The *rags*, Joe. Socialite rags, and shit. Had they been together for any real length of time, or shown up to enough public events together, their faces would have been splashed all over that shit. You know how they are here in Chicago. It's even worse in New York."

"Ah, yeah."

"So, how long?"

"I wouldn't say more than a couple of months, but maybe a little more."

"Is this all you've found?"

"I wish," Cory muttered under his breath. "From the people I know and talked to, they said they heard some bad shit went down between Liliana and Rich one night when they were heading to a private party."

Joe blinked at the clock on the wall. "What kind of bad shit?"

"No one said for sure—nobody saw Liliana directly after, either. Cops *were* called, though, so a police report *had* to have been filed. Thing is, there's nothing."

Joe thought about the Chief of Police he was supposed to kill, and wondered if that was the reason why the man needed to be killed—had he done away with evidence?

"Are there *rumors* about what happened?" Joe dared to ask.

"A guy knows a guy in the Marcello organization. Low fuck, mind you, but still."

"Cory, spit it out."

His brother sighed again. "Said the guy beat the shit out of her in the back of a limo, Joe. He suggested more, but didn't know for sure, and wasn't willing to say considering who she is and all. From other people—kind of sounds like Rich was fucking obsessed with her. Saw her dance at a show or something, and that's how he met her. Anyway, this is what I've got."

"So, why do they want me to kill the father and the Chief of Police, and not the stupid fuck who hurt her?"

"Maybe they're a means to an end," Cory suggested.

Huh.

Joe hadn't considered that.

"And I mean, if that were Mon," Cory added, referring to their little sister, "and there were guys who helped to cover up what he did to her, you know we'd put every single one of them in the ground."

"Yeah."

To say the least.

"Thanks, man," Joe said.

"You got it."

After he had hung up with his brother, Joe made one more phone call. On the third ring, Lucian picked up.

"Lucian here."

"I'll put the first hit through tonight—the father, he's gone."

He didn't explain why, or anything about his choice. He didn't bother to question Lucian on the things he knew, either.

Joe didn't *want* to ask Lucian.

He had someone else to talk to.

She should tell him.

It was Liliana's story, not anyone else's.

Joe was regretting putting off these hits for so long, and being as difficult as he had. No doubt, Lucian had looked at this situation the same way Joe was now seeing it. It wasn't the Marcello's man's place to out his daughter's personal business, but especially not something traumatic.

It took Lucian a second to speak, and his tone came out as flat as Joe's when he said, "Good. I've been waiting for this to get started."

Yeah, Joe bet.

"Watch the news, Lucian. It'll look like an accident."

Unfortunately.

But if he was going to do these hits on high-profile men, Joe was going to do it *right*. And safe.

They deserved worse.

TEN

"WHAT ARE YOU doing right now?"

"Soaking my feet, drinking coffee, and watching the morning news," Liliana replied.

Cella laughed. "Multitasking."

"It's the only way I get anything done."

"You sound … better today."

Sure, to Cella. Her sister was only getting the sound of her voice on the phone call, though. She couldn't see that Liliana's eyes were dimmed because she hadn't been sleeping well the past couple of days, and she didn't know that her sister couldn't keep still. Fidgeting, and always needing to *do* something.

Anything but think about—

"So, are you going to tell me what happened with Joe at the charity event, and *after?*" Cella asked.

"Well, I wasn't."

"Um."

"And then you brought him up," Liliana grumbled.

Taking another sip of her coffee, Liliana kept an eye on the television. As usual, the anchors were first going through the highlights of the day before, and she wasn't interested in any of that. She went back to her sister instead.

"He's working for Dad—or Dante," Liliana corrected quickly. "I'm not really sure which one; hell, it could be both."

"Working for them *how?*"

"Watching me, I guess."

Cella made a noise under her breath. "Ouch."

"Yeah."

See, her fucking sister got it.

Why couldn't Joe get it?

All he needed to do was *tell her.* Liliana wasn't asking for a lot, but if his involvement in her life was work-related, then that would have been great to know before they jumped into bed together.

"Had he just told me before everything else," Liliana said, "I feel like maybe we could have gotten all of that out of the way first, and then it

114

wouldn't have been sprung on me. I wouldn't have to feel like that's the only reason he was around, you know?"

Cella cleared her throat. "I don't think that was the *only* reason he was coming around, Liliana."

"Oh, no, I'm sure the fact I was spreading my legs for him was another reason."

"*Damn*—wow, not what I meant, either."

Liliana rolled her eyes upward. "That's all it's been, Cella."

"Not really. You had *moments*."

"Don't say it like that."

"Like what?"

"Like they were some earth-shattering, ground-moving events in my life. They weren't."

"I didn't say it like *that*," Cella argued.

"Kind of did."

"You did have … something, though. Do you know how many females were sitting at the table at that first dinner? Quite a few—he only talked, and looked at you. And he *smiled* at you, too. Anyone else, and he might as well have been carved from ice."

"*After* he probably got the job to watch me, Cella."

"You assume—you don't know for sure."

True, but still …

"I'm not saying my anger isn't irrational," Liliana muttered.

"Good because you're acting like a child."

"I am *not*."

"And that right there *really* helps your case, Liliana."

She blew out a hard breath.

Cella let her silently stew for a while.

Liliana was grateful.

"Listen, just the day before I found this out, I asked him to that event, and he refused me with no explanation. You know *when* and *how* he refused me?"

"Uh … no?"

"I was naked, and on my knees, Cella."

Her sister made a low keening noise, and then said, "TMI."

"Point is—that's kind of hard to take, all right. What woman is going to take rejection from a guy in that kind of situation easily?"

"Well, what did you do after all of that?"

"Asked him to leave," Liliana said.

"And did he?"

"Yep."

Wise of him, too.

"Have you ever thought that maybe your experience with Rich Earl has ... screwed you up a little bit when it comes to guys?" Cella asked.

Liliana's brow dipped. "I don't—"

"You either don't trust men—*any* men, unless they're family—or I guess in Joe's case, you take any hint of something you might not like as a rejection against you personally. So you've got walls up high, and when something does come up, it feels bigger than it is because you've been prepping and waiting for it like it *had* to happen or something. Like it's fucking unavoidable."

Christ.

Why did her sister have to know her so well?

"Daddy did say that Joe had been told ... not to tell me," Liliana muttered. "And I am quite aware that I look for failure because it's easier to take when I'm expecting it, thank you. Don't need you to shrink my head— Daddy paid someone to do that after the whole Rich thing."

"For the record, the therapist came in when you were dealing with that mess, and not when you were anywhere near ready to date guys again, Liliana. That was not the topic of discussion at your sessions—I know, you told me."

"Yeah, well."

"I don't think making conversation with only you, paying attention to only you, calming you out of a panic attack, going to see your show, and fucking you was part of the job for Joe," Cella said dryly. "If anything, that's the kind of thing that would probably make him lose his job, and his life."

"True," Liliana said under her breath. "But—"

"You *know* you acted a little on emotions, and you could have given him the chance to explain better. Or something, Liliana."

Fine.

"You know, I've run off on him, kicked him out of my place, and whatever else; he's probably looking at me like I am some kind of crazy mess that he doesn't want to deal with."

"You're *not* crazy."

Ouch.

The bite in her sister's tone was enough to sting Liliana all the way through the phone. So, maybe with their brother being bipolar, and often getting teased growing up because they had to walk behind the path he left of destruction, chaos, and uncertainty, crazy was a slur in their house. A word people tossed around without care, and in some cases, used it as a way to harm.

Cella was particularly sensitive to it.

"I know I'm not crazy," Liliana said.

"Listen," her sister said after a long pause, "if I find a guy who looks at me the way Joe was looking at you the night you two met, then I would

116

consider myself lucky. Guys who look at girls that way are going to keep coming back, trust me."

"He wasn't looking at me like any—"

"Yes, he was, Liliana."

"No—"

"Yes."

"*Cella.*"

"I swear he was," her sister said firmly, not offering more room for argument. "You just don't look for that kind of thing in guys anymore, and if you do, it's secondary to everything else that you're looking for. Think about it."

She did.

Now, Liliana looked to see if a guy was a little too sweet, or if he got close to her too fast for her comfort. She tried to look for any signs of jealousy that might rear its ugly head, and she was careful to watch how a man treated others when he didn't think people were looking. She was always trying to find signs of manipulation—of her, or others—because that's where she fucked up the first time.

That's what almost killed her.

"You know," Liliana said quietly, "I never really looked for any of that with Joe, but I was still maybe … protecting me, too. I run; or I push someone away when things get uncomfortable. Except with Joe, uncomfortable only meant if I thought he was discarding me in some way."

"Maybe you knew you didn't need to look for it in Joe."

She had felt safe with him.

From that very first second.

"Yeah, I mean, maybe that's—"

Liliana's words cut off as a breaking news banner scrolled across the screen of the television, and interrupted the anchors discussing the awful downtown traffic, and an accident that had caused it. She only stopped to take notice because of the large mansion that was showcased from an aerial view as a helicopter flew overhead.

A mansion she recognized.

She'd visited it several times.

Before.

"Liliana?"

She heard her sister, but she couldn't answer.

Not yet.

The video spanned wider—it showed a circular driveway filled with emergency vehicles, a black limo, and luxury cars.

Liliana's throat tightened.

Her chest ached.

"A breaking story this morning," the redheaded anchor said, "we've just received news that Republican Senator George Earl was found dead from what investigators say they believe to be an accidental drowning in his pool. We will keep you updated as more information develops."

Liliana blinked.

Cella was still calling her name. "Hey, where did you go?"

"George is dead."

"What?"

"George Earl—Rich's father. He's dead. Accidental, they said."

Cella made a noise under her breath. "Good fucking riddance. The world won't miss that enabling piece of shit."

They said accidental. And yet, Liliana still wondered …

Her father had promised the man, after all. Lucian promised death, and he said no one would know the difference. No one would suspect a thing.

Was he keeping that promise?

She didn't know her father to break promises.

Yeah, they *said* accidental.

Liliana still felt cold.

"Well done today, Liliana," Gordo said.

Liliana stiffened at the sound of the director's voice coming from the door of the women's private rooms. It was where all the ladies changed, showered, and kept their belongings. It certainly wasn't a place for *men*.

Men had their own.

None of the other ladies getting dressed seemed to mind Gordo's presence, but Liliana was just a little too sensitive to shit like that. It didn't matter that Gordo had never once tried anything inappropriate on her, or someone else—as far as she knew.

It still put her on edge.

"Thanks," she tossed over her shoulder.

"You know I wasn't sure you were right to be the lead of *Swan Lake*, but you're proving me wrong."

Liliana wasn't sure if that was meant to be a backhanded compliment, or not. Her entire ballet career was muddied by the fact she hadn't gotten a position in a company until later in her life than most other dancers, and people often mistook that as her being incapable, or a lesser dancer.

Their mistake.

She didn't care to explain.

Tossing her bag over her shoulder, Liliana slammed her locker shut, and turned around to face Gordo. "I'm glad you feel like you've made the right choice."

I guess.

What else could she say?

"Of course." Gordo smiled, and tipped his head to the side. "Also, someone dropped off a little gift for you. You'll find it at the front desk."

"What gift?"

"You'll see—I'm sure you'll love it. All women do, it seems."

Liliana frowned. "Who dropped it off?"

Gordo only shrugged.

Knowing she wasn't going to get anything out of this man, Liliana simply passed him by. She answered the echoing goodbyes of the dancers with a wave of her hand over her shoulder. She was ready to get home, and relax.

Maybe, if she could convince herself to stop acting like a child, she could even call Joe. Apologize … or something.

It might have taken her a couple of days—and a difficult conversation or two with her sister—but she recognized that *perhaps* she had overreacted. Or at the very least, she owed Joe the chance to explain himself.

Even if she didn't treat Joe like every other guy since the whole Rich debacle, she was still letting negative things bleed into her perspective. She was going to try to do better with that whole thing.

Try being the keyword.

"Oh, Liliana," the girl behind the front desk said. "Come to get your beauties before you go?"

"Yeah, Gordo said someone dropped something off for me?"

Margie smiled widely, and waved at the huge bushel of white roses on the side of her desk. Liliana stared at the ostentatious bundle for a long while, and then reached out to stroke one of the silky petals between her fingertips.

Joe, maybe?

"Any card?" Liliana asked.

Margie shook her head. "Nope—the guy just dropped them off, and said they were to be delivered to you before you left for the day."

Likely Joe, then.

If he was watching her—*still* the one watching her—then she suspected he would have her schedule, and know she was at the studio.

"They're a little big for me to be carrying home."

Well, she would take a cab. Still, she didn't want to hold that huge bushel in her lap the whole way, either.

"I could have them sent over," Margie said, picking up on Liliana's dilemma.

"Would you?"

"They're too lovely to keep them here. Gordo hates flowers, anyway. He'll just complain about them until someone throws them away."

Figures.

"That would be a shame," Liliana said.

Margie smiled in that way of hers again. "Exactly. Go ahead, and I will get someone to have them delivered to your apartment."

"You're a godsend."

The woman behind the desk laughed. "Be sure to tell Gordo that the next time he's in one of his moods."

"You know I will."

Really, though, when was that man *not* in a mood?

The sight of Joe leaning against Liliana's door made her pause as she rounded the final steps. With his shoulder against the wall, he looked like every woman's wet dream in dark-wash jeans, a white T-shirt, and his leather jacket. He kept his head tilted down, and his gaze on the small pocket knife he twirled between his fingers.

Bad.

Good-looking.

Dangerous.

Yeah, *literally* every woman's wet dream.

What little resolve Liliana had left about her anger with him was quickly bleeding away the longer she stared at Joe.

How strange that was …

"Aren't you supposed to be *trailing* me?" she asked. "If that's your job, and all, to watch me."

Joe lifted his chin a fraction of an inch, and his gaze found Liliana at the top of the stairs down the hall. He didn't look the least bit surprised to find her standing there; it was almost as though he knew she was there the whole time.

Maybe he did.

Who was she to say?

"Not today," he said. "Maybe not tomorrow, either. I have … other things to handle right now."

Liliana's brow furrowed. "Well, who is watching me then?"

Joe shrugged. "I'm not given those details."

And the better question ...

Something she had been thinking about for a couple of days—ever since she saw the news broadcast, anyway.

"*Why* are they having people watch me? Does it have anything to do with the Earl family, considering I've been approached twice now by them—or someone close to them?"

Joe's face gave nothing away when he said, "I think you should ask your father those questions, Liliana. It's definitely not my place to give out their business. They wouldn't appreciate it, and I'm sure you understand when I say the last thing I need to do is piss off any of those kind of men."

Liliana wet her lips, and looked away. "Yeah, that's fair."

"Are you going to stay down there, or come closer?"

"I haven't decided yet."

"Still pissed at me, then."

Liliana took one step forward, and then another as she said, "Maybe I should have let you explain, Joe."

His lips pulled into a smirk, and he cocked one eyebrow high. "*Maybe?*"

She sighed. "You're going to make this hard on me, huh?"

"Not really."

"Not—"

She was close enough for him to grab, and it seemed like that's exactly what he wanted to do with her. In a blink, she found herself pulled into Joe's embrace, and his arms wrapped tightly around her shoulders. It was like she couldn't help herself but bury her face into his chest, and hug him back.

A part of her *wanted* it.

Another part *needed* it.

"Been driving me crazy for days," she heard him mumble.

"I don't want to be a *job*, Joe."

She felt his lips press to the top of her head. "Yeah, I got that."

"So, I guess there's not much for you to explain," she said.

Joe let out a heavy exhale. "Nothing that I really can—nothing more than you already know. I get why it might have messed with your head, though. I didn't really consider that, so my bad."

"That's a shitty apology."

He laughed. "That's because it wasn't an apology."

His hands slipped under her chin, and he tipped her head back. Through her lowered lashes, she stared at Joe as he stroked her cheeks with the pads of his thumbs. And then, he closed the bit of distance between them, and kissed her soft, sweet, and slow.

Usually, he owned her with his kiss. Fast, hard, and deep. A lot like the way he enjoyed fucking her, really.

Not this.

Soft strokes of his lips. A gentle dance with his tongue. His gaze locked with hers.

Liliana smiled when Joe pulled away. "Was *that* the apology?"

"No."

"*Joe.*"

He grinned. "This is the apology."

"Get on with it, then."

"I'm sorry if I made you feel like anything less than the amazing, interesting, and perfect woman you are, Liliana," he murmured, stroking her cheeks again with his thumbs. "You've got this strange way about you—like a siren, or something. Captivating me, and pulling me in for more. That was all before I had to watch you, and I just considered the rest a bonus. I should have let you know, though. You may be part of the job I have to do, but when it's just me and you … it's just me and *you.*"

"And what does that mean—me and you?"

Joe tipped his head back and forth, considering. "I'm still trying to figure it out."

"But you want to."

"Hmm?"

"Figure it out."

Joe smirked. "With you, yeah."

Liliana pursed her lips, and gave him a look. "All right. Apology accepted."

"I thought so."

Cocky asshole.

She kind of liked it, though.

"Before I forget," Joe said, digging into the pocket of his jacket. He pulled out a small white card, and offered it to Liliana. "This was taped on your door when I got here—someone delivered you flowers, huh?"

Liliana blinked as she took the card from him.

Already, her fingers trembled.

Worse, her heart thundered.

Frighteningly, she couldn't take in enough air.

If not him—she'd thought it'd been Joe who sent the flowers—then *who?*

Liliana flipped the card over.

Anxiety swelled.

She saw familiar handwriting.

Pain exploded in her chest.

No name was attached—it didn't need to be.

CAPTIVATED

Her vision blurred.

"Liliana, hey," she heard Joe say.

The panic attack came on hard, swift, and unforgiving.

Like it always did whenever Rich Earl took her off guard.

The fucking bastard.

Why wouldn't he leave her alone?

ELEVEN

SHIT.

Liliana was losing it.

Panicking—again.

Gasping breaths, heaving shoulders, and fists clenched so tightly he thought her manicured nails might be cutting her skin. She had to be seeing tunnel vision because she sure as hell wasn't seeing him even when he stepped in front of her, and called her name. Even tipping her head back, and speaking softly didn't help.

Yeah, *shit* was right.

Carefully, Joe pulled the little card from Liliana's clenched hand. He didn't need to look over the words—he'd already read them when he yanked it off her door. At the time, he'd been more focused on the fact *someone else*, who wasn't him, had been sending her flowers. He felt a little fucking stupid for that, now.

"Hey, hey," Joe said, keeping one arm tight around Liliana's trembling shoulders. "Remember that thing we did on the street?"

Subtly, he saw her nod.

"You try that, and I'm going to grab your keys."

Another nod.

She wasn't speaking, but at least she was giving him something. Nods were better than fucking nothing. And he really needed to get her breathing under control, or she was going to black out from the way she was huffing.

Tears streaked lines down her face, and Joe took a quick second to wipe them away. It didn't do very much good, though. Not a blink later, and more of her tears fell. A never-ending stream, really.

Jesus.

"Touch, see, feel, smell, and hear," he told her. "Say them out loud, or in your head, but focus on that for a minute."

Joe slipped the messenger bag Liliana had been carrying up from the floor, and dug through it. It was just his luck that he had to search through to the bottom of the bag to find the goddamn keys.

Once he had them, though, all was good. He unlocked her apartment, and practically kicked the door open as he turned the knob. Her dark studio apartment smelled like that cinnamon and cupcake candle he'd seen on her table once.

With the door at least opened, Liliana calmed a bit.

Not a lot.

Just a little.

Good enough for me.

Comforting, familiar places did wonders to sometimes help soothe anxiety. It could shorten the time of a panic attack for some people, too. He figured that was probably Liliana's biggest thing—something, or some*one* familiar could help pull her out.

"Let's go," Joe said.

He didn't wait for Liliana to respond, or move. No, he just slung an arm around her waist, pulled her into his side, and easily hoisted her up over his shoulder. He grabbed the other shit on the floor, and picked it up, too.

Inside the apartment, Joe kicked the door shut behind him, and looked for the closest—and most comfortable—place for Liliana. The couch near the windows seemed like a good place. Even when he moved to set her down on the cushions, her small hands grasped firmly onto him, and her fingers all but dug into his shoulders.

Nope.

He could practically hear her screaming the word inside her head.

Nope.

She was not letting him go.

"All right," Joe muttered.

He turned, and sat his ass down on the couch. The very second he was settled, Liliana slid down into his lap, and buried her face in her hands. No matter what he tried to do, or how he spoke, or what he said, she just wouldn't look at him.

It kind of killed him.

Joe figured it wasn't about him right then, though. And he wasn't about to make it into something for him, either.

Still, Liliana seemed comfortable to stay right where she was on top of Joe. That didn't bother him. Hell, she didn't weigh more than one-twenty soaking wet.

Tall, and willowy.

Thin, and delicate.

In moments like those, he thought *fragile*, too.

Yet, he knew better. He knew this woman only looked fragile, and sometimes, the cracks in her beautiful porcelain mind started to show. Everybody had cracks, though. Some just weren't as visible as others.

"Why won't he leave me *alone*?"

Her low, keening words made Joe's fucking heart clench. And his rage soared at the same time. It was a strange mixture of emotions—sadness and fury. The two fed off one another at the same time they warred against each other.

Joe didn't have any reason to believe she was talking about Rich Earl—as she didn't offer a name, or details to say it one way or the other—but he just *knew*. Somehow, he knew given everything that was going on. Two and two always made four, after all.

"Who—Rich?" he asked.

He figured it was better to let her tell him, than to blurt out what he knew. Who fucking knew—maybe getting her to talk about it would help her a little bit?

"I thought he was gone," Liliana mumbled into her hands. "He hasn't bothered me for almost a year, and now ..."

Joe cleared his throat, and pulled his girl into his embrace again. Liliana said nothing, and didn't fight him, either. She just settled into his hold and chest like that was the safest place for her to be, and she didn't want to go anywhere else.

Frankly, he didn't want to let her go.

Here, she *was* safe.

Here, she didn't hurt.

Here, he could take care of her.

"Now he's showing up a lot more, huh?" Joe asked.

Liliana said nothing.

Joe decided he kind of needed her to talk, or that festering rage of his was going to boil over. The last thing he needed right now was to go off half-cocked, and make a fucking show of himself. Or worse, a mess he couldn't clean up.

Pulling her hands away from her face, Joe said, "Look at me, sweetheart."

Nope.

Nothing.

"Liliana," he murmured, nuzzling his face against her temple. His lips grazed her hairline, and then over her cheekbone. He was sure he felt her smile just a little, but he couldn't be sure. "Talk to me—*look* at me."

Finally, she did.

Tipping her head back, he found wide, watery eyes staring back at him. And fear, too. He saw her fear.

"I had someone ask me once," she whispered, "how I fell for a guy that ended up almost killing me."

Joe frowned. "Why would someone ask that?"

Liliana shook her head. "I don't know—I don't think they knew, either."

"Humans do suck that way."

Her tiny smile made him grin, but it quickly faded away.

"It's like people expect you to know who the monster is even though they blend in really well, and they don't show you the bad until it's too late. I didn't fall for a guy who beat the hell out of me—I fell for the guy who approached me after one of my shows, and couldn't keep his eyes off me. I was drawn to the man who took me to one amazing thing after the other, and made me laugh."

Liliana glanced down at her clenched hands. "And then one night, he got jealous over a friend of mine—another dancer at the company. I went to dinner with him after rehearsal. We were just friends, and it was *dinner*."

Joe cleared his throat. "And what happened after that?"

She shrugged. "I didn't even know how he *knew* I was out with the guy. It was the first time I learned he was having me tailed."

Jesus.

"First red flag," Joe said quietly.

"It was waving high and I missed it," Liliana replied.

"That's hindsight, babe. Everybody misses shit, and can find it a hell of a lot easier when we look at it from a different perspective."

"Maybe."

"No maybes about it, Liliana."

Her sigh came out shaky, and unsure. "Things moved really fast—I dated him for almost three and a half months, but it just went *fast*. Intense, too. The jealousy thing got worse, and one night he ripped a dress I was wearing because I wouldn't change before we went to a gala."

Joe scowled, but Liliana didn't see it. She was still too busy staring at her hands. He wished she would at least look at him when she talked, but he wasn't going to push anything.

Not yet, anyway.

"Maybe it was because everything had gone so fast, or maybe it was the way he made sure to take up all of my time and attention, but I'd stopped coming around my family and stuff. So, I didn't really have someone seeing these things going on. I didn't have someone to look at me, and say it wasn't right … it's not their fault, either. They didn't *know*."

Joe pulled her closer to him again, and kissed the top of her head. "Not your fault, either."

He said that because he could hear the guilt. He could hear the way she placed blame on her own shoulders, and did it without even thinking about it.

That killed him, too.

"And then one night we were, uh … going to a party for something." Liliana barked out a bitter laugh, adding, "I can't even remember what it was for. I don't know if that's from the concussion, or because I blocked out things. Anyway, we had gone to dinner before that, and the waiter was a little too nice to me, I guess."

"So, Rich was already pissed off."

Liliana nodded, saying, "So, when I started getting texts from my cousin, Andino, that only made it worse. I told him it was family—I was *trying* to calm him down, but it just spiraled out of control."

Joe grunted.

It was the best he could do because in that moment, anything else was going to send him flying over the very sharp edge where he balanced. His control was tipping one way, and his rage was following right behind it.

How fucking *easy* it would be to end that man.

How *simple* ...

And fast.

Shit, Joe could be back by morning. It would only take a couple of phone calls to get the man's whereabouts—Joe didn't even give a shit if the hit was clean, or not.

Really, Rich didn't deserve easy *or* clean.

"He just started hitting me," Liliana mumbled. "And not like a slap, but closed fist punches. One after the other. I didn't even understand what was happening. I said *sorry*, Joe. I told him *I* was the one who was sorry."

Those tears came again.

Joe just held her close again.

What else could he do?

"I'm sorry," he told her.

Liliana shook her head. "Anything I said pissed him off even more, anyway. He just hit me harder. And I couldn't even hear what he was saying at that point—everything sounded like I was under water, and I couldn't see. The limo driver had pulled over, but I don't think Rich even noticed. He was trying to get on top of me—I don't really know what he planned to do, but he'd ripped my dress. It all went black for a minute."

"You remember what happened afterward?"

"Not really. I was told the driver opened the back door, and I got out. I don't really remember how I got to the hospital ... just my dad coming in, and he was crying. That's the only time I ever saw my dad cry. My sister didn't recognize me. The bruising and swelling was that bad—he'd fractured my orbital socket in two places."

Liliana's hand came up to touch her eyebrow, and her fingers drifted along the line. "You can't see it because the plastic surgeon is one of the best in the country, but there's a scar that runs through my eyebrow. I have a metal plate here now."

Now that'd she started talking, she didn't seem to want to stop. Joe didn't want her to keep hurting, though. And it was so fucking clear that she was hurting.

"You don't have to—"

Liliana shook her head. "A lot of stuff happened afterward. His father's a senator, and he's trying to get into politics, too. All of the charges that were filed disappeared. It was swept away—reporters were paid off, and stories never even got the chance to *run*. I didn't even get to talk to the detective who came to the hospital that night after that. The next time I went in, the Chief of Police was the one there. Martin Abraham, or something. He interrogated *me*. He made it feel like I was the abuser, and not the victim."

Joe now understood why that name was on his list.

"I found out after from my dad—or because I overhead him talking with my uncle, Dante—that the Chief of Police was who the Earl family had been using as protection. I guess. He was helping clean shit up, and sweeping it all away. He was threatening my dad, too."

Joe's brow lifted. "*Your* father? Lucian Marcello."

Liliana nodded.

"What kind of balls—"

"It doesn't take very much for a *mafioso* to get arrested in this city, and the charges almost always stick when it's something petty. I was scared they were going to take my dad away, so I asked him to stop trying to fight them. It was okay, I told him, because Rich was gone, and he was going to leave me alone."

"So, he did stop," Joe murmured.

Liliana shrugged. "Yeah. I moved out of my other place and into here. I saw a therapist for a little while. I got back to dancing once my face was healed, and the doctor said it was good. I just ... wanted to get back to my life. I didn't tell people. We kept it quiet. I didn't want everyone to look at me and be like, oh, there's the girl whose boyfriend beat the hell out of her."

"Liliana—"

"Please don't see me like that, Joe."

He stilled.

"What?"

She glanced up at him—all water gone from her eyes, and only a firm resolve staring back. "I know I'm kind of a flight risk, and I run when something seems like it's going to hurt me. I'm sorry I'm not perfect, but please don't see me as that victim. I don't want to be her."

Didn't she know?

Didn't she fucking *know*?

Joe grabbed Liliana's face in his hands, and drew her close enough for him to press three quick kisses one right after the other to her lips. "You're just Liliana to me, *Tesoro*. You're always going to be *my* Liliana."

She nodded with a shaky exhale.

Joe smiled. "It's going to be fine—we'll figure this out. Whatever stupid shit the guy is trying to play, it's not going to work."

He got it now, too.

Got why they called him in.

Why they waited.

Why they didn't *tell* him.

Frankly, Joe was stunned the Marcellos had tried to handle this situation on the up and up, anyway. Shit like this couldn't be handled on the level—on the right side of the law, in a goddamn courtroom.

Or maybe, they had done that for Liliana.

It didn't matter.

Now, they were going to handle it like it should have been from the start.

On the fucking streets.

In the shadows.

Liliana peered up at Joe from her bubble bath, and gave him a small smile. "You don't have to stay, Joe. I'm sure you have better things to do tonight than take care of me."

He scoffed, and leaned down to rest his arms along the edge of the tub. "No, actually. There's no other place I would rather be than right here with you."

"So, you *didn't* have plans?"

"Just to come here, apologize for being an asshole, maybe grovel a little bit if I needed to, and then I was hoping you'd either let me in, or let me take you to dinner. I figure I got what I wanted in the end."

Liliana didn't even try to hide her grin. "Mmhmm."

"That was the plan. Now, do you want music, or something? A book?"

She shook her head.

"Nothing?" he asked again, raising a brow.

"You, maybe."

Joe flashed his smile. "You've got me—I'm right here."

"Not *in here*, though."

Ah.

"I could do that," he said.

Liliana's teeth abused her bottom lip in the sexiest way. "You should probably do that, then. *Now.*"

"Yes, ma'am."

Her laughter colored up the bathroom as Joe stood, and quickly discarded what remained of his clothes. It never failed to amaze him how whenever he took off his clothes, Liliana couldn't seem to drag her gaze away from him. Like she was seeing him for the first time all over again.

Maybe he liked it.

A lot.

"Why the sleeve?" she asked, reaching up to stroke bubble-covered fingers over the tattoos on his arm. "And only a few on the other side—the heart is my favorite."

Joe glanced at the black outline of a simple heart on the inside of his left elbow. "I went and had my first tattoo done with my brother when I was seventeen, and he was sixteen." He pointed at the eagle on the top of his left shoulder. "That one, actually. Cory has a slightly different version. Our mom kind of had a fit—too young, she said. Dad just shrugged it off like he does. And that was how it started for me, I guess. One tattoo led to another, and then another."

"People do say it's addicting."

He shrugged. "I just don't put them in visible locations. No need to be caught on camera with something recognizable, you know what I mean?"

Liliana said nothing; Joe figured she didn't have to.

Stepping over the edge of the large bath, Joe sunk into the other side of the water. Across from him, Liliana lowered deep enough into the bubbles that only her head was sticking out. The water was so hot, steam had already fogged up the mirror. She had so many bubbles that with him inside the tub, they were starting to spill over. The heady scent of strawberries and cream clung in the air.

"I guess that's what my father meant, huh?"

Joe glanced over at her. "Pardon?"

"When people call you in, they don't want you to be seen. That's what you do, isn't it? A job where no one can see you."

"Yeah, babe, that's what I do."

Liliana was quiet for a long while.

Joe couldn't help but ask, "Does that bother you? You did say you couldn't see the monster coming before—I'm just another breed."

"Not even close to the same, Joe."

"How do you figure that?"

Liliana smiled softly, and tipped her head back to rest along the edge of the tub. "Because I *know*."

"Gonna have to give me more to go on."

"I know you wouldn't hurt me—*couldn't*, maybe. Something about you … I don't ever feel unsafe with you, Joe. You don't scare me."

"I should hope not."

Liliana picked her head back up, and met his gaze again. "What about the heart tattoo—my favorite one. What's that for?"

"My parents."

"Oh?"

"My first understanding of love, yeah," he murmured. "Of two people loving each other, and how they love us. Felt right to memorialize it."

"How could they not love you, Joe? You're a beautiful soul."

Her words came out barely above a whisper, and yet, he still heard them. Just the way she stared at him was enough to make him hook a wet finger at her—a silent demand for her to come closer.

She did just that.

His sweet girl.

His *good* girl.

Liliana climbed into Joe's lap, and her arms snaked around his neck. This time, it was him who tipped his head back to rest along the edge while Liliana stared down at him.

"Thank you, Joe."

"For what, sweetheart?"

"You know what."

He did, but he also didn't need her to say it. Not even the thank you, either. He didn't need recognition for doing what was right, or giving a shit about her. He just … didn't.

She knew.

That's what mattered.

Liliana resituated on his lap with a little wiggle of her hips, and there was no hiding the way his semi-hard cock settled in just the right spot between her thighs. Joe didn't even bother to hold back the rumbly groan that escaped his mouth.

"You're making it difficult for me to act like a gentleman, Liliana."

Her grin was salacious.

Daring.

Promising.

"Who asked for a *gentleman*?" she replied, that sexy glint in her eye. "You think me getting you in the tub was innocent?"

She *pfft'd* under her breath.

"Not even close," she added. "I had plans, Joe. And now look at you—naked, and probably willing to give me whatever the fuck I want. Yeah, I had plans."

Oh, he could see that now.

Liliana rocked back and forth on his lap. It made that pussy of hers grind against his length until it was fully hard, thick, and throbbing.

Goddamn.

This woman was something else.

Liliana laced her fingers together at the back of Joe's neck, effectively keeping him locked in her barred embrace. Not that he minded. He certainly didn't mind the sweet, soft kiss she dropped to his mouth, or how with nothing more than a nip of her teeth against his bottom lip, that kiss turned into something else entirely.

Like a little spark blown into a flame.

He couldn't get her close enough when she kissed him—couldn't get his hands on enough of her skin, and he certainly couldn't get enough of those little tremors rocking her body. He kind of loved the way she tried to dominate their kiss, but she always let him win out in the end.

Joe's hand slid up Liliana's slick spine, and tangled into the damp waves of her hair. Tugging a bit to tilt her neck back, he took his time kissing down her throat, and tasting the salt on her skin. The spot beneath her ear was his favorite—she always gave these sweet, breathless moans when he sucked on that spot just hard enough to *almost* leave his mark behind. She couldn't even stop herself from grinding on him the longer he loved on her throat and neck.

"So perfect," he breathed against her ear. "Don't you know that, *Tesoro?*"

"With *you.*"

Her response did something to him—like a kick in the fucking heart, but not one that really hurt. It felt strange, and good, and fucking terrifying. Absolutely everything about this woman kind of terrified Joe for reasons he wasn't even sure he knew.

It was Liliana's deft hand sneaking between her thighs to grab his cock that brought Joe back to the moment. The way she rubbed the head of his dick through her folds, and teased him with her touch, and the promise of her cunt.

"Say you *want* me," Liliana teased.

Joe grinned. "You know I do."

"Say it."

He popped another kiss to her mouth, quick and fleeting. "I want you, Liliana—*Ti voglio, cara bella.*"

Through her lowered lashes, he saw her gaze darken. "You're going to bring the Italian out on me *now?*"

"I save it for special occasions."

"That's unfair."

"What is?"

"I can't control myself when you talk like that, Joe."

He shrugged. "*Colpa mia, principessa.*"

My bad, princess.

"*Joe.*"

Her grip on his dick tightened, and Joe let out a low grunt.

"*Badare.*"

"I am being careful—*you* stop this game of yours," she warned.

He smirked. "*Perdonami?*"

Liliana wet her lips.

Her control was slipping.

"Forgive me," he said again in English, "and I promise to have that pretty pussy of yours purring, Liliana."

"You are … terrible."

"Terribly good, maybe."

Joe bucked his hips upward, and the action made Liliana's hand stroke his dick. She gave him another one of her fake glares, but it quickly faded away when he caught her mouth with his own again. A deeper kiss than before—hotter, too.

How it was possible, he didn't know.

"Killing me," he whispered against her lips. "You better get my cock in your cunt before I get us both out of this tub, and put you on your knees."

"That doesn't sound so bad, either."

"I could make you *wait*, too."

Liliana's eyes widened. "For what?"

"To get my cock—to *come*."

"You wouldn't."

"Hurry up then; time's running out."

Joe was lying through his teeth. He was in no better spot than her. All he really wanted was to be buried nine inches deep into her pussy, and fucking them both to bliss. She didn't call him on his bluff, though.

No, instead she simply said, "Promise to do that after?"

Yep.

Dead.

Deceased.

He was done for when it came to this woman.

"Promise," he said.

Liliana lifted from his lap to fit his cock between her thighs, and then lowered just enough to make her pussy swallow the head of his dick. He felt her delicate inner muscles clenching—teasing him again; she *had to be teasing*.

"*Liliana*," he growled.

"Slow," she said, leaning in close to whisper the words along his lips. At the same time, she lowered painfully slow on his length until he was buried balls-deep, and his world felt *right* again. How did that even happen? *When* had that happened? Then, her fingertips dragged sweet, gentle lines over his skin. "And soft, Joe."

"Is that what you want?"

Bitten-red lips.

A tight, warm pussy.

Lust in her eyes.

"For now," she murmured.

So, that was exactly what he gave her. What she asked for—how she wanted it. None of his usual tricks. Just them, sex, sin, and *perfection*.

There was nothing quite like the feeling of her pussy around his cock. All tight, and dragging him deeper with every thrust. Like this, he could feel even more. Bare, and taking her slow, he felt *everything*.

He didn't tell her his dirty things when he was too caught up in the sounds falling from her lips, and the way his name curled around her tongue. She sounded so damn good when she was begging him for more.

Nice and slow strokes until her low whines turned into gasping cries. Soft kisses dotting her lips and cheeks and even her fingertips until he felt her shuddering breaths and the tremors rocking her hands.

Soft and slow until she came.

Soft and slow until she asked for more.

Then, he gave her that, too.

Joe leaned against the *barre*, and in the corner of his eye, watched Liliana through the opened bedroom door across the room. She was still sleeping contentedly in her bed even though he had crawled out of it a good ten minutes earlier.

He didn't want to disrupt her.

He didn't want to bother her.

At the same time, Joe had things to do now.

Things he *needed* to do.

It couldn't wait.

"Rossi," came the voice thick with sleep on the other end of the call. "Lucky I bothered to pick up this late at night."

Joe glanced out the window, and took in the dark, quiet street down below. "Lucian—evening."

"What do you need?"

"You should have told me."

Lucian cleared his throat. "Since I know where you are tonight—don't bother to ask *how*—I am going to assume you mean about my daughter."

"At the very least," Joe continued, ignoring Lucian altogether, "you could have told me *why*. It would have saved me trouble."

"I didn't owe you an explanation that wasn't mine to give, Joe. I think you can understand that, especially if you know now what happened. Do you know?"

Joe grunted uncommittedly. "You had to know I had affection for her."

"You have no reason to assume that, and even if I did know, I told you once that it's not up to me where Liliana and men are concerned. I meant that."

"I have every reason to assume, starting with the moment I asked to take her out."

Lucian made a sound under his breath before saying, "I knew the night you met her at the mansion, actually. I could see it—it's not my fault if people don't pay as much attention to me as I do to them. It's served me well over the years."

"So again, you *did* know. You didn't think letting me know—at the very least—that she had a bad experience with a man?"

"It wasn't my place. I hired you to do a job, Joe. I would really appreciate if you would finish that job now so that I could … finish my part of it. I assume now that you realize why I left a particular name off your marks, hmm?"

Yeah.

Rich.

The fucking bastard.

It didn't surprise Joe a bit that Lucian wanted to go after the man himself. Joe would give the man every dollar in every single one of his bank accounts if he let him do it instead, but he doubted Lucian would go for that.

Joe's jaw ached from clenching so hard. "Rich sent her flowers today. She didn't react well to it."

Lucian's tone came out cold and sharp when he said, "I will add someone else to her watch since I assume you're going to take care of other things. As for Rich, he's a suspicious little rat by nature. That's going to work to my benefit—I *want* him to see me coming. I made a promise, after all. I like to keep those."

"That's a dangerous game to play with a dangerous man, Lucian. And it kind of seems like he's playing his own game with Liliana right now, and I don't like that at all."

"What do you suggest, then? Because I *will* be following this through, Joe. One way or the other—I owe it to my daughter."

Joe glanced back across the studio apartment, and found Liliana still sleeping. "Let's remove the queen from the board altogether, and keep her out of his reach while the rest of this is finished. We'll start with that."

Lucian hummed.

CAPTIVATED

Joe waited.

"I like it. Now, do your job, Joe."

TWELVE

"WAKE UP," Liliana heard murmured in the background of her dream. "Wake up, *Tesoro.*"

It was his kisses dotting up her naked arm that did finally wake her up, but Liliana was still pretty determined to keep her eyes firmly shut. Why risk opening her eyes, and Joe dragging her from the bed when instead, she could get him back *into it?*

This just seemed like a far better plan.

"You can't stay in bed all day."

"On the contrary, I *can* do exactly that, Joe."

"Shouldn't, then."

"Who says? A break from life might be exactly what I need," Liliana mumbled into the pillow. "You could even join me on this break. Doesn't that sound fun?"

"It sounds like something. Get up."

"Nope."

Liliana refused to open her eyes, and even grabbed the black comforter, and pulled it up high over her head. Then, she could ignore the fact it was morning ... or pretty damn close to it, anyway.

"Liliana."

His voice was muffled, now.

She pretended she didn't hear.

"*Liliana.*" A beat of silence passed, and then, "You asked for it, *donna.*"

Liliana didn't know what exactly she asked for, but she hoped it was something good. Knowing Joe, it probably would be.

Nope.

No, it wasn't.

It was him ripping the fucking blankets away.

Even the *sheet!*

That left Liliana naked on her bed, chilled from the cool air hitting her exposed skin, and glowering at Joe from her back on the bed. At the footboard, Joe just grinned in that smug way of his as he held her blankets in one hand.

"You *ass,*" she said.

Joe shrugged one broad shoulder, naked but for the boxer-briefs he wore. "Time to get up, I said."

It was only then that Liliana noticed that it was the light in her bedroom that had been turned on, and not the usual sunlight filtering in from the window. In fact, by the looks of the darkness shadowing the slightly open curtains, the sun hadn't even rose in the sky yet.

Jesus.

Liliana rolled to her stomach, and reached for the alarm clock. Sure enough, the time showcasing how early it was made her want to scream. "It's five in the morning, Joe!"

"Yep—time to get up."

"Are you *crazy*?"

She snatched a magazine off the bedside stand, and tossed it at him. Joe gave her a lopsided smirk as he easily caught the magazine with his hand, and then with a flick of his wrist, threw it to the foot of her bed like it had never been a problem to him in the first place.

"I have to go," Joe said.

Liliana sunk into the bed. "What?"

"I have to head out, and I didn't think you would appreciate it very much if I didn't at least wake you up to let you know."

Damn.

She probably wouldn't have reacted well; she couldn't help the way even the idea of a slight from this man made her want to run for the hills. She understood that wasn't his intention, but her only way of protecting herself now was to just … well, *run.*

"Figured you might want to say goodbye—it'll be a bit before we'll see each other. Business, you know."

Liliana's brow furrowed. "What business?"

Joe only smiled. "Some things to finish up, that's all."

"Oh."

"So, are you getting up, or what? Because I didn't make breakfast for it to fucking go cold, *donna.*"

She laughed, and pushed up from the bed. "When you put it like that …"

Joe's hand smacked hard against her ass as she passed him by. She didn't jump from the surprise, but she did give him a little wink over her shoulder as she headed for the bathroom. He only grinned right back.

This man …

What was he doing to her?

Whatever it was, Liliana *liked* it.

A lot.

"And put on some clothes, you're going to have a guest shortly," Joe called just as she slipped into the bathroom.

"What, who?"

"Not important."

"Joe—"

"Food is getting cold, Liliana."

Fine.

Once she had made use of the bathroom, cleaned up a bit, and put on something moderately appropriate considering the time of day—and the fact *someone* was coming over—Liliana found Joe getting three plates ready in the kitchen.

"Pancakes are my favorite," she told him.

"Good—you'll have to find whatever you want to put on them."

"Jam for me."

He grinned. "I would have thought whip cream, or something."

Liliana nodded. "Sometimes."

He'd gotten dressed while she was using the bathroom, too, it seemed. Although she'd pulled on simple sweats and a beater, he was dressed back in his entire outfit from the night before. Leather jacket included.

That was Liliana's first sign he wasn't going to be there for very much longer. Her second was when he rolled up a pancake, and took a bite off the end. He probably wasn't going to be there long enough to even eat with her, apparently.

Joe, seemingly noticing how quiet Liliana had turned, finished off the pancake, and then reached for her. She let him drag her into his embrace, and then he pressed a sweet kiss to the very top of her head.

"You trust me, right?" he asked.

She didn't even have to think about it.

Liliana leaned back, and stared up at him. "Yeah, I do, Joe."

"Good. Promise me you won't ask *too* many questions today. Just do what you're told—it's all done because it's for the best, love. It's what's *safe.* Once everything is settled, one of us will explain everything because it won't matter then. Okay?"

The entire time he spoke, Liliana was quiet. A knot had formed in her lower back, though. A ball of tension that said more shit was going on around her than she realized. She was not, however, a stupid woman.

"This is all about Rich, isn't it?"

"Questions, questions," Joe said, cocking a brow. "And maybe that's not one I can answer right now."

She sighed.

"Fine," Liliana returned, "after it's done, will it be about him, then?"

Joe barked out a laugh. "No, everyone will be so over him by then, Liliana. Take that however you want, love."

She didn't need to.

He gave her the answer.

It was a knock on the apartment door that sent the two moving apart. However, that lasted just long enough for Joe to grab another pancake, and then press a quick kiss to Liliana's lips.

"I have to head out now—you eat that food, and *enjoy* it, too," Joe murmured against her mouth.

She couldn't help but smile. "I will."

"And no questions."

Liliana tipped her hand back and forth as if to silently say, *We'll see.*

He chuckled, and kissed her again. "I'll be seeing you soon, *Tesoro.*"

But how soon?

Liliana didn't ask.

She was a little scared of the answer.

Joe left her side when another knock on the apartment door echoed. She didn't think to be bothered by whoever was at her place this early, but only because Joe said someone would be coming over. She didn't turn away from her plate of pancakes on the counter until she heard Joe greet the person waiting.

"Morning, Lucian."

"Joe. Give me a call when you can."

"You got it."

Liliana turned around in just enough time to see Joe's eyes connect with hers before he disappeared out of her apartment door. And only then did she glance at her father who was closing the door behind him.

"Daddy."

Lucian smiled. "Morning, sweetheart. A little early for us, isn't it?"

"That's what I told *him.*"

Her father only chuckled.

She couldn't help but notice how Lucian didn't question why Joe was at her place, or anything like that. Then again, he never had been the type to do that with his daughters. He let them live their lives, and only stepped in when things were unsafe.

"Joe made you a plate," she said, waving at the pancakes beside hers.

Lucian crossed the floor, and picked up the plate with an appreciative nod. His gaze darted back toward the door where Joe had left only moments before. "I like him—a little. That's more than I can say for a lot of other people."

Liliana grinned, but hid it by taking a bite of her pancake covered in jam. "What are you doing here, anyway? I think I remember hearing you tell Ma once when someone called for you early in the morning that you don't roll out of bed before eight for less than a hundred grand."

It was one of her fondest memories, and she had *no* idea why.

Lucian chewed on a bite, and shot her a sly grin. "That did happen, too. You were probably ... maybe, *six.* And you remember that?"

She shrugged. "I keep hold of the good things, Daddy."

Because there had been bad things, too.

Scary things.

And those times were blank spaces—memories painted with a black brush, and she couldn't see through it to remember what happened. A lot of it was because of her brother, and the spirals he had gone through, but she didn't blame him for that. She just … needed her space now.

"Yes, well," Lucian said, sighing, "I don't get out of bed before eight for anything less than a hundred grand, but today is for something priceless. Precious, even, *vita mia*."

Liliana glanced up at her father, and knew he was talking about her. "Oh?"

"Mmhmm." Lucian ticked a finger at her. "Someone told me I was playing a dangerous game, and they were right. I'm going to make it a little safer, now."

"This is about Rich, isn't it?"

Her father's smile was cold, and calculating. Joe hadn't really answered her question, but gave her something else to fill in the blanks. She wondered if Lucian would answer her, instead.

"From the moment he put his hands on you," Lucian said, "it was only a matter of time, and it has always been about that bastard. You'll need to pack a bag. Say, enough for a few days at the very least."

Liliana glanced up. "What, why?"

"You're leaving the city today. I need you somewhere safe for a while."

To where?

She thought to ask, but …

Joe's words remained in the back of her mind. Not to question too much. There was a reason for everything, and probably that, too.

Liliana asked nothing.

"Okay, Daddy. After we eat."

Lucian smiled widely, and waved a bite of pancake. "He's a damn good cook, too. Thank his mother for that. I've met the woman—this is all her, trust me."

Thank her, he'd said. Not *if you get the chance*. Or, *maybe someday*. No, just *thank*. Like there was no doubt in his mind that Liliana would be doing exactly that.

Huh.

"Well, he's definitely good at something, yeah."

Her father gave her a side-eye.

Liliana only grinned.

Liliana stepped off the escalator at Chicago's O'Hare, and her gaze was immediately drawn to a man she had seen once or twice with her uncle, Giovanni, over the years. She wasn't entirely sure of his name—he'd never really been properly introduced, and didn't stay long enough for someone to ask when he did come around.

She figured he was probably the one waiting for her, but it was only compounded by the sign he held in his hands.

It simply read, *L. Marcello*.

The man was handsome—in an aging well kind of way—but she guessed he had to be around the same age as her father, or somewhere in there. His light brown hair had been dragged back as though he had been pulling his fingers through the strands, and his brown gaze drifted over the crowd, but not looking for anything in particular.

In his three-piece suit and shined shoes, he looked entirely out of place with the rest of the waiting people who were dressed rather casually, for the most part. Not that it seemed to bother him, really.

"Still trying to figure out who I am?" the man asked.

Liliana smiled.

He hadn't even looked at her.

"A little," she said.

"Theo DeLuca," he offered.

Liliana nodded, still not entirely sure why *he* had been the man picked to grab her from the airport once she landed. Never mind the fact she didn't know what kind of business he did here in Chicago, but she figured it didn't matter.

"Liliana Marcello," she replied.

Theo did turn to look at her, then, and with a sly smile. "Oh, everyone knows who the Marcello *principessas* are, sweetheart. No worries there. Do you have a bag to grab from the arrivals carousel?"

"Just one."

"Follow me—we'll grab it, and then head out."

"To where?"

Theo only gave her another smile, and extended his arm for her to take. She did, and then he was directing them through the crowd with a confident stride that said he knew the airport and its layout quite well.

"Your father wants you to call him once you get settled in tonight," Theo said.

Liliana nodded. "Okay, but I don't have a phone."

Theo cleared his throat. "No, I imagine they took that from you to keep you from being traced, didn't they?"

She realized then that this man knew quite a bit about whatever was going on. Clearly, more than she did, and all her knowledge was based on guesses and assumptions.

"Yeah, that's what I was told," Liliana finally replied.

"No worries," Theo said, waving a hand as if to dismiss her concerns. "I will pick you up a burner, but there is also a landline at the house you can use."

Liliana gave him a look. "A house?"

"That's where you'll be staying, yes. A house in Melrose, to be exact."

"*Your* house?"

Not that Theo DeLuca didn't seem like a nice man—and she was sure he was—but Liliana didn't quite know how she felt about being made to stay with someone she didn't know personally. She would much prefer to lock herself away in a hotel, or something.

Theo chuckled. "As much as my nephew likes me, he made it very clear where you're to be staying, actually."

"What?"

"Oh, here we are. Look for your bag—they can go pretty fast. I'll grab it when you point it out, Liliana. You don't need to be carrying it."

For the moment, Liliana's attention was distracted by the bags swiftly moving on the baggage carousel. Her blue leather, rolling luggage ended up being somewhere in the middle of all the mess.

Theo easily plucked it out while a couple of others missed their chance to move between the people to grab their own. He said nothing as he flicked out the handle, and the wheels hit the ceramic tiles of the airport floor with a *click-click*.

"Ready?" he asked.

Liliana shrugged. "I don't really have much of a choice, do I?"

Theo laughed. "Oh, if I had to guess, I think you'll enjoy your stay in Chicago. Sure, it's a little different than New York, and you don't know very many people, but that's not really the point of you being here. Is it?"

"No, I guess not."

"And besides," Theo said, moving forward and gesturing for Liliana to follow along, "I think you'll meet a few people who have been ... well, curious about you."

"Why would people here be curious about me?"

Theo smiled. "You'll see."

It only took maybe twenty to thirty minutes before Theo had pulled his black Rolls-Royce in the small driveway of a moderately-sized Melrose home. The white, two-level home with an attached three-door garage seemed dark and maybe empty given there didn't seem to be any life inside, and yet ... Liliana still felt strangely welcomed.

Theo was right, too.

Chicago didn't seem to be all that different from New York in a lot of ways. Sure, his accent was a little different, and she didn't recognize the streets. The wind picked up more when she stepped out of the car onto the black-tarred driveway, but she didn't feel at all cold.

"I'll walk you in," Theo said, "but I need to get back to my wife before she thinks I forgot about her show tonight."

Liliana turned to him. "Her show?"

"She owns a gallery. I like to be there."

"Oh. Sorry to take you from her."

Theo chuckled. "No worries. This is part of the job sometimes. Eve knows that better than anyone."

The two climbed the front steps, and Theo handed over a key to Liliana.

"For you to use while you're here," he said.

"It's not *my* house."

Theo's expression didn't change. "You have free run of the place while you're here. He wanted you to be comfortable."

"My father?"

"Not even close. Open the door."

What was with these strange men sometimes?

Liliana shook her head, and then proceeded to unlock the door. Once it was open, and the two were inside, Theo set both of her bags to the corner.

She took the moment to look around the hallway, and some of the pictures hanging on the earthy-toned walls. The cherry hardwood floors gleamed, and the small decorative table still held a bowl full of knickknacks, gum, and even a set of keys.

Like the person who lived here had expected to come back shortly after they left, or something.

"You good?" Theo asked.

Liliana looked back at him, but a photo hanging above a tall plant sitting on a small rug caught her eye. It was the man in the picture, and the other man clinging to his back like a fucking monkey that made her smile. The two couldn't deny that they were somehow related—brothers, likely. Both wore three-piece suits, wide smiles and in the background, white chairs had been set up.

Maybe a wedding?

Anyway, she finally figured out who lived here. And, of course, why this house had felt comforting to her at just the sight alone despite the fact she didn't know anything about it, and had never even seen it before.

"This place is Joe's," she said.

Theo nodded. "Welcome to Chicago, Liliana."

"Knock, knock! Anybody home?"

Liliana jumped away from the books she was perusing on the shelf, and sloshed her morning coffee on her hand at the same time. "Shit."

Thankfully, it wasn't hot enough to burn.

"Jesus, Cory, stop acting foolish," came a man's voice.

"I don't know why you bother," followed a woman.

"Someone has to tell him."

"It's too late for Cory."

"Hey, there she is."

Liliana spun around to find a man—younger than her, definitely—standing in the doorway of Joe's living room. She only needed one look at his face to know exactly who he was. Cory Rossi—the same man in several pictures inside the home, and Joe's younger brother.

"You busy, girl?" he asked.

She blinked. "What?"

"You ... busy ... now."

An older gentleman, with similar features and kind eyes, slid in beside the young man, and at the same time, smacked the back of Cory's head without ever taking his eyes off Liliana. The same man who she had first seen at the Marcello mansion when she met Joe, but he hadn't stayed long enough to have dinner with the rest of them.

"Quite enough of that, Cory."

"Ouch, Dad. *Fuck*."

Dad.

Joe's father?

So that must have meant the woman pushing between the two men with a wide smile and food in her hands was Joe's ...

"Lily Rossi," the woman greeted, "and you must be Liliana."

Liliana smiled. "I am."

"I have been waiting quite a while to meet you."

A part of Liliana wanted to feel awkward, but how could she when this sweet woman with her blonde hair and brown eyes was smiling like they were the oldest of friends?

"Why?" Liliana asked.

She wiped her hand off on the side of her pants to get rid of the coffee she had spilled while Lily talked.

Shooting her youngest son a look, Lily said, "Someone doesn't know how to keep his mouth shut, that's all."

"Not entirely *all*," Cory grumbled.

Lily shrugged, and grinned. "And maybe I pestered Joe a lot when he called yesterday to explain some things."

"And you came over here?"

"Who wants to eat breakfast alone in a big house?" the older man asked.

"Like Damian said," Lily added, "we just wanted to say hello, maybe have some food, and make you feel welcome."

But *why?*

"Is that her? *Move.*"

A small girl—maybe ten or eleven—with her mother's eyes, and her father's hair, who looked a hell of a lot like the feminine version of Joe and Cory, pushed through the people. She wore an oversized sparkly, pink sweater and black leggings. Her Nike sneakers were also pink and black, and her dark hair curled in perfect ringlets.

The girl peered up at Liliana with curious eyes.

"It is her, right?" she asked Lily.

"Yeah, Monica," Cory said.

Oh.

Joe's little sister.

Monica smiled widely at Liliana. "My brother says we have to be nice to you, Liliana. So, Ma made you food, Dad will take you out to get you anything you want, and Cory's not going to be a *shit*. Mostly."

"Mon!" Lily cried, "Language."

Well, this made a hell of a lot more sense, now. Liliana thought it was terribly sweet that Joe had thought to ask his family to make Liliana feel welcome during her stay, so she wouldn't be so alone. And honestly, it gave her a chance to get to know the people who he came from.

It made her heart swell, really.

Beat fast and hard.

Only Joe did that for her. Only *he* could do that without even being there. The realization that came down on Liliana in that moment was kind of terrifying, but at the same time, it wasn't scary at all.

She would just have to wait a little longer to tell Joe what she knew now. Hopefully, not too long, though.

Liliana couldn't suppress her grin if she tried. Bending down so she could be at least close to eye-level with Monica, she asked, "Is that what Joe said?"

"Yep."

"And why would he say that?"

Monica did a little bounce in her shoes. "I guess 'cause you're his person, you know? He said we'll *love* you."

Liliana stilled. "Is that so?"

The girl smiled widely. "Guess so."

The room went quiet.

Or maybe that was just her.

His person.

His. Person.

Huh.

THIRTEEN

"NO ONE TOLD me we were having a buffet," Joe said from the dining room entryway.

Dante, who had been lost in conversation with his brother, looked to Joe with a smile. "Yes, well, that wasn't the plan. My mother likes to cook when she's nervous, though. Come in and grab a plate. Don't let it go to waste, Joe."

"Where's Lucian?"

Because that's the only reason why Joe showed up to the old Marcello mansion this afternoon. He'd spent the day before fielding phone calls to make sure Liliana was settled into his place in Chicago, and gathering the last bit of intel he needed on Martin Abraham to make the Chief of Police's hit successful, and clean.

Joe was not going in on that mark half-cocked.

It would be stupid.

"Lucian took a phone call from Liliana in the next room," Giovanni said. "Sit, Joe, and tell us what you have. We can pass the message along if he doesn't get back in time."

Joe wished it was *him* taking the call from Liliana. Right now, though, she was just a distraction he couldn't afford to mess around with. He needed to be as detached as possible from his mark, but especially when he finally went in on the man. That way, there was little chance of his emotions taking over the kill, and fucking up the whole *clean* aspect he needed to maintain.

They all needed to make it out of this unscathed, after all.

Problem was, should Joe talk to Liliana, he was going to hear her voice. And then he was going to remember the way her voice sounded when she told him how a man had helped to cover up the fact Rich beat her, and then that same man proceeded to threaten her family and father's freedom to keep her quiet.

And *yeah* …

Joe didn't need to be focusing on that right now. He needed to remain disconnected from the reason why he was doing this in the first place, even if that reason had been overtaken by Liliana, and what happened to her.

"Well?" Dante asked.

Joe came into the dining room as he spoke, and grabbed a plate to start filling with food. "Tomorrow—Saturday—Martin will be heading to his vacation home in Long Island. I guess he has a pond, or something where he fishes. Relaxing, I bet."

"The point?" Giovanni asked.

"Well, he's not going to make it there, but it'll look like he was trying."

Joe didn't really like giving the details of his plans when it came to the actual murder. Mostly because some men in this business got off on that shit, and he wasn't killing for the excitement of others. He killed because it was a job that needed to be done more often than people cared to admit, and he was fucking good at doing it.

He'd been damn good at it since his first at fifteen when an enforcer called his aunt, Abriella, a whore, and Joe beat the man to death after luring him into the backyard. The guy hadn't even seen him coming. Joe didn't even *think* about it, really. His uncle, Tommas, hadn't said very much about it, but he did tell Damian to take Joe to confession.

That was the first time he ever *used* confession.

He usually went back a couple of times a month, now.

Dante rested back in his chair, and steepled his fingers. "And you're certain this will be as clean as the hit on the Senator?"

"Cleaner, maybe," Joe replied. "With that stupid fuck, I had to avoid security cameras and shit. Martin doesn't even have that in his home, and no security around the perimeter. He's just a fucking cop—and no different from other cops, despite his title, at the end of the day."

"His wife—"

"Heading to a breakfast with some friends at the golf club she frequents," Joe cut in. "I called in a favor, and had a friend hack into their Wi-Fi. That then allowed us into their phones, and their digital calendars. The woman has breakfast with the same three ladies every Saturday unless it's a holiday, or some other occasion. At least, according to her calendar."

"Tomorrow could be the day she wakes up sick, and decides not to go," Giovanni pointed out.

Joe passed the man a look. "You must think I'm a dumbass."

"No."

"Then, you must think I'm new to this."

Giovanni cleared his throat, and passed Dante a look. "I'm not sure how many marks you've successfully carried out hits on."

"One hundred, twenty-two," Joe said, "since I began at fifteen, anyway. On average, that's six a year, if you're curious. To be fair, some were done in small groups of several. Some were brought to me to see what I could gain from them first."

The man cleared his throat.

Joe figured, *Point made.*

"I know you think I work *only* in Chicago because that's where I live, and whom I work for, but fact is, I go wherever Tommas Rossi sends me to remove someone who might be causing him trouble. He's got problems making more problems all over the goddamn world. Point is—I'm not new to this."

Joe fell into a chair at the far end of the table, and a good twenty chairs down from Dante and Giovanni. Really, he was kind of surprised at the large size of the table as he had yet to see the entire family fill it. Although, he knew by the size of the Marcello family that they absolutely could fill the table.

Digging into the food on his plate, Joe enjoyed the moment of comfortable silence that he was afforded by the only other people in the room. *Shit*, cinnamon and sweetness saturated his tongue with every bite of the French Toast sticks.

Cecelia Marcello was—by far—one of the best cooks Joe had ever gotten the pleasure to sit at their table. He reminded himself to tell the woman exactly that when he saw her the next time. She deserved to be told.

"*If* the wife doesn't go to breakfast," Joe said, finally deciding it was time to bring the conversation back around to the point at hand again, "then I will carry out the hit at the vacation home. She doesn't go there—not that I've found, anyway. Maybe once or twice a year, but not during Martin's weekend trips."

"Still just as clean, right?" Dante asked.

"I know you just want to *be sure*," Joe murmured, "but it's offensive when people question my tactics or ability at every turn. Just for the record."

Dante sighed a little.

Giovanni chuckled.

Joe shoved another bite of food in his mouth, and chewed. Behind him, he heard footsteps enter the room before the man even spoke. And he could tell exactly who it was by the comfortable smiles the two brothers at the other end of the table wore at the sight of him behind Joe.

Lucian.

"How's Liliana?" Joe asked before Lucian could speak.

The man moved around him, and up the table to take a seat closer to his brothers. "Pretty well, all things considered. She's got a lot of questions, though, but I'm putting them off for now."

Joe nodded. "Better to explain after, I suppose."

"You could say that."

It was only the ringing of one of two burner phones in Joe's pocket that took his attention away from the men at the table. He made a move to leave the table for a second to take the call, but Dante and Giovanni stood before he could.

"Stay, and enjoy your food, Joe," Dante said.

"Give us a call when the hit goes through," Giovanni added.

Then, the men were gone. That left Joe with Lucian as his phone rang again, but he didn't mind answering the call with him there. It was the phone designated for his family, anyway. He figured it probably wasn't sensitive, or about business.

Tugging the phone out, he put it to his ear as he took another bite. "Hello?"

"Are you talking with your mouth full?"

At the sound of his mother's amused chiding, Joe quickly chewed the bite and swallowed it a little too fast. It half-lodged in his airway, but then scraped its way all the way down to his stomach.

"No," he croaked.

"Liar," Lily said, laughing. "When are you coming home? You're forgetting your manners being away this long, and I don't like it."

"Or you miss me, Ma."

"Yeah, that too. And your father. *Cory*. Mon."

"Cory misses pestering my ass."

"What are little brothers for?"

They had been telling him that his whole life. Thing was, Joe enjoyed the pestering as much as his brother enjoyed handing it over. He just wasn't going to tell Cory that.

"I don't know when I'm going to be back, Ma," he settled on saying.

"Oh."

"What, Ma?"

"I think your little *friend* here is missing you, that's all."

Joe smiled at the way his mother twisted the word *friend*. That's what he'd offered to her when he called to explain what he could about Liliana, and her stay in Chicago. And then his mother pressed and pressed more until he admitted she was a little more than a friend to him.

A hell of a lot more.

His *person*.

That one person his father talked about—every man had one, Damian liked to tell him. *You just have to find her, son.*

Well, he had.

And now she was a couple of states away.

"I like her," Lily added when Joe stayed quiet.

"Do you?"

"She's wonderful, Joe."

"I knew you would, Ma."

"I bet." Lily sighed. "Well, that's all I really called to say. Oh, and Cory is planning to go over and keep her company tomorrow morning."

"Tell him not to be an annoying ass."

"Call him, and tell him yourself."

His mother hung up.

Well, *damn*.

Chuckling, Joe set the phone back to the table, and the food on the plate regained his attention for the moment. His mouth was full of French Toast sticks and a strip of bacon when Lucian cleared his throat down the table, and then began to talk.

Smart man.

Catching Joe when he couldn't reply.

"Thank you, by the way."

Joe raised a brow, silently asking, *For what?*

Lucian smiled faintly. "Well, I could vaguely say all of this, I suppose, but it's more than that. For sitting here, and eating with us. For indulging my family, and my brothers when it's clear they get on your nerves because I guess we don't work the same way you do. Something like that, anyway."

Just how long had Lucian been listening outside the dining room before he came in?

"Even if it's just a little bit more than when you first came here," Lucian added, "you've dropped your walls down, Joe. We see more now of you than the blank slate you showed us time and time again, so thank you."

Joe swallowed his food, and sat straight in the chair. "No offense, but I can't say that was intentional."

Lucian shrugged one shoulder, saying, "And yet, here we are."

Yes.

How had that happened?

And *why?*

Joe stuffed his hands in his pockets, and puffed on a cigarette that hung from the corner of his mouth. The quiet Queens suburb was barely awake at only a little after seven in the morning. People were just starting to wake up on a Saturday morning with their whole day still ahead of them. Most probably had plans. Unlucky fuckers would head off to work.

Him, though?

Joe had a job to do.

He was one step closer to it, now.

He stopped at the end of a driveway that led up to a quaint beige bungalow with a black roof. The shutters on all the windows matched the roof color, as did the front door with the frosted glass.

Joe didn't really *care* about the house. He cared more about the man rolling a tire from the back of his SUV to the front.

Flat tire, it seemed.

The guy was in his late fifties, if Joe had to guess. Although, frankly, he didn't have to guess at all. A little bit of gray at his temples, but the rest of his thinning hair was still black as tar. His tanned skin spoke of vacations on beaches, and the wrinkles around his eyes and mouth as he squinted and grimaced at his flat tire told Joe he'd lived a long life.

Maybe even a *good* life.

That life was just about over, now.

"Need help?" Joe called.

Martin Abraham glanced up over the tire he was attempting to fit into the front driver's side. "Somebody must have left a damn nail in my driveway. Came out to it flat this morning. Fucking kids."

Kids, right.

Joe sauntered up the drive, and finished his smoke on the way. He made sure to crush the butt of the cigarette, and stuff it into the pocket of his jeans—just in case … He bent down near the tire, and gave the man a smile.

A welcoming smile.

A friendly one, even.

"I don't mind helping," Joe said. "New to the neighborhood, and all. The wife keeps saying I should make friends."

The Chief of Police laughed. "Yeah, wives think a lot of things, don't they?"

Joe only shrugged.

"I think I'm good," Martin added.

Nope.

Joe couldn't let him off *that* easy. He still needed to make this as clean as possible, after all. "I recognize you—Chief of Police, right?"

Martin grinned.

Proud and pleased.

Hook, line, and sinker.

"I am, young man," Martin replied, rocking back on his heels. "Proud to be a part of the Blue Line."

Yeah, Joe bet.

Cops always were a special kind of *proud.*

To say the least.

"Really, let me handle this," Joe told him, "and you can finish packing up your gear."

The man's gaze narrowed—suspicious in a blink. "My gear?"

Joe nodded toward the porch of the house. "Fishing gear. It's sitting on the deck. You do that often?"

At the mention of fishing, Martin was fine again.

Pleased again.

Stupid again.

"Every weekend," the man murmured, pushing up to stand. "Thanks for this, I appreciate it. I swear, these young people nowadays wouldn't know how to lend a helping hand if their lives depended on it."

You're one to talk.

Joe said nothing, only gave the man a nod, and then got to work on replacing the tire. It took him maybe fifteen minutes to get the tire on, and fit all the lug nuts, too. He was done before Martin had even finished hauling all his shit to the back of the car.

That seemed like a hell of a lot of gear for a day—or even *two*—of just fishing. But who was Joe to say?

Leaning against the back of the SUV, Joe swung the tire iron to and fro with the tips of his fingers. Martin eyed the swinging tool as he came with the last of the bags.

"That was fast," he said. "Thanks again."

Joe nodded. "No worries."

He could have easily swung that tire iron, and killed the man. Probably crushed his fucking skull into bits in the process, too. He would have enjoyed the sight of the blood pooling and splattering, if only because he could imagine this man had *seen* pictures of what Rich Earl had done to Liliana, and he chose to help hide it.

Monsters were everywhere.

They came in all forms.

Not all were easy to spot.

Instead of hitting the man like his heart screamed to, Joe handed the tire iron over with a smile. "I'll let my wife know I did what she said, and made a friend. I'm sure it'll make her day."

Martin chuckled. "You do that."

"Maybe you know her."

The man glanced up from the bag he was pushing into the back of the SUV. "Pardon? Why would I know your wife?"

Joe shrugged. "She does a lot of things—charity, and whatnot. Made her rounds around the block shortly after we moved in, too."

"Oh, well, maybe."

"Liliana Marcello—ring any bells?"

Martin stilled.

Joe watched the color drain from the man's face.

That fear was like a drug to Joe. He soaked it up because for no other reason, that fear was going to keep Martin company on his drive. A drive that would only end in his death.

"Shit," Joe said, glancing at a watch that wasn't even on his wrist, "I've got to run. Have a good day, Martin."

Joe didn't wait for the man to respond. He jogged down the driveway, and headed up the block. He only shot a look over his shoulder just long enough to see Martin fumble with pulling the hatchback down on the SUV, and then scramble to get inside his vehicle behind the wheel. He didn't waste any time pulling out of his driveway, either.

That was fine.

Joe would follow behind.

He slipped into the black sedan the Marcellos had provided him to use, and pulled out on to the road to tail close behind Martin Abraham. Soon, the two were on the highway, and Joe was *feet* from the man's bumper the whole time.

Even when Martin sped up, and glanced in his rearview mirror, Joe smiled and kept driving just as fast. He sped up, too. He took the turns on the exit ramp just as sharply.

Joe made his first call then.

"Nine-One-One, what's your emergency?"

Joe rattled off the road name, and then quickly added, "There's a man in a brown SUV driving erratically. I'm concerned he's drunk or something. He's been weaving in and out of vehicles, and I know he's going at least twenty over the speed limit."

"License plate, Sir?"

Joe gave the number—he was close enough to read it clearly, and if he pushed the gas, he would be so close that his own bumper would actually cover it.

"Thank you, Sir. Could I get you to stay on the line—"

Nope.

Joe hung up the phone.

An exit ramp came up on the right, and apparently, Martin must have thought that if he took it sharply enough, he might lose the vehicle trailing him.

Stupid fucker.

That tire couldn't take that.

Joe had *barely* tightened the nuts. Just enough not to make it noticeable while the man was driving, but loose enough that the tire would fly off at too high of speeds, or reckless driving.

And it did.

Spectacularly.

Joe swerved in behind Martin when he took the ramp, and then yanked his wheel to the other side when the tire came off as the SUV entered the sharpest turn on the ramp. At the speed, and the curve the vehicle was turning on the ramp, the SUV was top heavy, and couldn't take it. It hit the gravel, and then it flew.

Six turns on the pavement.

Over, and over, and over. It crushed the top of the SUV in from the force, and Joe swore he saw Martin's head snapping back and forth.

That alone was enough to kill a brain, or break a neck.

Joe had hit the brakes, and watched the accident happen. Like slow fucking motion. Kind of beautiful, really.

All of the glass exploded out of the SUV's windows, while smoke started to puff from under the hood when the SUV finally came to stop on its totally destroyed roof. Other vehicles had come to a stop behind Joe, but he didn't bother to get out. Someone else did—running over to the SUV, and sticking their arm inside the window.

Checking a pulse, it looked like.

He saw the shake of the man's head when he turned to the woman who had followed behind him, and the way his face whitened.

Dead.

Joe made his second call as he carefully moved forward, and maneuvered his vehicle around the wreckage and people on their phones. One woman was crying. The man who had checked on Martin was white-faced.

Like he'd seen death.

"Lucian here," the Marcello said when he picked up Joe's call.

"Two down," Joe murmured.

He swore he could see Lucian's smile when the man replied, "One to go."

"You called?" Joe asked.

Lucian didn't bother to look up from the newspaper he was reading. "I did. Sit, Joe."

Joe took a seat in the high-back leather chair, and realized he could see the whole private bar from this position. "Didn't expect you to call me somewhere during daylight hours."

"No one but my brothers know I frequent this place. I find it calming."

He could see why.

The bar, with its dark wood and rich colors, was a quiet place. The patrons—all well-dressed, and lost in discussions with those around them—couldn't seem to be bothered with what was going on around them.

It would be the perfect place to get lost.

Maybe.

"What did you need?"

Lucian handed the paper over to Joe, and he took it. "Front page, down toward the bottom."

Quickly, Joe found what Lucian was talking about. It seemed Martin Abraham's death was front page news in the *New York Times* this morning. Shit, it had only been a day.

"Read it," Lucian said.

Joe already had. "They're making him out to be some kind of hero for his whole life's work, or some shit."

Ignorance was the best kind of bliss.

Or so he had been told.

Lucian sighed. "They did the same thing for the senator. Made sure to list each and every one of his achievements—if you could call them that—in his political career, and even named charities people could donate to in his honor. And then his kids and wife …" Beside him, Lucian's mouth curled up at the edges in an almost-sneer before he added, "They got on the television and *cried* for him. It all disgusted me."

"I get why."

And he *did*.

"But," Lucian said with a wave of his hand, "I resigned myself to the fact they got what was coming to them, and I don't need the rest of the world to know it, too." He pointed to his temple, and gave Joe a cold smile. "What matters is that I know it up here, and they knew it before they died. Sometimes, karma isn't some invisible force, but rather, a man you pay to do the deed."

All of this was fine and great, but Joe was still wondering why in the hell Lucian had called him here to begin with.

"Do you need something?" Joe asked, figuring it was better to get right to the point. "I was going to head out to Chicago—had a flight booked for tonight, actually."

The earliest fucking flight he could get.

He *still* hated flying.

Lucian glanced over at Joe. "Spend time with her before you bring her back, I imagine."

It wasn't even a question.

Joe wasn't in the business of hiding his intentions. "I would like to be able to do that away from all of this. Actually … I don't know, take her out, and let her have fun."

Lucian nodded. "I like you, Joe."

Yeah, he kind of figured that out.

He still wasn't sure how he felt about it.

"But," Lucian said, "if you were willing to wait a day or two before getting back to Chicago, and Liliana, then I had an offer for you. I felt it was … appropriate, all things considered."

Joe cocked a brow. "What kind of offer?"

Because at the moment, nothing was worth to him what Liliana was.

"One last mark," Lucian murmured. "Rich, I mean. I'm sure he knows by now—he has to; he's not stupid—that I'm coming for him. So, he'll be looking for me, Joe. I expect him to be waiting or running from *me*."

Ah, Joe was getting it now.

"And if I delivered the stupid fuck, what would you do for me?"

"Well, it won't be very hard for you to deliver him, mind you. I've had someone watching him for a while. But I think he knows the guy is tailing him, too." Lucian grinned. "I would let you have a little fun with him, and allow you to watch me kill him. Poetic, maybe. Or … maybe I just need a little more God in my life. That's what my mother would tell me."

Joe chuckled. "You drive a hard bargain."

Because *yes*, Joe wanted to take that offer.

More than anything.

"Counteroffer," Joe said.

Lucian frowned. "This isn't that kind of deal, Joe."

"Fact remains, I am giving you one. I give her the news."

"Mmm."

"What?"

"All of it, or just the Rich bit?"

Joe shrugged. "All of it."

Lucian considered that for a moment, and then nodded. "Better you than me, I think."

"Why's that?"

"Well, she already loves me, Joe. And while she *may* love you, she has to still love all of you, too. Even the parts that scare her. So yes, better you than me."

"Sounds—"

"Lucian."

Lucian glanced away from Joe at the Marcello enforcer that approached. "What, Jacob?"

"We have a problem."

"What kind of a problem?"

"Giovanni called—let me know the boss gave him a shout when the lead he had tailing Rich went to shit this morning."

Lucian stiffened in the chair. "And what does that mean *exactly*?"

Jacob swallowed thickly.

Dread colored up his gaze.

"Means we lost him, Lucian."

For the first time in a long time, Joe felt something he hadn't experienced in a long while. It felt cold, and heavy. Like strong hands wrapping around his throat, and choking him to death without concern or care.

Fear.

That's what he felt.

Fear.

"Joe," Lucian hissed, "there's no possible way the man knows where Liliana was taken to. We made sure of that—you chose it for *that* reason."

Could the man read his thoughts?

Or was his fear that visible?

Maybe it was just because it was *her.*

And he hid nothing for her.

Still, Lucian continued even through Joe's haze of anxiety and fear. "I was talking to her an hour ago—she was *fine.*"

It didn't matter.

Joe was already pulling out his phone, and dialing the number to his house back in Chicago. She should be there; he kept up with what she had been doing since she got into the city, although he had yet to call her.

He was still trying to keep disconnected.

Detached.

At least, up until *now.*

"Are you calling her?" he heard Lucian ask.

Joe gave a short nod, but nothing else.

It was all he could give.

"Hello?" Liliana asked when the call connected.

"Hey, *Tesoro,*" Joe replied.

The relief was sweet.

Too sweet, even.

"Joe?"

"That's me, ballerina."

Liliana's laughter coated his black soul.

Like a shadow meeting the light. He couldn't hide with her.

She lit up every part of him. Every single dark part.

"Why haven't you called? I missed you."

Joe cleared his throat, saying, "Yeah, sorry about that. You'll see me soon, though. I promise."

"How soon?"

Beside him, Lucian said, "Are you going to help us track him, or not, Joe?"

Liliana was safe.

At least, for a day or two.

Joe had to finish this fucking business here, so he could get back to his girl. His girl that he waited so fucking long to find.

"Joe?" Liliana asked when he stayed quiet. "How soon?"

"A couple of days, maybe."

"Oh."

Her sadness cut him deep.

She didn't *know*, though.

This was for her.

"But it's still soon," he added.

"Guess I'll just keep snooping through your stuff, then."

Joe laughed. "I hope you find something good."

"I already did, and I didn't need to be here to find it, Joe."

FOURTEEN

LILIANA FLIPPED THROUGH the journal she had found tucked under the pillow on Joe's bed. The house had two spare bedrooms—both decorated—and yet, she found herself compelled to sleep in the room she knew was *his*.

The journal didn't seem like much on the surface with its matte black leather wrap, and a single cord wound around the cover. Joe clearly made no effort to make it safe from snoopers—like *her*—but she figured there was a point to that.

Like the fact she couldn't understand what in the hell was written inside. Oh, she could read it perfectly fine, sure. Making sense of it was a whole other matter.

Initials.

Dates.

And then a checkmark, X, or line might be drawn beside the information. It was like he was logging something, and she couldn't quite figure out what it was.

"Where did you find that?"

Liliana's head snapped up, and she found Cory Rossi leaning in the arched entryway of the kitchen. Mostly, she liked Joe's younger brother even though he was the complete opposite of his brother. Cory was loud, and Joe was *not*. Cory seemed to thrive in having the spotlight, and Liliana had watched Joe move away from attention more than once.

And yet, whenever Cory talked about his brother, it was clear the two cared a lot about each other. *He always has my back*, Cory had said about Joe.

It reminded Liliana of her and Cella, in some ways.

"Come to annoy me again today?" Liliana asked, going back to flipping through the pages of the journal. "Coffee's hot, by the way."

"First, I don't *annoy* you. Jesus, you sound just like my brother."

"Bet you annoy him, too."

She joked, mostly.

Cory just gave her a wide grin as he passed the island by, and headed for the coffee pot. "Joe would say I absolutely annoy him, but for the record, if I didn't, he would have nobody to get him out of this house when he isn't doing a damn job. The man is a hermit—he would happily live alone for the rest of his life, and never need human contact. He even has his groceries delivered."

Liliana frowned as Cory came to sit on the stool beside her with a cup of black coffee. The mug was swallowed by his large hands, and steam curled upward from the hot, bitter liquid. It kind of amused her that from the corner of someone's eye, the Rossi brothers looked so similar that they could *almost* be considered twins.

She could see the difference.

It was obvious to her.

But *still* …

"So, what, Joe doesn't have a life is what you're saying?" Liliana asked.

"Joe has a life," Cory mumbled, lifting his coffee up for a sip. "He just … prefers for that life to be quiet, we'll say. He's always been like that."

"Huh."

She wasn't really *surprised*. She didn't think that would be the right word to use. After all, she had gotten the best insights to who Joe really was when it was just them alone, and no one else around. With others, he almost always turned into a statue with a mask of nothing by way of opinion, emotions, or otherwise.

"So that's where I come in," Cory said, setting his cup down and smiling. "I get him the hell out of this house, whether he likes it or not, and he goes because I'm the little brother who he feels like someone has to watch out for just in case I blow myself up or some other stupid shit."

Liliana blinked. "But would you?"

"What?"

"Blow yourself up."

Cory made a noise in the back of his throat—considering. "I mean, I've done some stupid shit. As my father reminds Joe whenever he asks why he has to keep an eye on me, anything is possible when it comes to me. I just need shit at my disposal, a little bit of time on my hands, and some inspiration. Give me all or a combination of any of those things without someone to keep me in line, and people are asking for trouble. Who knows what might happen?"

She smiled a little.

At least he was honest.

"I guess that means you're the reckless to his serious," Liliana said.

Cory glanced over at her, and smiled. "You could say that, yeah."

"How would you say it?"

"I would say that where I push my brother to be a little less controlled in literally every aspect of his life, he reminds me why it's good to be responsible, too. Or, something like that. He thinks *he's* keeping me busy and out of trouble with all these businesses we keep opening up together, but truth is, maybe it's me who's making him get out of the house a little more."

Liliana laughed.

Cory smirked, and shrugged. "But we won't tell him that, will we?"

"Suppose not."

It amused her to no end how these two brothers clearly liked to mess with the other, and at the very same time, take care of one another.

She was glad Joe had Cory. And his sister, too. Monica clearly adored her big brothers. That was before Liliana even got in to Joe's parents who also seemed to love their kids more than the sea, earth, and air combined.

"Are you going to ask about that?"

Liliana's brow furrowed. "Huh?"

Cory pointed at the journal she had closed, and sat down on the island countertop as the two of them talked. "The journal. Are you going to ask about it? Snooping is a bad habit, you know. Should quit that before you find something *scary*."

She scoffed. "Nothing scares me anymore."

Mostly.

Or, that's what she kept telling herself.

"Besides," Liliana added quickly, "Joe *told* me to snoop when he called the other day. So, I think it's fair game for me to … look around."

"Oh, that's what you're calling it?"

"Yep."

"I see," Cory murmured. "So, are you?"

"What?"

"Going to *ask*."

Liliana picked up the journal again, and weighed it in her palm. She opened the front cover, and flipped through a couple of the pages. Something about the fact Joe was carefully logging something made her think maybe it wasn't any of her business, or rather … she should ask the source, not his brother.

"Not really," Liliana said.

"What does that mean, exactly?"

She set the journal aside. "It means, I don't want to ask about *that*, but I do have other questions you might be able to answer for me."

Cory sipped from his coffee again. "Shoot."

"I've been here a few days. When is *he* going to get here?"

"Don't know."

Liliana frowned. "Do you know what they're doing right now?"

"Who is *they*?"

"Joe, my dad … people in New York, I guess."

Cory cleared his throat. "I know just enough to tell you I can't say anything because it's not my place, or my business. I'm reckless, not stupid."

Fair.

"Your dad—"

"Damian, yeah," Cory interjected.

"He's pretty high up in the Chicago mob, right?"

"Outfit, Liliana. We call it the Chicago Outfit."

"I know what it's called."

Cory passed her a look. "Then, use the right name."

"Touchy." She stuck her tongue out at him, and he did the same thing right back to her. Then, she asked before she lost her nerve, "So, I guess that means you and Joe are probably connected, too, right?"

She understood vaguely that Joe had a job in the mafia, and what little bit of information she had been given was enough for her to draw her own conclusions. But really, she didn't like doing that. She would much rather just be *told*, and then she knew for sure.

"You could say we're *connected*," Cory said. "More me directly than him, or I'm working on it."

"Oh. And people keep saying he's the Shadow, right? So, what does that mean exactly?"

Cory chuckled. "A part of me thinks it's better for you *not* to know all the details about what Joe does in this business, girl. And another part of me thinks … you probably wouldn't give a fuck if you did know."

"Probably not," Liliana agreed.

"Still ain't going to tell you, though."

Asshole.

Annoying as hell.

"You're lucky Joe loves you," Liliana mumbled her empty half-threat.

Cory grinned. "I could say the same for you."

Except … Joe hadn't told her that yet.

"I was thinking pizza for dinner—Chicago-style," Cory called from the living room. "How does that sound for you?"

"Sounds—"

It was the banging thrash of the front door being thrown open that stopped Liliana from saying more. She jumped up from the table where she had been flipping through a magazine at the same time she heard Cory curse.

"What the fuck?"

"Liliana!"

Her fear instantly bled away.

Joe.

He met her in the hallway at the same time Cory came out from the living room.

"Hey, man," Cory said.

Joe's gaze was only on her, and Liliana wasn't entirely sure that she liked what she saw staring back at her. Cold and distant Joe was back, it seemed. She could see it in the darkness of his features, and the stiffness in his posture.

He tossed his brother a look. "Pack me a bag, and grab her shit, would you?"

Cory didn't even bother to ask questions.

He wasn't like Liliana.

"You got it, Joe," Cory said.

The younger man headed for the stairs, and Liliana turned back to Joe. "What's going on?" she asked.

Joe shook his head, and grabbed her jacket hanging on the hook by the door. "Here, put this on. We need to move you again."

No, Liliana wasn't going anywhere. At least, not right now. She didn't like that all of the sudden he showed up at *his* home with nothing more than a demand for her to leave. Likely to leave with him, sure, but *still.*

Something felt wrong.

Off.

"What's wrong?" she asked.

Joe held out her coat.

Liliana refused to take it.

Letting out a harsh sigh, Joe said, "Just … I need you to listen to me right now, Liliana. Not question me, or anything else. Just *listen.*"

"And I'm not moving until you tell me what in the hell is going on, Joe."

She wasn't entirely sure how much time passed with the two of them staring at each other, and daring the other one to move or say something. A few seconds, but maybe more. Long enough for her to hear Cory moving around upstairs.

Definitely not like his brother.

She would never know Joe was anywhere around if he didn't want her to know it. Cory didn't seem to give two fucks who heard him.

"Where's your phone?" he asked instead.

Liliana pulled the device Theo had picked up for her out of her pocket, and instantly, Joe snatched it from her. He didn't even look away from her when he swung the device, and smashed it into a useless bunch of pieces against the wall.

Her gaze widened, and flew back to Joe. "What the fuck, Joe?"

"Someone might be tracking it. It needs to go."

"It's a burner phone, Joe. It's not even my real phone!"

Joe only shrugged.

"Okay, now you really need to tell me what in the hell is going on."

"Liliana—"

"Please just tell me, Joe," Liliana said. "I've been sitting in this house for days wondering why I'm even here, and what's going on. No one will tell me anything. I don't like feeling alone and afraid, okay? And I think, so far, I have done really well about not being a bitch regarding all of this. I haven't *really* demanded anything, or whatever. So, *please*, just tell me. It's about me, right. It has to be, so I think, at the very least, I deserve to know *something*."

His fist clenched.

His throat bobbed.

Finally, he spoke, saying, "Rich Earl has gone off the grid."

Liliana stiffened.

The cold spike of fear driving into her spine was only matched in force by the heavy weight of dread sinking low in her stomach. A feeling so thick and harsh that it made the bile in her stomach rise to the back of her throat. She could practically taste it on her tongue, and it made her want to be sick.

It tasted like hell and fear.

Like old blood in her mouth.

Felt like a broken eye socket, and a busted mouth. Like black eyes, and bruises on her body. Like a sting in her scalp from her hair being ripped out, and a ringing in her ears that lasted almost two weeks before it started to fade away. Like an ache in her thighs from where they had been forced open, and scratches on her back from when she had practically fallen out of the car onto the pavement to get away.

Just like that, with seven words from Joe, Liliana was thrust into a chamber of memories, and fear. Neither of which she wished for, or needed.

And yet, here she was.

"Hey, it's all right," Joe murmured.

He'd come forward, and wrapped her in his embrace. Tight, secure, and snug. Warm, and safe. His coldness bled away, and he took those few seconds to stroke her face with his thumbs, and skim the top of her head with his lips. He tipped her head back, and his fingers wove into her hair to.

"It's *fine*," he whispered, "we're just going to move you until we can get eyes on him again, and finish this nonsense out."

"Why did you have eyes on him in the first place? And finish *what*, Joe?"

Joe stiffened that time.

Liliana didn't miss it.

"I *really* need to know what's going on," she said.

"I know you do, but—"

"No buts. No excuses. Just tell me."

"You know I was hired by your father ... or your uncles ... what does that matter, anyway."

Liliana frowned up at him. "Yeah, to watch me."

Joe's lips pressed together into a thin, grim line before he shook his head subtly. "Not at first, no. That came after when the man who had been watching you for quite a while was found dead in his place—your dad didn't tell you because he didn't want you to worry. You had the show coming up, and he just wanted you to focus—"

"Stop rambling, Joe."

"I don't want to scare you."

Ice slipped through Liliana's veins.

Fear walked with it.

She suppressed as much as she could. Right now, she had something else she needed to handle. She needed to know *everything* before she let it consume her.

"Scare me with what?"

"With me," he said quietly.

That had not been the answer she was expecting.

Not at all.

"Keep going," she said hoarsely.

"I wasn't given details about why I was hired to take out George Earl and Martin Abraham; I was given the file for their marks, and I took them on."

"Take them out."

Joe just kept staring at her.

Liliana barely even blinked.

"*Take them out*," she repeated thickly.

"It's what I do. I remove people, and problems. It's what I'm good at, so that's what they brought me in to do."

"Why those two men, though?"

Joe's gaze flashed with something Liliana found difficult to recognize. "Because your father made a promise after what they did, and what Rich did—Lucian doesn't really seem like the type to break his promises, does he? Because they *knew*, Liliana. Because they covered up what he did to you. Because they needed to go."

"And you did it," she said. "You killed them."

She wasn't entirely sure how she felt about that.

Concerned.

Frightened.

Amazed.

Comforted.

She didn't know how to deal with it.

"I did it," Joe said, "and I would take care of Rich, too, but right now, I have to worry about you. So, please make this easy on me, and let me get you the hell out of here. We have no reason to believe he knows you're here, so we can safely assume moving you again will just take you even further out of his path."

Liliana's throat tightened at what Joe *wasn't* saying.

But she wasn't dumb.

"You think he's coming for me," she whispered.

Was that why Rich had started approaching her again? Making himself known again in her life? Terrorizing her like he had?

Because he was *coming back for more?*

"I don't know anything except how to keep you safe," Joe said, "and so that's what I'm going to do, if you'll let me."

It didn't seem like she had a choice. Not that she would have made a different one if given the chance.

"All set," Cory said as he came to stand beside the two, and dropped the bags next to Joe. "You need me to come along?"

Joe didn't look away from Liliana.

She was still in his arms.

Still safe, despite knowing what he was.

Who he was.

"No, not for this," Joe said, never taking his eyes off her while he spoke. "Just keep an eye out here for anything off, Cory. You know how to get in contact with me, should you have to."

"Whatever you need, Joe."

"You okay?"

For the first time in the two hours since they had hit the road, Liliana dragged her gaze away from the passenger side mirror. "Yeah, Joe."

"You sure?"

"Why wouldn't I be?"

"Because you haven't said one word since we left."

It was just easier to stare at the passing scenery than at Joe right now. She was still trying to connect the man who had touched her with the sweetest hands, and treated her like something precious to the man who she now knew killed people for money.

It didn't change who he was, sure.

He could be *both*.

It just ... quieted her, for a moment. It took her through a series of revelations about her life, and the people in it. Of course, she knew her family was full of criminals. Of course, she knew her father—a man she loved and adored—could be someone else entirely when he left his home, and family behind.

There was still a strange, small part of her that kept thinking ... *I never expected to fall in love with one, though.*

Because she did.

Love Joe.

Entirely.

"Why did you send me to Chicago?" Liliana asked. "And not *just* Chicago, Joe, but to your home and your family?"

His gaze drifted away from the long stretch of highway in front of them. "You need an answer for that, love?"

"Maybe I would like to hear you say it."

"I wanted them to meet you."

"Your family," she pressed.

Joe nodded, and put his attention back on the windshield. "And for you to meet them, I guess. You also needed to get the hell out of New York for a while. It felt like a win-win, you could say."

Huh.

"Where are we going?"

He shrugged. "Just far enough to stop for the night before we move again."

"And what are we going to do when we get there?"

"Guess we're going to find out."

Liliana glanced away from him to see a sign for an upcoming exit ramp, and then a larger sign for a hotel not far beyond it. "I want to call my dad."

"As soon as we settle in, you can do just that."

"Okay."

What else could she say?

Liliana didn't even know how to *feel.*

It didn't take long for Joe to get them off the highway, and settled into an Illinois hotel for the evening. Although frankly, *motel* would have been a better term.

She wasn't going to be a snob.

Or picky.

She just ... needed to think.

Sleep, too.

While he had booked them a room, Liliana was made to stay in the SUV, and out of sight. She didn't mind.

"Here," Joe murmured, passing over his phone. "Press two and hold it—your father's number is already on the speed dial. It's the phone they gave me to contact them during the job. He'll answer it."

Liliana took the phone with a small smile. "Thanks."

"We'll only be here for the night, and then we're moving again."

"All right."

Joe nodded, and then he slipped into the small bathroom connected to the equally tiny bedroom. That's really all there was to see inside the room. Old furniture—things that needed updated, for sure and a rug that really needed to be ripped up and replaced. Even the old blinds on the windows had seen better days.

But it worked.

She supposed ...

Liliana pressed two, and held the phone to her ear when it started ringing. Her father picked up just as Joe came back out of the bathroom, but he barely even looked at her. In fact, he put as much distance in between them as he could, and let her have space.

She didn't know whether to be sad, or grateful.

What did she even want?

"Hello?"

"Daddy, hey," Liliana said.

She kept her focus on the phone call, but her eyes on Joe. He fiddled with some maps on the bedside table, and then turned the lamp on.

"Liliana." The relief in her father's voice was palpable. It made her heart clench. "I take it Joe got to you if you're using his phone."

"Yeah, you could say that."

"Good. I didn't want to scare you."

Liliana laughed weakly. "Seems like you've done a lot of things with the intention of not scaring me, Daddy."

"And what does that mean?"

"I just ... you know I love you, right?"

She swore she could see her father's smile when he said, "I have always known that, *mia principessa*."

And she knew he loved her.

That's why he had done what he did.
Why he was *doing* what he was doing now.
Her gaze drifted to Joe.
She wondered if it was the same thing for him, too.
She wasn't ready to ask.
Liliana was still trying to process, think, and *feel*.

FIFTEEN

JOE WAITED FOR the ringing of the phone to click in his ear, signaling someone had picked up the call. Taking one last drag from his cigarette, he flicked the butt to the ground, and watched sparks fly when it hit the pavement. Leaning back against the hotel door, Joe stared up at the sky when he finally heard the call connect.

"*Ciao*, Lucian here."

"Wanted to give you an update," Joe murmured.

"Moved again?"

Joe cleared his throat, and nodded. "Moved this morning   drove for twelve hours, and then I found a spot to settle in again."

"Good."

He appreciated how Lucian was smart enough not to question Joe about where he and Liliana now were, or anything like that. The less people knew, the better. It was far more unlikely that information would get out that way.

"How is she today?" Lucian asked.

Joe chuckled dryly. "Same."

"Well, that's better than nothing."

"And not talking to me at all."

Lucian quieted.

So did Joe.

He wasn't even entirely sure why he had admitted that to Lucian, as it wasn't like he wanted the man to know, or thought that he could do something to help. Shit, maybe he just needed to *voice* it, to handle it.

Who knew?

"I take it she knows things, then," Lucian said.

Joe shrugged. "Some things—the important bits."

"Things that make her reevaluate."

"What makes you say that?"

"Kind of obvious, isn't it, Joe?"

"Is it if I asked?" he shot back.

Lucian laughed lowly. "My apologies. I *meant*, men who may seem like strangers—or in some way, scary—to Liliana, she keeps a distance. Maintains a safe, respectable space between her and them."

"I'm not a stranger."

Or scary, he added silently.

At least, not to her.

"But perhaps the things she knows about you contradicts what she's seen or knows," Lucian offered quietly.

Joe scowled.

He hadn't thought of it like that.

"Like I said," Lucian continued thoughtfully, "it might have made her feel as though she needed time to reevaluate. Maybe she could have done that quicker had she been able to put some distance between the two of you, but here you are."

Distance.

Joe hated that word.

Distance wasn't possible right now.

Or ever.

Joe figured it was time to get off this conversation, and move onto something else entirely. "What good news do you have for me?"

"Very little, actually."

"Stab that knife deeper, huh?"

Lucian chuckled darkly. "Trust me, you have no idea how much I wish I had good news on my end."

"Rich is still MIA, then?"

"Entirely, but it's worse, too."

Joe didn't like the sound of that at all. "How so?"

"The Marcello name has now been dragged into this," Lucian muttered, his distaste and hatred coating each and every word.

Stiffening against the door, Joe scrubbed a hand down his face. Fuck, he needed a shave like nothing else. And a good night's sleep, too. Half decent food, a good fuck, and a change of clothes. He needed a lot of things right then.

This was not one of them.

"*How?*" he asked again.

"Rich's mother—the senator's wife—made a public plea that her son has gone missing, which brought the fucking police in on it over the last day or so. There's talk the FBI might move in, too."

"I don't see how that brings the Marcello—"

"She suggested that she didn't believe her husband's drowning was accidental, despite the reports to the contrary. Said she had it on *good faith* that it was intentional, and even dared to add he didn't drink."

Joe barked out a laugh at that statement. "He was already drunk when I got there that night. So was she—so much so, that she didn't hear a thing when I dragged him out of their house, and to the pool in the backyard."

"We *all* know what the senator was like, Joe."

"Then, get to the point."

"She *purposely* brought up my family's name, and that leads me to believe she knows exactly what is going on, or has a good suspicion about it. Probably because of Rich."

Joe frowned, and his gaze narrowed into the darkness in front of him. "You did want him to know you were coming for him, Lucian."

The man on the other end of the phone sighed. "Point is—this felt like a last-ditch effort on the wife's part."

"What, like maybe if she invoked your family's name in a public forum, it might save Rich's life? Keep you all from going after him?"

"Exactly that."

"See how well that works out for her, I suppose," Joe mused.

"You're missing the point, Joe."

"Sometimes, I do that."

He had jokes tonight.

Well done to him.

"The *point*," Lucian stressed thickly, "is that as clean as this has been working with you to get rid of the others, it's now dirtier than sin."

Ah.

Yeah.

Joe hadn't considered that. His mind was focused in on other things—Liliana, most importantly, and keeping her as safe as he could for the time being.

"When Rich goes—"

"And he will *go*," Joe interjected.

"Of course," Lucian said, "but *when* he goes, our name is already tossed into the mix. They'll be looking at us for a while. Attention will be hot, and heavy. We had prepared for that, anyway, sure, but maybe things are a bit more complicated now, considering you and … well, *her*."

Shit.

Yeah, difficult.

"That's one way to put it," Joe mumbled.

"We'll need you to go underground, or get back to business in Chicago, Joe. Stay out of sight, and have absolutely no connection to the Marcello family until this dies down, or at least until they have no reason to suspect you were the means we used to pull this off. We don't want to purposely give them something or someone to dig into. That's how it all comes crashing down. I know I don't have to explain *why*, but—"

"Nature of the business," Joe cut in.

"It might not be for very long that you would have to stay away."

But it could be.

Days, certainly.

Weeks, more likely.

175

Months … *probably.*

Joe didn't really want to talk anymore. "I should get back."

He didn't offer anything else.

Lucian didn't ask. "I'll be seeing you soon, Joe."

One could only hope.

That meant this would be over.

Joe's gaze drifted from the flat screen television on the wall to Liliana's towel-wrapped form as she slipped out of the bathroom. This much larger, and expensive, hotel was likely more up to her tastes than the first one they had used for a night, but she had never said a thing. She didn't offer him a single complaint.

She only really talked when she wanted food.

He kept her in his peripheral vision as she moved across the room, and sat on the edge of the bed. Her hair hung in damp waves down her back like she had run a towel through it, but still left the strands a bit wet. He knew she had taken her things—an outfit change, and whatever else— into the bathroom with her, so why she came out wearing nothing but a towel was a mystery to him, and not one he wanted to prod into.

She said nothing.

Joe was used to that.

He went back to watching the basketball game playing on the television. Basketball wasn't really his sport, but it was the first thing he found when he turned on the TV. It would do for his purpose of distracting him, and he wasn't in the mood to channel surf until he found something more appealing.

"I'm sorry."

Joe stiffened.

He wasn't sure he heard her right.

Turning a bit to stare at Liliana, he asked, "Pardon?"

"I said," she clarified louder, "I'm sorry, Joe."

"*Why?*"

He wasn't sure what she was apologizing for, or even why. He didn't think she had anything to apologize for, really. None of this was her fault. He thought she already knew that.

"For me and you," she muttered. "Us, and this, I guess. I'm sorry."

Joe blinked. "I still don't know where you're going with this."

And he had the distinct feeling he wasn't going to like it, either.

She waved between them, although she never lifted her gaze to look at him. He probably hated that the most, but didn't have time to think on it for long when she was already moving onto the next thing, and speaking again.

"This ... us," she said again, "it's a little confusing for me. Relationships, maybe. I never really had one of those before—not a *serious* one, you know what I mean?"

Joe shrugged. "Sure, me either."

Liliana did glance up at that, and her gaze met his with an intensity that had him stilling in place when she asked, "Really, never?"

"Nope."

"Oh."

"I guess I just never found someone I wanted to have that with ..." Joe trailed off before adding quieter, "Until you, that is."

Liliana peered down at her twisting hands. A nervous tic he recognized that she did whenever words were failing her, and she was struggling to come up with the right thing to say. He wished she wouldn't do that at all—but hey, she was talking, and that was something different than she had been doing for far too long.

He wasn't about to ruin it.

Not by pushing her.

"The one man I thought did love me in a romantic way ended up hurting me," Liliana said, "and I think that still fucks with my head a lot. And then I get this stuff about you shoveled onto me, too, and it's not the Joe I knew, or the one I met. It's not the one who came to my place at night, or the man who watched me dance. It's not the one who made me feel safe, or *perfect*."

Joe swallowed hard.

He made her feel perfect.

She should feel perfect.

"You are perfect," Joe murmured.

Liliana looked up again, but a line of water had dampened her gaze. "Except it is the same man, isn't it? The things you do, who you are, and then what you are with me—it's all the same person, just in different shades of your life."

Joe nodded.

What else could he do?

"I give myself whiplash trying to figure out how I feel," Liliana said sadly.

Joe chuckled. "Me, too."

"I don't mean to."

"It's okay," he assured. "Only one thing really matters to me at the end of the day, *Tesoro*."

"And what's that, Joe?"

"Would you let me in—would you let me love you, Liliana? When all this is over, and life is back to normal, can I come back again, say hello, and start this over? Would you let me *love* you?"

She didn't wait a second.

Not even a breath.

"I would."

That's all that he cared about.

The rest was inconsequential.

"Okay," Joe said.

Liliana cocked a brow, and smiled a tiny bit. "Just okay?"

"Yeah, *just* okay, love. Go get dressed. I ordered you that red velvet cake you liked from the restaurant. It should be here soon. Don't need to give anybody a show, huh?"

Her laughter coated his dark soul, and Joe swore he still heard it long after she had disappeared back into the bathroom. More than anything, he had wanted to get up, and go to her. Get her back on the bed, lose himself between the heaven of her thighs, and show her just how much that *okay* really meant to him, but he couldn't do that ...

Not yet.

She had to come to him this time.

He had to let it be on her terms.

Not his.

It was only later in the evening, when all the lights were off, and Joe was hovering in the space between wakefulness and sleep that Liliana finally reached for him again. It started with an innocent whisper from across the bed that had his eyes flying wide open.

"Joe?"

"Hmm, *cara?*"

"Do you really think that's what I am—*darling?*"

Joe tipped his head to the side on the pillow, and grinned at her through the darkness. He could just make out the outline of her features which meant she had to be able to see him, too. "You've always been darling, Liliana."

"Mmm."

She went silent again.

So did Joe.

And then she reached for him. One hand snaking under the blankets, and coming to rest on his midsection. Her fingers traced the railroad pathway of his abdominal muscles, making each and every one of them jump at the touch.

She came closer under the sheets.

He didn't move an inch.

"Joe?"

"Hmm?"

"You know it's okay if you kiss me—*touch* me. Right?"

Joe only replied, "Only if you want me to, love."

And he meant it.

Damn, did he ever mean it.

"You know I do; I always want—"

She didn't even get the rest of her words out before Joe was reaching for her. He pulled his sweet ballerina on top of him in a flurry of laughter, and mussed blankets. Her body rested flat against his as he thrust his fingers into her hair, and yanked her in for a kiss he had been dying for.

He missed her taste.

The softness of her lips.

The way she kissed him.

How her tongue warred with his.

Oh, he missed it.

Her.

The thin cotton boxer-briefs he wore did little to hide the way his cock grew the longer she let him love her mouth. His erection was only urged on by each wiggle and shift of her hips until Liliana had straddled him completely, and was shamelessly grinding her pussy against his dick.

Fuck, he loved that, too.

"I can feel you already," he mumbled against her lips. "You're already hot and wet, aren't you?"

He *could* feel it.

Her dampness.

Her heat.

Liliana nodded, and her whispers melted into a low moan when he snuck a hand between her thighs. She lifted just enough for him to slide two fingers under the gusset of her panties, and through her slick folds. Her answering shudder when his digits dove into her cunt made him chuckle, but it was the way her pussy hugged his fingers tight that damn near drove him insane with need and want.

He knew what she wanted, too.

"Is that what you want?" he murmured in her ear. "You want me to pet this pussy, Liliana, and make it purr for me?"

"God, yes."

Her words came out breathless, and spun.

"What do you want, then, my mouth or my fingers first?"

She hesitated.

Her hazel eyes—darkened with lust and locked on his—drifted over his lax, lazy grin when she said, "Both."

Joe's smirk was wicked.

Sinful.

"That's my girl. Get those clothes of yours off, and turn around."

She still remembered what he had told her that first time—listening would get her everything she wanted, and more when it came to him. She wasted no time moving off him just long enough to shed her panties, and tight tank-top. She slid back on top of him, but this time, he had the perfect view of her ass.

Joe slid his hand from the curve of her backside, to the middle of her spine before he pressed down firmly with his hand. His position, with his back and head slightly raised against the headboard, gave him ample room to do what he wanted like this.

"Head down, and ass high. If you want, you can make that mouth of yours useful, and get my cock ready for you. Got it?"

"*Jesus*, Joe."

His hand landed down on her right ass cheek with a firm swat, and pinked the skin. She stiffened at the smack, but her back relaxed when the sweet sigh she released.

"*Yes*," she quickly corrected, "I understand."

"Good. Take me out, and then give me your hands."

"W-what?"

He'd made her stutter on her words when he stroked that sleek pussy of hers—all pink, and wet for him—as she spoke. It looked good enough to eat, and he knew she was going to taste hot and tart on his tongue once he really got her worked up good.

He looked forward to it.

"Take me out," Joe said, working two fingers in and out of her pussy and enjoying the wet sounds her cunt made for him with every stroke, "and then give me your *hands*."

Joe knew Liliana was struggling.

To trust, or not to trust.

To compare, or not to compare.

And yet, he didn't think that she even realized her heart had long ago made the choice that her brain had not. Because she didn't question him at all as she freed his hard cock from his boxer-briefs, and then extended her arms back to him to lock in tight at her lower back within his large grasp.

"Ask me for it," he said softly, "use words, babe."

"Please, Joe. *Please* give me your mouth and your fingers, and then your cock, too. Please."

"Good girl."

It wasn't like he was actually going to *refuse*.

Liliana's warm, silken lips encased his dick at the same time Joe lowered his face to the heaven between her thighs. He hadn't been wrong—that first taste of her was like nothing else. A flavor unique to her, and it only got better the more she shook, and the hotter her body became. The initial stroke of this tongue through the slit of her sex to tease and test her had Liliana moaning hard despite his dick being halfway in her mouth.

Fuck.

It took everything in him not to jerk his hips upward, and get her swallowing all of him.

Due time.

All in due time, he told himself.

Her first.

His tongue worked her slit and into her pussy while his one hand kept her arms locked firmly at her back, and his other hand worked at her clit. Just two fingers—light pressure, and small, tight circles against the throbbing bud.

It was more than enough.

He loved the way her body responded.

All wet, warm, and shaking.

The faster he ate her pussy and worked his fingers against her clit, the more she made those sweet little sounds around his cock while she sucked him off. It practically vibrated through his whole body, and made him high and drunk all at the same time.

He didn't need drugs or a drink for that.

Just her.

"Take that cock," Joe murmured, pulling away from Liliana's wet sex just long enough to kiss the curve of her ass cheek. He bit the same spot, and felt her jerk from the surprise shock of pain. He did it again just to feel the way her throat constricted against his dick with her gasp. "Do you wanna swallow my cum after I fuck you, ballerina? Get a taste of you on my dick again?"

She sucked harder.

Her teeth scraped along sensitive flesh.

She did that shit on *purpose.*

Joe couldn't take it, and she knew it.

He forced himself to focus on getting her off with his mouth and fingers at least once before he bent her over, and gave her what she wanted the most.

And what *he* wanted the most.

Joe didn't relent the second his mouth was back on her pussy. He was the starving man, and she was the fucking feast spread out before him. Her pretty pink pussy spread open for him, and needy. A lot like her, really.

Needy.

Wanting.

Aching, probably.

Liliana released Joe's cock with a *pop* when her body tensed, and then the shaking started. "Going to come—shit, don't stop, *please.*"

He let go of his hold on her arms when she did fall over the edge, making Liliana fall forward to catch herself on the bed. He grabbed tightly to her ass, letting his fingers dig in to the firm flesh as he lapped up every bit of her arousal that flooded his tongue.

Goddamn.

Yeah, she tasted so much hotter when she came.

Like candy, really.

Joe pulled away from Liliana before she had even stopped gasping his name. He slid higher on the bed, grabbed her around the waist, and pulled her into his lap. She was already widening her legs for him, and grabbing the base of his cock with her warm palm. She was the one to fit the head of his dick at her pussy, and she lowered down on him faster than he expected her to.

He kept her tight to him—her back to his chest. His mouth on her neck, and his arm tight around her chest. His palm came up to cup her throat so he could feel every noise she made before it even escaped her parted lips.

He bit her neck and shoulder, kissed the same spots, too, as his other hand slid between her thighs, and found her warm, wet cunt swallowing his dick. He flexed his hips every time she lifted or lowered on him—the push and pull. He wanted to get deeper, fuck her harder, but he also wanted to *feel,* and to *taste.*

All of her.

Every fucking inch of her.

"Christ, I can feel you," he growled in her ear. "So fucking *wet,* babe."

His fingers graced the length of his dick when she raised on him again, and he used the wetness from her arousal to drag up to her clit. He toyed, while she fucked. Her answering breathless whines came out high, and sweet.

"Almost, *almost,*" he heard her whisper.

The promise of her coming again goaded him.

Teased him.

Promised him.

"Fucking give it to me," Joe demanded. "It's *mine,* Liliana."

"*Yours.*"

The stiffness in Joe's back as he felt the sun streak across his skin had him grinning into the pillow instantly. Usually if he woke up sore, he wouldn't be very fucking pleased about it. Not today, though.

Waking up sore meant good things happened the night before, and he was more than willing to stay right where he was for just long enough to relive it in his memories. That round with Liliana had been one for the ages, and it lasted *well* into the early morning hours. He slept like the dead because of it. He doubted an elephant walking through the room would have woken him up.

Maybe he had needed that sleep.

Fuck.

What time was it?

Joe checked his watch with one hand, and then reached for Liliana with the other. His hand came up with nothing—air on her side of the bed—at the same time he realized it was closing in on ten in the morning.

Ten.

In the morning.

What the fuck?

"Liliana?"

Joe turned his head, but found the same thing his hand had. Nothing and no one was on Liliana's side of the bed. Only crumpled blankets, and a pillow with the indent where her head had once rested.

He sat up.

"Liliana!"

He wasn't going to panic.

No need to fucking panic.

Not yet.

"Liliana?"

Silence answered him back. The fucking hotel room wasn't that big. It was only the bedroom and sitting room as one damn room, and the bathroom. That was *it*. It wasn't like she couldn't have heard him if she was in the bathroom. And she wasn't.

He knew it.

The bathroom door was open, the light shut off, and he didn't hear *anything.*

Jesus.

Fuck.

A part of him kept screaming, *It's fine, it's fine, it's fine.*

After all, no one but her father knew where they were, and Joe hadn't even given Lucian a proper location. There was no possible way someone had found them here—they weren't registered at the hotel under their real names, and they'd barely left the room for the whole day and half they had been there.

It just wasn't possible.

Another part of him … a part that somehow just *knew* … was screaming louder.

She's gone.

She's gone.

She's gone.

A mantra he couldn't escape.

Joe kicked the sheets off, and snatched the phone from the bedside table. He didn't know why he thought to call down to the front desk, but he figured if Liliana had left for whatever reason, she likely would have used the front entrance.

Two rings later, and the concierge picked up.

"Mr.—"

"Room 202," Joe barked, "did you see the woman from room 202 leave this morning?"

"Um … just a second, s—"

"Just *think!*"

The guy stumbled over his words, and then Joe heard something rustle against the phone. Likely the man's hand covering the speaker. Seconds later, he was back on.

"A young woman ordered breakfast a couple of hours ago, but no one answered the door when we knocked."

Joe deflated.

His heart *shattered.*

Two hours ago?

If she had ordered breakfast, and it hadn't been delivered two hours ago, but she *still* wasn't in the room with Joe … that only meant bad things.

Terrible fucking things.

"No one saw her leave?" Joe asked. "She's hard to miss—tall, willowy, dark blonde hair half way down her back, and hazel eyes? No one saw her at all?"

The man pulled the phone away, and Joe heard him barking questions to whoever else was around. He knew the man's answer before he even came back to the phone. And yet, when the concierge delivered those words Joe already fucking knew, they still killed him like a knife driven straight into his heart.

And then the blade was *twisted,* too.

"Not through the front, sir. Is something wrong?"

Was something *wrong?*

Oh, no.

No … just his entire life being gone.

His soul ripped to shreds.

Nothing fucking *big*, or anything.

"How many exits are in this building?"

"One for every floor, sir, and one for every room."

Joe's gaze drifted to the small patio that was connected to their room. Yes, it, too, had a small metal ladder that could extend to the ground if needed. Shit.

"How much would it cost me to get a look at your security footage for this morning?" Joe asked.

"Excuse me?"

"I didn't fucking stutter. *How much?*"

SIXTEEN

THE POUNDING BASS drum beating inside Liliana's skull was unlike anything she had ever felt before. Painful enough to keep her from speaking, but still allowed a strangled groan to slip past her dry lips.

Dry … like her mouth.

And her eyes when she tried to peel them open.

She tried to focus on just one thing. Either the pain, the way her lips peeled off whatever they had been pressed against, the haziness in her mind, or … all the rest. It felt like everything was mixing together and only getting worse the longer she tried to fight whatever was happening to her.

And Christ …

What was happening?

Her vision was as thick and hazy as her mind. As though she were looking through gray clouds to focus on whatever was behind them. Black leather, she thought. A handle, maybe? Also black, but that was just about all she understood.

She tried to reach out to touch whatever it was just in front of her face, but found her strength was seriously lacking. Even moving like she had took every bit of effort she possessed, and when she couldn't reach whatever was there, her body just gave out.

Done, again.

Why did her stomach feel empty?

Her mouth tasted like vomit.

And her *head* …

Jesus, her head *hurt*.

"No, no, no," she heard.

The words came out sing-song.

Teasing.

Amused.

Pleased.

And that voice.

Oh, God.

That voice.

Every part of Liliana screamed internally at that voice.

Rich Earl.

"Don't wake up just yet," Rich said somewhere behind the clouds and the haze and the pain. "I'm not happy enough to talk with you yet, whore."

That *tone*.

That *warning*.

That *man*.

Liliana squeezed her eyes shut as whatever she was resting on swayed a bit. In a car, maybe. Soft leather, and that distinct *rental* smell. It had to be a car, didn't it?

How had she gotten here?

The memory flooded ...

"Anything in particular?"

Liliana hummed as she looked over the menu, and glanced back to where Joe was still sleeping on the bed. He was fucking out. Like a damn light, or something. A hurricane wasn't about to wake that man up, and some silly part of her found that most amusing.

She could have slept longer, too, but she woke up hungry.

And horny.

The horny bit she would deal with once Joe was awake, and she had food in her stomach. Jesus, she needed to have some kind of priorities where this man and sex was concerned, or she was going to end up starving herself because she would much rather stay in bed and fuck her days away with him.

That's what he did to her.

"Could we just get a spread?" Liliana asked. "A little bit of everything, but nothing extravagant. Just basics."

"Eggs, bacon, toast, pancakes, waffles ... "

The guy on the other end of the phone downstairs at the restaurant kept rattling food off like Liliana didn't understand what basics *meant when it came to breakfast foods. Yes, she understood. That's why she asked for it.*

"Make it two or three different kinds of eggs," Liliana interjected, stopping the guy from saying more. "Buffet-style, okay?"

"That'll be about an hour."

"No problem. Thanks."

At least, that gave Liliana a little bit of time to clean herself up, and try to pull some clothes on to look decent. She didn't feel like giving anybody but Joe a show. And since he was still sleeping ...

She gave him another look.

Yep, still sleeping.

She headed for the bathroom, and shut the door behind her to keep the noise of the shower from filtering out. It took her all of ten minutes—maybe fifteen—to put the shower to use, and then step out to dry off. She had just finished rinsing her toothbrush when she heard the faintest knock echoing from the bedroom.

No way the hour had passed by that quickly.

Maybe it had.

Liliana didn't even bother to check the clock as she left the bathroom, She headed for the door, and quietly said over her shoulder as she reached for the doorknob, "Joe, get up. Food's here."

He didn't even stir.

Huh.

Maybe it was more than just them fucking like rabbits into the wee hours that put him into such a deep sleep. Maybe it was something like everything going on around them, and the stress he was dealing with. He never complained—never said a thing was wrong, or bad. He just did what he had to do.

And damn …

Liliana loved him for that.

She was coming to learn—although she hadn't told him yet—that she loved Joe Rossi for a lot of reasons, and for a lot of things.

Most importantly, because he was him.

And he loved her.

"Joe," Liliana said louder as she pulled open the door.

"Say his name again," came a low, threatening voice, "and I'll kill him before he can roll over, Lilibet."

Lilibet.

It was the nickname first, and the voice second that she recognized. A part of her didn't want to turn and face the man waiting behind the door because the idea of facing him again when he wasn't even supposed to know where she was terrified the hell out of her.

"Look at me," Rich ordered.

She tore her gaze away from Joe.

Not because she wanted to, but because she needed to keep Rich's attention away from him for now. That much she was most sure of. On a fucking cellular level, Liliana knew she was in trouble, and so was Joe.

So much trouble.

Bad all the way around the board.

"Rich," Liliana greeted.

Kindly, *too.*

Although how she managed, she wasn't sure.

He looked the same—still tall, lean, and handsome. His dark hair was a bit more disheveled than usual, but his suit still looked like he pulled it out of a fucking magazine somewhere. His grin seemed warm and welcoming, but Liliana wasn't so stupid to let that trick her. She knew what overlooking this man could do and bring her way.

He could not be trusted.

But hell, that's what good looks, money, and a charming smile could do for a fucking monster. It could turn him into someone else entirely—someone the best of people didn't recognize for what he truly was.

"Step out with me," Rich said.

He didn't pose it as a question.

Not an offer, either.

Liliana didn't move. "You need to leave."

Rich tipped his head to the side, and that slow smile morphed into something else entirely. Something far more cold, and terrifying. The sneer made her feel like a block of ice in an instant, and her hand on the door tightened in preparation to slam it.

It would give her a second to lock it, maybe.

A moment to do—

"Close the door on me, or make a sound, and this will get far worse. I have people waiting. I will take you by force, and him, too. Make it easy on me," Rich said like he was offering her something sweet to take between her lips and taste, "and I will leave him here alive. Consider it, Liliana. It's just you two here—your family isn't going to protect you today, and certainly not that father of yours."

The way he said father, *like he was spitting it from his mouth, made Liliana cringe. She felt the fear fighting its way up her chest like bile spilling onto the back of her tongue. Not one single part of her wanted to go with him, but what she didn't know terrified her more.*

Did he have people?

It wasn't just her and Joe to consider, either, because the hotel was full of other guests. How many innocents would be harmed in Rich's effort to get her away from Joe?

Although, Joe was the most important to her. And nothing was worth him being hurt.

"Also know that should you make this difficult," Rich added, "I have plans for him, too. Starting with having him watch me fuck you, and depending on how he takes that, we'll go from there. Good torture takes patience, and skill, after all."

Rich's gaze cut back to Liliana, cold and detached in a blink. "So, surprise me, Lilibet, and show me what you've learned since our time apart. I've been very patient, you see. Waiting for this ... don't disappoint me."

Jesus.

Liliana stepped out of the hotel room, and closed the door behind her. The form that rushed her from the side the moment the door was closed had a scream rising in her throat. It died in the hand that covered her mouth, and the sharp prick that found her neck.

A needle.

Coldness slipped through her veins. Blackness found her soon after.

"Drink."

The bottle of water was pushed into Liliana's hand when she refused to take it from Rich. She squeezed the water tight, and despite her throat being so dry it was protesting in pain, her desire to drink from the straw sticking out of the bottle was little to none. He handed it to her opened, after all.

Who knew what the bastard put in it?

She wasn't making this easy on him.

A man stood behind him dressed in all black—apparently, the guard for her. Should she run, he was going to be the one coming after her.

Or, that's what Rich explained.

"It's just *water*," Rich snapped, his exasperation clear.

The condensation on the outside of the bottle wet Liliana's fingers. The water promised reprieve, and relief. For her throat, aching stomach, and maybe even her pounding head.

"Where are we going?" she asked.

Liliana hadn't forgotten a few tricks about Rich. Like the best way to get the man off one topic was to distract him by making him talk about something else. Even better if that something had to do with him, or something he wanted to do.

It could also calm him down.

Relax him.

"A little place I bought," he said, smiling again.

That warm smile.

The charming one.

He used it on her the first night they met, and then again right before he almost beat her to death. She hated that fucking smile, and quite frankly, wished someone would cut it off his face, so he couldn't use it on her or some other poor woman, ever again.

It would be doing the world a favor, really.

Rich leaned closer to where she was sitting with her legs hanging out of the back of the car. The small rest stop and gas station was all but empty save for one or two cars. Nobody was even looking their way.

He reached out, and Liliana forced herself not to move when the tips of his fingers came in contact with her eyebrow. The scar hidden by her eyebrow stung like hell with a phantom pain when he dragged his finger across it, appraising it silently.

"The plastic surgeon did good work, I see," he noted.

She did tense at that statement.

Rich moved fast—and *harsh*—when his hand moved from her brow, down to her chin. He grabbed tightly to her face and his fingernails dug into her skin hard enough to either break the skin, or bruise. He forced her to look at him, and that smile of his had been replaced by a thin, grim line.

"Smile, Lilibet."

Liliana *couldn't*.

"Smile," Rich demanded again, "and stop the sulking. You know I hate it when you fucking *sulk* like a baby."

She swallowed hard.

And *smiled.*

Her best fuck-you-smile.

Rich couldn't tell the difference. "Well done. Aren't you curious at all?"

"About what?"

The only thing she *really* gave a shit about right now was getting the fuck away from him, and then making sure he never came back for her again. She had never wished for someone to die as much as she was willing it for this man in front of her.

"How I *found* you," Rich said.

"Not particularly."

Rich scowled, and tipped his head to the side. A warning if Liliana ever saw one. She was not interested in getting his desires beaten into her, so she decided to play along. If only for a few minutes, and maybe it would keep them in place for a while longer.

That way, they were standstill, and not still on the move.

It was *something.*

"You know what, yeah," Liliana said. "How did you find me?"

"It started with *him*, actually," Rich replied.

He couldn't even *say* Joe's name. Liliana could practically feel Rich's jealousy and disgust radiating from his body. It was a dangerous game to play with him because the wrong step or word would find her bleeding on the backseat of the car while he forced her to apologize.

She'd done that before.

She wasn't doing it again.

Rich didn't seem to notice Liliana's distraction because he was too busy talking about all his amazing accomplishments where she was concerned, and his disconcerting obsession with having her back.

Surprise, surprise.

"And so yes, I had been watching you for a good while—a year, or so," Rich said. "From the moment that bastard let you out of the limo, I had been keeping an eye on you … waiting."

The driver, he meant.

Liliana swallowed her discomfort. "He was trying to *help* me, Rich."

Rich's gaze cut back to her, silencing her instantly. "Yes, and his *help* earned him an early grave. He had no business stepping in, and worked for our family long enough to know his place."

Jesus Christ.

This man was sociopathic.

He waved a hand, adding, "And then I noticed you had a ... *friend.* The first one since me, it seemed. Here I was thinking you were pining over me, but no, you were just biding your time before you skipped off to play the whore again."

Liliana clenched her hands into tight fists, and forced herself to stay quiet. Even though every part of her wanted to tell him to shut his goddamn mouth.

"I saw him on the street with you, and had reports he was going into your building at night. Showed up at your shows, and even visited your family. The charity event was my final straw—I needed to know who he was, so I ... had someone look into him, we'll say."

Nothing had been safe, she realized.

All of her father's plans, while possibly not known to Rich, had been being crept on from behind anyway.

"Joe Rossi—Chicago, affiliated to the mob," Rich said dryly, giving Liliana a raised brow. "Color me fucking surprised. Is that what gets you off, darling—you're a mob whore? A made man gets you hot, and wets your cunt? All you want to be is a *fucking mob wife?*"

"No," Liliana whispered.

Because that *was not* the case at all.

She loved Joe for Joe.

Not because he was mob affiliated.

"Good," Rich murmured, "because I have *far* better plans for you. You're meant to be much, much more, Lilibet."

Yeah, she bet.

"I had leads put on you, and those around you that I could reach," Rich said, continuing his little story. "Wires tapped into the phones at the ballet studio, and even paid the girl who makes your bagel and coffee every morning to make a call whenever you came in ... or didn't, for that matter."

Her heart *clenched.*

Shit just added up and it was like a light bulb going off in her head.

"Now you get it," Rich said, grinning again. "You made a call while in Chicago—to Gordo about your dancing. You needed a few weeks, you said. Apologized because you knew how important the upcoming shows would be. He had the stand-in waiting, though. They always have someone to replace you, don't they?"

"That's the nature of the business," she replied, keeping her tone level and emotionless.

"Shame," Rich muttered, "he should know better, Lilibet. No one can be as captivating as you on that stage. You know that's what drew me to you, don't you? The way you danced, and *moved.* So graceful, and beautiful. Free, really. All I thought about was how I could *cage* you."

Don't respond.

Don't react.
Don't give him anything.
Liliana stayed silent.

"Anyway," Rich said, waving a hand, "I got the call, too, since I had the phones tapped, and the number you called from which was how I knew it was Chicago. Given I already knew about your fancy with the Chicago man, it didn't take too long to put it all together. It was just shit luck that I showed up in Chicago about an hour late to grab you before he did. Couldn't get a flight in time, you see?"

"Didn't think of using a private jet?" she asked.

Rich's gaze flashed with something Liliana didn't understand. "If you must know, I thought I had time to spare. My mistake—don't think I'll make another."

Duly noted.

"But I was not so far behind that I couldn't follow you both, or *try*," Rich said, finishing up his tale, "and so here we are. You with *me*, and him *without*. I like it better this way. Don't you?"

Not at all.

And where was Joe?

Had he woken up, yet?

Figured out she was taken?

Or … thought she just left him?

Fingers snapped in front of her face before Rich's aggravated features clouded her vision. "Are you paying any attention to me at all?"

"Not really, no."

Honesty *was* the best policy.

Except in Rich's case.

His hand came up faster than Liliana expected it to. The slap connected hard with the side of her face, and sent her head spinning to the side, and crashing into the passenger door. Blood bloomed in her mouth, and the coppery taste made her want to puke.

Before, she might have cried.

Asked him to stop.

Begged, even.

Apologized, likely.

Not this time.

No, this time she laughed, and straightened a bit in the seat. She laughed, knowing he was sadistic and easily provoked. She laughed even fully aware that it would only goad him into hitting her again and again until she *stopped*.

It didn't matter.

Because she kept laughing.

Rich's narrowing gaze left her for a brief moment as he tried to right himself, but that was his fucking mistake. Liliana bolted out of the back seat, and launched herself at him. Her fist connected with his mouth at the same time her other hand ranked bleeding lines down the side of his face.

"Don't touch me, you bastard," she hissed.

She was *kicked* back into the car by the guard who decided to step in two seconds too late.

Rich leaned in right after, hovering above Liliana with a bleeding mouth, and a sore-looking face. It terrified her, but it also brought her the greatest sense of satisfaction, too. She never would have fought back before, fearing it would only get worse.

It was probably still going to get worse.

She didn't care.

She wasn't lying down like a *dog* for this man.

She wasn't his *bitch*.

"Keep those surprises coming," Rich murmured, blood staining his teeth, "they get me hard, Lilibet. And you remember what my cock feels like when it's hard, and I'm shoving it into one of your holes, don't you? It's been too long since you got a taste—too bad you're going to have to wait."

Rich slammed the door.

Liliana kicked it right after.

Fuck him; fuck all of him.

And fuck his stupid nickname, too.

She *hated* that nickname.

"Welcome home, my queen."

Liliana looked up from her hands to see a gate opening to allow them entrance to a long, twisting driveway that led up to what looked like quite an estate. She didn't recognize the place, and since Rich had forced a hood over her head for long portions of the drive when he became sick of talking to her, she really had zero fucking idea where she was.

She might have been impressed by the estate were it anyone else showing it to her, but instead, all Liliana could really feel in those moments was a heavy sense of dread settling into her stomach. She *didn't* know where she was. The estate was quite private, by the looks of it. Several guards stood around the property as the car was parking.

How in the hell was she going to get out of this one?

"A home fit for a queen," Rich said.

Queen, like the Lilibet thing. Actually, that's how he came up with that stupid fucking nickname. She despised people calling her Lily—kids used to tease her when she was younger because of her brother. They said Johnathan was crazy when he acted out, and then stories spread like wildfire. They'd call her Silly Lily, and she *hated* it.

Rich liked Lily.

Instead, he settled on Lilibet, like the old former queen's nickname, because that's what he told Liliana she was going to be. His queen.

And then he beat the hell out of her.

"Please stop calling me that," Liliana muttered.

It was the only thing she could think to say.

Rich passed her a dismissive glance. "What, you'll wear their princess title, but not the queen's crown when it's all but handed to you?"

"It's *principessa*," Liliana uttered, "I am a *principessa della mafia* and it would do you well to remember that, Rich."

Except he didn't care, she knew.

That was half of the problem.

This man believed he was untouchable.

"Get out of the car," he deadpanned.

Fine.

Whatever got her farther away from him, she was game.

Unfortunately, the second she got out of the vehicle, she was dragged to Rich's side again. She couldn't even try to hide the shiver of disgust that wreaked havoc up her spine at the feeling of his hand gripping tight to her waist, never mind the taste of bile growing stronger in her mouth when he kissed the side of her head.

Her fists twitched.

She was going to hit him again.

If he kept that shit up …

"Let me show you around," he said, "and then you can get yourself familiar with whatever rooms you prefer. It's all made for you—every room, every floor. All the things I know you love, and things I *love* to watch you do. For a while, I'm sure it'll seem like a prison to you while you work out your problems, and we work out our issues, but that'll pass."

Their *issues*.

He expected them to live together, and work out their issues.

"You're delus—"

"Happy," he interjected, squeezing her side hard enough for it to hurt. "I am incredibly happy because right now, I have everything I want, Liliana."

Oh, God.

The disgust was back.

It burned her throat.

"Don't try to run—you won't make it far," Rich told her as they climbed the stairs to the entrance of the large mansion. "And despite what you may think, I don't like it when you force me to teach you a lesson."

Liar.

Bastard.

Monster.

"You first," he sat, patting her on the *ass*.

The door was opened, and Liliana moved inside. Anything to get the fuck away from him, or at the very least, put a few feet of space between them. It might help her to control herself, if nothing else. She needed to stay alive, after all. Provoking Rich into some kind of physical altercation was *not* going to keep her alive and breathing until Joe or her father could find her.

Rich took great pleasure in showing Liliana around. It kind of stunned her how a lot of the layout of the place reminded her of her grandparents' mansion. She had mentioned once to Rich how much she loved their home and how comforting it made her feel when she visited. He'd gone with her once or twice to the Marcello mansion, as well, and clearly hadn't forgotten anything.

"And I think you'll like this room quite a bit," Rich said, turning to face Liliana as he leaned against the wall. Waving at the entryway to the space, he added, "Go ahead, and take a look."

She peered in.

Her stomach dropped.

It was a dance studio—*barres* along one wall with floor-to-ceiling mirrors behind them. Large windows covered the other wall. Lights hung from up above, and the brightness made the cherry oak floors gleam.

"I've missed watching you dance," he murmured.

Jesus.

He was right in her *ear*.

How had he gotten so close?

"Our room is down the hall," he added, "and you have your own closet full of clothes, shoes, bags, and whatever else your heart might desire. Care to take a look at it with me?"

Like fuck.

She wasn't stupid enough to put herself in a room with a bed—certainly not with this man, anyway.

"I'd rather not, actually," Liliana said.

She didn't tamper her tone, or the disgust. It all came spilling out in that one sentence with those four fucking words.

She should have known better.

She had pressed his patience.

She had tested his good nature enough.

Liliana didn't even see his fist coming until it was too late, and by the time she realized what was happening, she was being dragged down the hall by the hair on her head. The stinging in her scalp and the ringing in her ears reminded her of being in the backseat of the limo, and she swore it was like her body froze.

Unable to fight.

Unable to breath.

Unable.

And then she did snap out of it just long enough to try and get out of his hold. She kicked and fought, despite the way it probably ripped hair right out of her head from his unrelenting grasp. She clawed marks down his arms, and called him every name she could think of.

It didn't bother him at all.

He barely reacted.

Like he *expected* this.

Rich stopped walking long enough to *throw* Liliana inside a room—she got one good look around, and it scared her. Bare mattress on the floor. One blanket, no pillow. Boarded up windows, and no lightbulb in the light hanging from the ceiling.

He stood in the doorway while she laid on the floor, prone and in shock. Her ears were still ringing, too. She bet her face was swollen, or at least, bruised all to hell.

Rich probably liked that.

"Maybe a few days in here will make you more agreeable," Rich said.

Then, he slammed the door.

Liliana heard the lock twist, too.

She was alone.

It was dark.

He couldn't see her.

She could be quiet.

At least like this, she was safe.

And finally … *finally* … she cried.

SEVENTEEN

JOE WALKED FASTER.

They still *talked.*

He didn't have any need or reason to open his mouth and verbalize the same thing the rest of them were—this was bad.

Bad, bad, *bad.*

"What's the stats?" he heard his uncle, Theo, say. "After forty-eight hours, the survival rate drops in half, right? We're approaching that, Damian."

"Could you *not* right now?" his father growled.

"I'm just saying—"

Joe could practically feel his father's eyes nailing to his back. "Well, don't, Theo. Jesus Christ."

"He wants her alive," Joe muttered.

He didn't even bother to turn around when he offered that statement. He really didn't see the point in looking at them while he talked. Besides, he had better things to do, and he felt that them coming to New York and taking time away from his effort to find Liliana was nothing more than a waste of his time.

More men in the pit.

More ideas they couldn't use.

More loud voices.

Except … maybe Joe was wrong about that, and his father and uncle would be of great help. He really didn't know, but his mood was too fucking low to care about anything else except for his own goddamn agenda.

And his agenda was getting Liliana *back.*

"He didn't go through whatever effort he went through," Joe continued, "just to get her back, and then kill her within forty-eight to seventy-two hours. He *wants* her. He likely wants her so that they can pick up right where they left off."

"Good point," his uncle said.

"Joe—"

"Please, don't."

His father cleared his throat. "All right, son."

A sweet, small sense of relief flooded Joe even as his father's hand came up to pat him on his back. It was a traitorous feeling—he didn't deserve to feel anything except rage and fear until he got Liliana back, and *only* then could he worry about the rest.

Yet, he felt it then.

Because his dad was there.

Damian understood Joe.

It *mattered*.

His father came into step with him while his uncle stayed a couple of paces behind. "Cory is working resources—pulling whatever he can to help. He'll give us a call should he find something worth using, or that might take us to the Earl man. He *said* he could do that work here, too, but I know when it comes to you your brother can be a little ..."

Distracting?

Intense?

Difficult?

All of the above, but Cory would also feel the need to get Joe's mind into a better place just *because* of what was happening. It was his younger brother's *thing*. He was wild, but he was also a fixer when it came to his family. And it would only make Cory feel like shit when he realized this couldn't be fixed.

No, it was far better for Joe to be here, and for Cory to stay in Chicago at the moment. They could each focus on what they were good at without one feeling like they had to compensate for the other, and then they could meet together in the middle again at the end.

That's it, that's all.

"How hard was it to keep him in Chicago?" Joe asked.

"I threatened to lock him in a cage," Theo muttered behind them.

Joe's lips twitched.

An itch of a smile.

It didn't come all the way.

Pain seared through his chest—a random sensation he had been feeling ever since he woke up in that hotel room, and realized Liliana was gone. The pain happened if he was thinking for too long, talking too much, walking too often, or shit, *breathing*.

It happened because she wasn't here.

And he fucked up.

He should have *never* stopped looking for her from that point forward. He could have been on their trail, or caught up to them later. Instead, he followed the direction to get back to New York, and now he was even further behind Rich and Liliana than before.

This fucking *sucked*.

And he was useless like this.

Completely fucking useless.

Joe stopped in the hallway, and put his back to a wall. He stared up at the ceiling, and wished that if even for a second, it would come down and swallow him whole. Take him away to somewhere else where he didn't have to think or *feel*, and then maybe his brain would work like it was supposed to.

Maybe *then*, he would find her.

Or he would know *how*.

"*God*," Joe grumbled, dragging his palms down his face. "I need a second."

"All right."

Through his fingertips, he saw his father nod at Theo, and then gesture toward the hallway. The two men walked the rest of the way to Dante Marcello's office themselves, and Joe only took his hands away from his face after he heard the door click closed.

He stared upward again.

He couldn't see the heavens here, but then again, he wasn't one of those people who looked up at the sky and thought that was it, too. He'd only ever felt close to heaven and God in church, and ... well, with Liliana, too.

For entirely different reasons.

Give her back, he prayed, holding tight to the rosary hanging from this neck. *Give her back to me. Please, give her back to me.*

He didn't bargain.

He didn't offer this for that.

That's not how God worked, anyway.

Besides, now that Joe had taken a second and said his peace to Him—for what felt like the hundredth time today—he was slightly better again. At least, for a time. That pain in his chest had stopped, but Joe knew it would be back.

It kept coming back.

He didn't have time to think about it right now.

Moving down the hallway, he didn't even bother to knock on the office door before he walked into Marcello pandemonium.

Or *chaos*.

Two men were arguing with one another. Another—although far older—man was sitting by himself. The Chicago men were on their phones. A redheaded woman stared out the window with her arms crossed, and her expression pensive.

It was only Lucian, leaning against the far wall and ignoring his arguing brothers, quiet father, and distant sister-in-law, not to mention, Joe's father and uncle. It was only him who looked to Joe when the man came into the office.

Of course, Joe recognized them all. He *knew* them all. He just didn't care right now. Until one of their thoughts or phone calls manifested into some kind of fucking information about how they could *safely* retrieve Liliana, he didn't give a shit.

"Anything?" he asked Lucian.

The man shook his head, quiet and cold. Joe didn't think he'd ever seen the man this blank before. His control was ... frightening.

Yeah, that was as good of a word as any.

"I think we're looking in the wrong spot," Lucian said.

Joe's brow furrowed. "Pardon?"

"We're looking where we expect him. Just like when we watched him before, and trailed him. We did that *knowing* what we were looking for, or looking at. And I think we missed something because we inadvertently overlooked something else. Do you understand what I'm saying, Joe?"

He did.

But what had they missed?

And *when?*

"So, you've got *nothing?*" Joe demanded.

Cory sighed. "I have aliases, man, and it's going to take us a bit to go through shit for that, too. What do you have on your end?"

"A forty-eight hour mark that passed ten minutes ago."

His brother sucked air through his teeth, and then murmured, "You know it'll be fine."

"I don't know anything at all, actually."

"*Joe.*"

Well, it was the truth.

Horrifying, but true.

Joe didn't respond to his brother, and finally Cory got irritated enough that he asked, "What are you doing right now, anyway? I know Dad and Theo are looking into some shit."

"Threatening people, you mean."

"Yeah, well, that's what they do best."

Joe rolled his eyes as he came up to a coffee shop he recognized, and sighed. It was his third stop of the day, and he likely wasn't going to get *shit* from here, either. Just like all the other places he had gone to in an attempt to backtrack Liliana's steps in New York. He had to try something different, and he had to keep moving.

Otherwise, he felt useless just sitting the fuck around and waiting for something to happen. That wasn't his style.

Instead of going into the coffee shop while he was still on the phone, Joe opted to end his call first, and then continue on with the rest of his business. Cory would understand … eventually.

"Listen, I have to go, but call me if—"

"Have you considered the alternative to Rich following *her*?" Cory asked suddenly.

Joe stiffened. "I don't understand what you mean."

"The obvious answer, Joe, is that Rich is obsessed with her. He was probably following your girl. Maybe you didn't see him, or maybe he just outsmarted you all. That's the *obvious* answer to how this happened, right?"

As much as Joe hated to admit it—and *fuck*, he hated to think it, too—Cory was right, as usual. "Thanks for the info I already know, but I don't need you shoving that fuck up in my face right now. It's already obvious enough without you doing it, too."

"No, *listen*, fuck-head."

Jesus, save him.

Because Joe was going to kill him.

"I'm saying," Cory continued, "that it's easier to look at the obvious because that's typically where the answers are, Joe, but what if in this case, that's the wrong place to look."

Joe hesitated, and then asked, "How so?"

"What if while everyone was busy looking at her and him, he was looking at you."

"Cory—"

"I know, *I know*, Joe," his brother rushed to say, coming off snappish and defensive, "you're the fucking Shadow, and nobody sees you if you don't want them to. But you're not goddamn invisible, Joe. All right? You're not. And you got mixed up with a woman who clearly had some baggage that you weren't made aware of going in which might have made you a little more careful in some of the shit you did with her. So, tell me if it's not remotely possible that someone was watching you, and you weren't aware because of that."

Well …

Shit.

"It's possible," Joe settled on saying.

But he didn't like it.

"You don't think it's the case, though," Cory argued, "I can hear it in your voice."

"Wrong—I don't want to *think* it was the case. Big difference."

"Why not? It could mean you might find something someone else hasn't found, Joe."

"It also means I fucked up again, Cory."

"You didn't *fuck up*, man." Cory sighed when Joe didn't respond. "Where do you go from here, then?"

Well, that answer was easy.

He needed to stop retracing her steps, and start retracing his.

"I have to go," Joe said, offering nothing else to his brother before he hung up the phone. He didn't even let the screen blank out before he was dialing another number—Lucian's. The man picked up on the second ring, unsurprisingly. He didn't let Lucian speak before he was saying what was forefront on his mind. "I need ... something."

"Something like *what*, Joe?"

"Feeds—surveillance. From my hotel, and from Liliana's show. That charity event, too. The coffee shop I used down the street, and hell, even the convenience store where I picked up my smokes."

"Why would—"

"Can you get those videos, and have someone survey them, or not?" Joe demanded.

Lucian cleared his throat. "We've got someone. A hacker."

Joe rattled off dates to make it easier. "That's what I need ... and any clips with me in them, I need sent *to* me."

"It's going to take a while."

"Pay to make it *faster*, Lucian."

"Don't assume I wouldn't, Joe."

Yeah ...

Damn.

"Any news on your end?" he thought to ask.

"No, but the mother was on the television tonight. Blaming us again," Lucian grumbled.

Huh.

"Maybe I'll start with her," Joe said.

"Joe, that's dangerous. She might not know your name like she does ours, but she will recognize your face if someone thought to put a goddamn picture in front of her. You're going to force yourself into a worse position, and what might have been a short while away until the dust clears could be far longer."

Worth it, he thought.

As long as he got Liliana back.

Nothing else mattered.

Tick-tock, tick-tock.

Joe swore he could *feel* the fucking watch on his wrist counting down time, and it was driving him fucking crazy. Each time that second hand moved, it felt like a jolt of electricity against his wrist. Had the watch not been a gift from his mother last Christmas, he probably would have ripped it off and thrown it in the fucking garbage.

Other shit to do, Joe. Focus on other shit.

Yeah, right.

Other shit.

He stood leaning under the street lamp, and despite knowing he should do literally *anything* else, he lifted his wrist up to stare at the watch. The second hand passed the twelve, and then the minute hand moved along with the hour hand.

Seventy-two hours.

Liliana had been gone for seventy-two hours.

And they were still no closer to finding her.

Fuck.

That pain was back in his chest—deep, aching, and thumping hard. He had at least been able to breathe through it the days before, but now it had turned into something else entirely, and even breathing didn't help.

Nothing fucking helped.

Joe forced his gaze away from the watch, but only because something else had caught his eye. The woman stepped out on the front porch of her large, tucked away home. The quiet suburb just outside of the city limits was, for all purposes, as safe as it could possibly be.

Except when it came to people like *him.*

The woman fixed her jacket, and took a cursory glance around her front yard, but little else. She certainly didn't look far enough down the street to see Joe standing under the lamp light. For the most part, he wasn't even trying to hide.

He *meant* to be seen.

At least, by this particular woman.

The senator's wife.

Rich's *mother.*

Marcie Earl tugged on the leash connected to the collar of a small Pomeranian. The little dog looked like a giant ball of fluffy hair as the animal practically bounced down the steps. Its fucking legs weren't even long enough to get from one step to the next—it actually had to jump to get down.

Kind of amusing, really.

Joe never understood the point of having a dog that small. What else did it do but sleep on your lap, and bark too loud?

Anyway.

As Marcie headed down the block—a usual ritual for her to walk her dog at this time of night, according to information he'd gotten pulled on her—Joe pushed away from the lamp post, and headed after the woman. He kept his steps fast, but light. There wasn't a single sound coming from his shoes hitting the pavement, not that he wanted her to know he was following behind just yet.

Soon, but not yet.

Marcie barely took in her surroundings as she walked her dog, never looking over her shoulder, or checking for anyone else around. It was a sure sign that said she felt safe in this place, and thought of it as *her* environment.

People were predictable in that way. They had a way of assuming that nothing bad could ever happen to them as long as it was *their* space. No one would dare to intrude on their life in that way, as though their familiar, comforting places were sacred, or some kind of shit like that.

Wrong.

That's where everything bad happened.

Marcie only stopped occasionally when her fluffy little dog wanted to sniff, or piss in someone else's grass. Joe made sure to keep a respectable distance, but he never even needed to slip behind a vehicle to stay out of sight as the woman went about her nightly business.

She wasn't worried *at all*.

Stupid woman.

Once Marcie made it about halfway around the block, she stopped to sit on a bench while her dog finally seemed to take notice of Joe down the sidewalk. The little Pomeranian barked at him, but he wasn't paying it any mind.

Ankle biter.

What was it going to do to him, really?

His wrist was as thick as its *head*.

Marcie stiffened a bit on the bench as Joe approached, and then glanced away from him. She clearly didn't recognize him—which wasn't a bad thing for his side of the equation—but his presence obviously made her uncomfortable.

Good.

She was about to get even more uncomfortable.

Joe took a seat on the bench, leaned back to put his arms behind his head, and crossed his boots at the ankles. "Nice evening, isn't it?"

"I suppose."

Polite.

Strained.

Joe almost smiled.

She was clearly the type of person who would engage a stranger in conversation simply because she didn't want to be rude. A part of him found that both annoying, and amusing. Neither part of him cared all that much.

Marcie glanced over at him—the lines around her eyes and frowning mouth spoke of her age, but other than that, she was a pretty woman. Her pale blonde hair had been pulled back into a simple chignon, and her warm brown eyes took him in. He almost wondered if this woman even understood the kind of hell her son was.

She probably did.

That sort of behavior was learned, after all.

Boys didn't grow up hitting women.

They were *taught* to do it.

"Did your husband beat the hell out of you, too?" Joe asked.

Marcie stiffened. "I beg your pardon?"

"Your son—*Rich*—he abused Liliana Marcello, and given the shit I know, I can safely assume that wasn't a one-off occasion for him. There are probably others. More women he's abused, which means he likely witnessed the same kind of behavior growing up."

"I—excuse me," she said, moving to stand.

Joe couldn't let her do that. His hand shot out fast, and locked around her wrist to yank her back to the bench. "No, don't leave just yet. I'm just getting started. We haven't even gotten to the fun part, Marcie Earl."

She sucked in a sharp breath, and her gaze darted around as she hissed, "I will *scream*."

"And I will slice your tongue right down the middle, and sit here with you while you choke on your blood until you drown in it. I'll even give your dog something to chew on or play with while we wait. Now, be *quiet*."

Marcie blinked.

Joe smiled at her. "You know, I've taken some time over the last day to look into *you* a little more. I had all this information on your husband, of course, but I didn't care very much about you. Nothing about you was needed for my job, after all. And then I did need to look into you, so here we are."

"I don't know what you want me to—"

"You cake on the makeup, don't you? Heavy powder, too. So much so, they gave you the nickname Barbie because you always looked so plastic and fake with your hair in perfect waves, your makeup done up, and your false smile plastered on. Every photograph of you next to your husband was *exactly the same*."

"I—"

"I bet you used to wear your hair down because it helped to hide whatever marks were on your neck. And when you had to use a shade or two darker than your own skin tone to hide the bruises, you just used a little bit more so it wouldn't be as noticeable. And that smile? Perfectly practiced in front of a mirror every single night, so he wouldn't be able to tell how much it killed you when you did it."

"You don't know *anything*."

"He's dead now," Joe offered, "so protecting him, or whatever lie your life had been, isn't really needed, or necessary."

"I don't know who you are, but you need to go."

Joe laughed. "No. When did he start hitting you?"

Marcie swallowed hard. "What do you *want*?"

"Right now—to talk. Depending on what I get from you will determine a lot of things. Whether or not you get to live beyond tonight and find out what life is like without an abusive husband at your back. You put on a good show for the cameras crying about him, and pushing the hard line that it wasn't accidental, but I bet in private, all you feel is *relief*."

Marcie relaxed a bit.

Joe saw it even though she probably figured he didn't.

It confirmed everything she wouldn't say.

Yes, her husband had beat her.

Yes, Rich had *learned* it.

Yes, she was happy he was dead, but she still had a role to play, too. And he doubted this career-politician's widow wanted her personal business and her abuse shoved under the spotlight for the rest of the world to dissect, or mock.

Humans were terrible in that way.

"And it's okay to feel that," Joe added quieter, "because I sure as shit would, too."

"What do you *want*?"

"I want Liliana Marcello back with her family, and your son has her."

Marcie's head snapped to the side, and her gaze blazed as she stared—slack-jawed—at Joe. "How do you know Rich has her?"

"I know," is all Joe offered.

"Well," the woman spluttered, "*I* don't know that, so I'm not sure why you assume I have anything that might be useful to you."

"I'm sure you know someone who *might*."

The woman's cheek twitched.

Like her fingers.

And her eye.

She was going to lie. Joe saw all the signs.

"He's my son," she offered quietly.

Joe nodded. "And so, you want to protect him."

"Clearly."

Joe didn't *like* to lie, but he could, and he was damned good at it, too. Especially when it meant getting what he wanted. And right now, he wanted Liliana more than anything in the whole world. He wanted her back, so he could tell her that he loved her, and she was his one person made just for him.

He wanted her *back*.

So, he lied.

"Tell me who would know the information I'm seeking, and I'll let him live when I find him," Joe said.

Marcie took a breath.

And then another.

"Trevor."

"The assistant?" Joe questioned, remembering the man he had punched at the charity event. "You're sure that's the answer you want to give me?"

Marcie shrugged. "If anyone knows anything, it's Trevor Mason. He won't even answer my calls because he doesn't like to lie to me. He *knows* that I know something is wrong, and he has the answers. Or … some of them."

Trevor it was.

Joe stood up, and glanced back at the woman. "The slitting your tongue thing can still happen, by the way. This meeting never happened."

Streaks of color managed to break through some of the dirt and grime on the warehouse window, and left red and yellow lines on the ruddy floor.

Ruddy from dried blood.

Usually, Joe liked this time of day the best. A fresh start, and new beginnings. Each day could be something different, if that's what he wanted to do. On this day, however, none of those thoughts were forefront on his mind.

"One last chance to give me a name," Joe murmured, his knife twisting beneath the kneecap of the man tied to a chair, "or we start this all over again."

The guy was bloodied.

Battered.

His mind probably broken.

It had been six straight hours of getting the shit beat out of him in between various methods of torture. And shit, Joe had to give it to Trevor

Mason—he was tough. He hadn't wanted to break, but Joe was what he was.

And he was fucking *resilient.*

Relentless, too.

He was going to keep going.

He *could* keep going.

It had been a matter of a couple of hours from the time Joe gave Lucian a name to the point when Trevor was dropped off—bound, gagged, and with a hood over his head—to a lower Brooklyn warehouse for Joe to extract information.

And now it was morning.

He was still working on getting that info.

His control was being *tested.*

Joe heard the kneecap pop, and Trevor let out a gagging sob. He knew it then that he was going to *finally* get something useful from the prick.

"Ryan," the man gasped-sobbed, "Ryan Thompson. That's the alias he's been using for a while to do s-shit on the l-low."

Joe left the knife where it was stuck in Trevor's knee, and turned to his father. "Call Cory, and mention the name. See what it brings up."

His father cocked a brow, and didn't soften in his tense stance with his arms crossed over his chest. "Take a break, Joe."

Nope.

He shook his head. "I'm good here."

"Joe—"

"Leave him be, D," Theo murmured. "Let's make that call."

Joe stood straight, and stared out the grimy window a few feet away. Beside him, Lucian paced. At the other side of the warehouse, the other two Marcello brothers stood beside one another in silence.

So had been the way they worked all night.

"*P-please, please just … please.*"

Trevor's mumbled, slurred cries fell on deaf ears.

Joe just didn't care.

"What are you thinking?" Joe asked Lucian.

The man's pacing didn't stop. "Nothing you want to hear."

"I would want to hear it, actually."

Lucian sighed. "We're coming down to four days, now. Four days he's had her. So, what has he done to her in that time, Joe? We get her back alive, but *then what?* What can I expect to get back? Certainly not the same woman he—"

"Lucian," Dante murmured quietly from the other side of the warehouse, "don't do that, brother."

Lucian's jaw tightened. "Let me stew, Dante. It's all I fucking have."

Joe felt about the same.

"Like I said," Lucian told Joe, "you don't want to know what's in my head."

Nothing more or less worse than what was in Joe's. He had just been able to, for a time, put it aside while he handled this. Compartmentalize, if you will.

"Joe, listen," he heard his father say as Damian re-entered the warehouse.

Cory's voice filtered through the phone on speaker. "Ryan Thompson is one of the names that came up—we were going through other ones first, so we hadn't gotten to that one yet."

"Speed it up," Lucian barked.

"Sorry, yeah, so Ryan Thompson bought a private estate in Vermont six months ago, but renovations just finished on it last month."

"What do you mean, *private?*" Joe asked.

"I mean … deep in the woods, lots of land, and plenty of security. The records of that weren't all too hard to pull, but if I had to chance a guess, Joe, that would be it. That's where I would say he is. I've got the address coming through to Dad's phone."

"Makes sense," Lucian muttered under his breath.

Joe turned back to the blubbering mess of a man in the chair. Trevor was still firmly tied down, half-dead, and he wasn't fucking going anywhere. "If you gave me the wrong info, I will make it my personal mission to kill every single fucking person tied to your bloodline and name. Last chance to correct *anything.*"

"It's him—it's him, I swear!"

Good enough.

Joe yanked the knife from Trevor's kneecap, and with one hard swipe of his arm, the blade cut through the man's throat. Blood arched, and sprayed heavily. Trevor was dead in a few seconds, and his wide, glazed eyes stared up at the ceiling.

Just like that, Joe was done.

He dropped the knife, and turned on his heel to head for the door.

Calm.

Cold.

Ready.

He was done with this business, and ready to move on. Ready to finish the rest, and get Liliana back to the safety of her family, and *him.* He wasn't going to stand there and fucking dwell like an idiot about the dead man in the chair, or what might be happening in Vermont. He needed to keep moving—to keep getting closer to her—or he was going to fucking explode.

"Jesus Christ," someone—it sounded like Dante, but Joe couldn't be sure—said. "Damian, you ought to be mighty fucking proud of that man. I can't say any of us would be that collected in this situation."

"We are," his uncle, Theo, said.

"Very proud," Damian added. "And far more. Let's go get her, then."

"Yes, *now*," Lucian snarled.

Joe was already gone.

EIGHTEEN

LILIANA STARED AT the ceiling, and wondered what time it was. How many days had she been in this goddamn room now? She couldn't be sure—the guard assigned to her door only opened it once a day to throw two bottles of water inside, and then he promptly closed and locked it up again.

He never said a word.

Never even *looked* at her.

She couldn't tell how many days it had been by the rising or setting sun considering the windows in the bedroom were boarded up, too. She suspected it must have been at least two days, but probably three or more *if* she were going on the amount of times the guard had opened the door to give her water.

If that's what they called *throwing* the bottles at her.

She'd fallen asleep twice.

The second time, Rich had been watching her from the doorway when she woke up. His gaze had raked over her, and the absolute and total *fear* that climbed up her throat in those moments was enough for her to know … Liliana fucking swore she wouldn't sleep again after that.

It made her vulnerable.

Weak.

Liliana sucked in a deep breath, and exhaled slowly as she kept her gaze on the ceiling. Next to finishing off the last bit of her water—she only drank in small sips instead of gulping it down like her body wanted to do— her rhythmic breathing was the only damn thing keeping her awake, and her mind away from the pains in her stomach.

Aching, panging *pain.*

She was starving like nothing else.

Liliana refused to ask for food, though. She wouldn't shout, cry, or scream. And she most definitely was *not* going to beg at the door.

Something told her that was exactly what Rich wanted more than anything. To hear her pain, and terror. Then, he might think he had broken her.

She was far from broken.

It was only the murmurs outside the door that dragged Liliana's attention away from her current task of distracting her mind. Her mind said it was closing in on the time when the guard would open the door, and throw in more water, but she wondered if that was just her body envisioning what it needed, and not what actually *was*.

It was hard to fucking say.

And then ...

Shit.

And then she heard Rich's voice clearer when he said, "It's been a while—let's see if she's more compliant today, hmm?"

Liliana shivered.

Disgust rolled heavily through her body. Dread climbed up her spine with hard, punishing steps. Her hands balled in fists so tight that her fingernails nearly broke the skin, and her throat tightened with the promise of closing up entirely, so she wouldn't be able to speak at all.

Somehow, she managed to shove all of those reactions down. She was not going to let Rich see her fear—he *wanted* that. She was sure of it.

Once the door was finally opened, Liliana had already turned her head back toward the ceiling, so she was staring at anything but Rich. Still, his presence was a tangible fucking thing whenever he was within seeing distance of Liliana. Like her nerves and blood and heart were all screaming at the same time for her to *run, run, run.*

She had nowhere to run.

Not right now.

"Liliana, darling, how are you doing? Hungry, I bet."

His voice came off like brown sugar, and black coffee. Sweet, warm, and *bitter.*

She saw his comforting tone for what it was, and nothing more. Trickery to try and make her trust him, but she was far from fucking stupid.

"*Liliana!*" Rich's shout practically slapped her in the back of the head. "Speak to *me!*"

Fine.

"Hungry," she admitted.

"Are you in a better mood today?"

How quickly and smoothly he went back to his previous demeanor and tone. Nice, comforting, and *promising.*

Liliana still wasn't stupid.

"A little," she said.

She only kept talking to—at the very least—keep Rich from shouting at her. She knew what his shouts would lead to, and it was nothing good for her. He was vicious, and unpredictable. All of this had taught her that, frankly.

Somehow, Liliana needed to get out of this place, and get out *alive*. So, if that meant she had to play along with Rich's dumb fucking games for a little while, then that's exactly what it meant.

Surely, she could play along.

Even if it *killed her.*

Liliana turned to glance at Rich, but was surprised to find he had already come to stand practically right beside her. In fact, his hand was reaching out to touch her. She had all she could do not to stiffen when his fingers drifted through her dirty blonde hair to sift the strands between his fingertips.

"I hated when you cut those few inches off your hair," he murmured.

Jesus.

That was six months ago or more.

"I had some split ends," she lied.

Really, she had just needed a change.

"You'll let it grow out again for me, won't you?"

Her throat tightened.

No.

"Of course, Rich."

"That's my sweet girl."

Fuck you, you—

As though Rich could read her goddamn mind, his fingers grabbed tight to the hair at the base of Liliana's skull before he tipped her head back, and forced them both to stare at one another in the eyes. She couldn't look away from him while a snake-like smile slid over his lips, and his gaze drifted down her face, over her throat, and down her shirt where the neckline was cut with a deep V.

The disgust was back.

So was the *rage.*

The sting in her scalp made her eyes prickle with the promise of tears, but Liliana held them back. She wouldn't even let this asshole see her eyes glisten. He would get too much enjoyment out of it, frankly.

"You need a good change of clothes, some time to work on that face of yours, and probably a shower, too," Rich murmured.

Liliana nodded. "All of that sounds good."

To say the least.

It would likely get her away from him, too. She was not going to complain about that, either. The more time she got to herself while outside of this damn room, the more likely it was that she could figure a fucking way *out.*

"That could be arranged if you continue to *behave*," Rich said.

Liliana offered him a small smile.

It was the best she could do.

"Why wouldn't I behave, Rich?"

"You know, when you look like this, I am almost willing to believe anything you say, Lilibet."

That fucking nickname again. The nickname meant for a queen, but one she didn't want at all. She had to swallow her desire to tell him to stop using it … *again*.

"But then I remember you're still the same whore you were a week ago," Rich continued on, seemingly oblivious to Liliana's internal struggle, "and I can't possibly believe anything you say or do."

Liliana stiffened.

He grinned again. "Try not to think I'm stupid, girl."

"I don't."

Far from it.

"Good."

His murmur was followed by his lips crashing down on hers. The move was unexpected, and Liliana had all she could do not to push him away. She couldn't hide the way her lips twisted in a cringe when Rich's tongue forced its way into her mouth, or how her instincts made her try to back away from the kiss.

Wrong move.

She knew it was wrong the second she did it. She saw the anger flash brightly in Rich's eyes when he realized she wasn't responding the way he wanted her to. The apology was already on the tip of Liliana's tongue, but it was too late.

There was nothing she could do to make this better. No excuse she could use to distract him from the fact his kiss was the very *last* thing she wanted.

He disgusted her.

She couldn't pretend.

Not even to save her life, apparently.

Rich pulled back just enough to hiss at her, *"Kiss me, Lilibet."*

"I—"

"Kiss me, now."

He didn't offer her the chance to refuse him again, instead kissing her again without warning. This time, he let go of her hair, and grabbed her arms. She found herself dragged onto that bare, thin mattress on the floor with Rich's heavy body forcing its way between her legs.

No, no, no.

He was hard already.

His erection *there* already.

No, no, fucking no.

Liliana was not a weak woman—her strength came from years of ballet training, and she was more than capable of fighting back. And yet, all her efforts to get Rich off her were quickly shut down when he pinned her arms above her head with one hand while his other one slipped between her legs.

Still, he kissed her.

Touched her.

She had pants on, sure, but they would only last as long as she could keep them on. They certainly didn't stop Rich from rubbing his hand against her vagina, and they didn't seem to keep his erection from grinding along her thigh.

If anything, her fighting only seemed to spur him on even more.

The *pig*.

"Get off me," Liliana hissed.

She bit him, then.

It was the last thing she could think of, really.

Probably the wrong move, considering the rage that flooded his features when he pulled back with a bleeding lip. But it got him away from her for a spit second.

And then he was right back again.

With a closed fist.

His punch landed hard against the side of her head—right at her temple. For a split second, Liliana's gaze blacked out as she saw stars. By the time she was able to regain some of her vision and focus again, Rich was pushing away from her, and getting up from the mattress on the floor.

"I see you still need more time in here," he muttered, fixing his suit jacket.

No.

Not more time.

Not in here.

She needed to figure something out, and *fast*. She needed to get the hell out of this room today.

"I'll be good," Liliana heard herself say, "*Please.*"

He hesitated at the door.

She knew the begging would do it.

Predictable bastard.

"Fine," Rich snapped, "then get dressed, fix your face, and find me downstairs. Don't even *think* to pull some stunt, Liliana. It will not end well for you. I promise."

"Are you just about finished?"

Liliana ignored the guard standing in the doorway of the bathroom. He hadn't even left the spot when she stepped into the shower using only a towel to hide her nakedness. Now, she was fully dressed, and taking her sweet time to paint her lips a stark, bright red.

"I know you are not *deaf*," the man spat.

Liliana rolled her eyes. "No, I'm not done yet."

And she wouldn't be for a few more minutes.

At least.

The longer she could stay out of Rich's sight, the better. Even if that meant taking extra time and care to get ready. She usually wouldn't put this much effort into her makeup and clothes, but hell, a good face could take an hour to put on.

She used that to her advantage.

It was almost fucking creepy the time and effort Rich had put into getting this place ready for her, and making sure she had everything she might want or need. Including jewelry, and makeup. Clothes, shoes, bags, and *more.* Anything and everything that she might need to look beautiful and appropriate for Rich was in the bedroom, connecting walk-in closet, and attached master bathroom.

Right down to the right shade of foundation.

Yeah, *creepy.*

"All right, that's enough," the man at the door grumbled. "You're just fucking around now, and the boss won't appreciate it."

The boss?

Liliana couldn't contain her scoff as she moved past the man. "Yeah, sure."

"Excuse me?"

"Rich doesn't know what being a *boss* is, but you know, he signs your paycheck, so."

"Be careful," the man said at her back, "because he won't appreciate you saying something like that. I'm sure you already know this considering the bruise I just watched you spend an hour covering on the side of your face."

Liliana's heart stuttered.

Yeah.

There was that, too.

This was going to be harder than she thought.

The guard—who Liliana couldn't even be bothered to ask his name—directed her through the long hallways of the mansion, and down two flights of stairs. They were headed back through a hallway she recognized from first arriving that would lead to the dining room. The voices filtering down from the space made her slow in her steps a bit.

The guard didn't seem to notice.

Thankfully.

"This is *concerning*," someone said. "Why aren't you listening?"

"I am listening," Rich barked, "but it's not enough for me to think there's something happening, or—"

"Trevor isn't answering calls, and your mother? She hasn't made a statement in *days*. Something *is* happening, or it already has, Rich. You're messing with the wrong people, and I warned you. I fucking *warned you*."

"Then leave," Rich said simply.

"I beg your pardon?"

"Leave. Heed your empty warnings, and leave."

"Boss—"

"*Leave.*"

Liliana stepped into the entryway of the large dining room at the same time a man she hadn't seen before rushed out of it. He knocked into her on his way out the door, but mumbled a quiet, quick apology under his breath before he beat it down the hall.

"Fucking idiot," Rich grumbled under his breath. And then, at the sight of Liliana in the entryway, his wide, welcoming smile returned. *All lies.* "And look at *you*."

Liliana suppressed her shudder at the way his eyes raked over her. "Good evening."

Her gaze drifted to the window to see the sun was setting. Evening seemed appropriate.

Rich looked past her to the guard standing behind Liliana. "Thank you for making sure she wore a dress, and you can go now."

"You sure, boss?"

"Leave us."

With two words, the guard scattered.

Rich waved a hand at Liliana, and then gestured at the table where a spread of food had been set out. Her stomach threatened to revolt on her at the sight of the food. Like she was so fucking hungry that just the sight of the food was enough to make her get on her knees and beg like a foolish girl.

No.

She wouldn't.

She refused.

Rich smiled again. "Would you like to eat?"

"I could eat," she replied quietly.

"Then, sit and eat, but I don't want to hear you while you do it."

At that statement, he pulled out a newspaper from his lap, and opened it up to read. His gaze didn't even follow her as she moved to the table, and sat down.

What is happening?

"I have a gift for you," Rich said.

Liliana had been all too aware that about half way through her plate, Rich had started watching her again. The feeling was unnerving, but she pushed through and finished her meal. She certainly hadn't forgotten how the man used to point out every extra calorie Liliana shoved inside her mouth.

The world of ballet and dancers was already toxic enough for a young woman struggling with her body image and weight. Although, Liliana had never gone that far, thankfully—she had managed to find a man who was just as bad. Rich had nearly introduced her to the vile relationship that was an eating disorder during their time together, but somehow, it was the one thing Liliana never got trapped in with him.

Or maybe he just hadn't gotten enough time with her.

Who was to say?

"Do you want your gift?" he asked.

"Sure," she said.

Her mind screamed, *Fuck no.*

Rich stood from his chair, and pulled a small pale pink box with a white bow from the seat next to his. Liliana hadn't even seen it resting there, but then again, she had been far too caught up in shoving food into her mouth.

Who could blame her?

Coming close enough to stand right beside her seat, making it impossible for Liliana to do anything but sit there like an expressionless doll who wouldn't displease him, Rich set the box in front of her, and moved her plate away.

"Go on," he urged, "open it."

Yay.

Liliana tugged the bow from the box, and then flipped open the lid. Resting inside on white tissue paper was a pair of brand new pointe shoes. The soft satin ribbons and firm soles of the shoes felt like heavy weights when she plucked them out of the box.

Heavier than they should have been.

She *loved* dance.

Ballet was everything good for her. An escape that very little else provided for her in life. An accomplishment that was solely hers. Something she worked so very hard for, and was proud to say she had mastered.

And this man was going to ruin it for her.

He was going to destroy ballet for her.

She *knew* it.

"I was hoping you would dance for me," he murmured.

Liliana wet her lips—*find a lie*. "These are new shoes, Rich. They would kill my feet—they should be broken in, at the very least."

"Then break them in while you *dance for me*."

She closed her eyes.

Searched for an excuse.

Anything; something.

She couldn't.

"Right now, in fact," he said, "so, let's go."

He didn't allow her the chance to protest before he'd grabbed her arm, and pulled her up from the chair. She said nothing, and kept feeling that heavy weight in her hands as she looked over the shoes.

It felt like those hallways passed far too quickly, and in the next blink, Liliana was sitting on the studio floor in front of the row of *barres* to slip on the pointe shoes. She took her time tying the ribbons around her ankles and calves.

Perfect knots, like she had been taught.

Flexing her toes, to test the comfort.

"I should stretch a bit," she said faintly.

Across the room, Rich shook his head. "No, *dance*."

Of course.

Liliana dragged in a heavy breath as she stood, and began the few steps to a simple dance that wouldn't put too much pressure on her, and didn't require her to be *en pointe* for the majority of the moves. The shoes really did need to be broken in, and she did not want to break her goddamn toes in the process.

"Stop," Rich muttered thickly.

Liliana did instantly.

Turning, she found him staring at her with narrowed eyes. "What?"

"Not that dance—I want you to do another."

Her heart clenched.

"Which one?"

"The one from the time we first met—when I saw your show. That *one*. Do that one, Liliana."

"I—"

"Do it!"

Jesus Christ.

"All right," she whispered.

Back straight.

Legs tight.

Toes pointed.

Arms like wings.

Breathe in, and exhale slowly.

It was easier for her to hear her own voice in her head when she danced then because it kept her mind off the man across the room. Problem was, the dance he wanted her to do made her fucking feet *scream* in protest. She needed *her* shoes for this—not brand new ones that were too stiff, and difficult to move properly in.

"Shit," Liliana hissed, dropping out of her *en pointe* pirouette, and barely catching herself before she hit the floor. "Sorry, sorry."

She apologized out of *habit*.

Not for him, but because she fucked up a move.

A move she *knew*, and could execute perfectly with the right shoes.

"Get up and start again," Rich said. "I've seen you do this dance perfectly, so I know you can. Stop wasting my time, and stop whining. Wipe the scowl off your face, and smile for me like you give a damn."

"I can't," Liliana mumbled.

"Get *up!*"

"I can't dance in these shoes, Rich!"

"Or you don't *want* to, Lilibet."

"Stop calling me that!"

Her scream was as good as a slap, if the expression on his face was any indication. She should have known better, frankly, but she had been keeping that in for too long now.

He crossed the space in a blink, and Liliana didn't even have time to cover her head before he was attacking her. He didn't hit her, though. And maybe that's what was most surprising, and horrifying when he did abuse her.

No.

No hitting.

He *stomped* on her fucking foot.

Liliana doubled over in pain with a shout, and grabbed her foot. She swore she heard the crunch, and a sob caught in her chest when she realized trying to move two of her toes did *nothing* but cause immeasurable pain.

Vomit climbed high in her throat.

Fury saturated her.

"You bastard, you—"

He did hit her that time, but he didn't even give her the opportunity to cover her head for the next hit before he was dragging her up from the ground. He said nothing as he pulled her—despite her clearly broken foot, and the obvious pain she was in—toward the door.

"Let me go," Liliana cried.

"Time for you to *learn*, Lilibet. I have been *very* patient with you, but I am not waiting one more goddamn minute. We could have done this the easy way, and you could have just given it to me, but now ... I see that won't be the case."

"Let me—"

They were almost to the stairs, now.

She heard the first shot.

Gunshot.

And then the second.

One came from the front of the house, and the second, from the back.

Rich's head snapped back and forth, but his blank expression never changed.

"What was that?" Liliana asked.

He didn't respond, simply started pulling her up the stairs again.

"Rich, what was—"

"Shut the fuck up," he snarled.

Liliana turned just in time as they rounded the top of the stairs to see Rich's men scattering to different spots on the bottom level. Their guns were already drawn, and the black hats they wore were pulled down over their faces like masks with only eye-holes for them to see out of. She didn't get to see anything else, though, because Rich threw her into the closest room. The force of it made Liliana land on her broken foot, and she swore she heard another crunch.

Her gasp of pain was followed by another cry. Tears welled, and fell down her cheeks. She reached for her foot, but maybe that was her biggest mistake of all.

She should have been watching *him*.

The fucking bastard.

She heard the clink of metal a second before she heard leather hiss as it was pulled. Rich's belt coming out of the loops.

The belt hit her hard.

Once, and then again.

Again, and again, and again.

Stop, stop, stop.

She heard her own cries.

Heard her screaming.

And yet, she couldn't be sure it *was* her.

"You. *Will.* Listen."

Another smack.

Another cry.

"You. *Will*. Learn."

The next crack of the belt came down across Liliana's face—splitting skin, and blinding her for a second.

The panic welled.

The fear took over.

She was frozen for those seconds.

"What is that smell?"

It was Rich's distraction that allowed Liliana a few seconds of reprieve. A moment to gather her bearings, and look for something—anything—to *use*. To get her out of this, to help her fucking survive.

She realized she had been thrown into a bedroom, and while her one eye was impossible to see out of, the other one was just fine. There on the bedside table, she found a lamp that looked heavy as hell, and ... well, it was something.

And that was all she needed.

It took all of her strength, and every effort in her body to ignore the protesting pain in her foot and shooting up her leg, to push up from the floor, and grab that goddamn lamp. She didn't even think about it once she had it in her hands.

No, she simply turned with it and swung for all she was worth. She didn't even think she had aimed it properly, but the lamp still crashed over the back of Rich's head.

He swayed for a second.

His head swung back to her.

His gaze *glazed*.

Move, her mind screamed, *do something!*

In his confusion, Rich had dropped the belt, and his knees hit the floor. She didn't know if he was going to move again, or how long it might take for him to snap back to reality. She didn't know anything at all, and she couldn't think beyond her mind still screaming for her to do something.

Liliana grabbed it before he could reach for it again, slipped the end tail in through the metal loop to create a noose of sorts, and then threw it over his head. When it hung around his neck like a piece of jewelry, she pulled. She tightened it as much as she could, and pulled again until she heard him gag. Yanked and fucking *yanked* until she watched his legs kick, and his hands try to pull the belt away.

Liliana didn't care.

She got on the edge of the bed, and used the arm of the four-poster bed as leverage to help her keep that goddamn belt as tight as it could be.

Her pain intensified—she was probably damaging her broken bones even more. She could barely hold back the vomit. She didn't even smell the smoke, or hear the shouts and the gunshots; she just saw Rich dying.

She just wanted him to die.

Fucking die.

NINETEEN

"SHOT SUCCESSFUL."

The comm in Joe's ear crackled, threatening a breakup of communication with the others, but he was laser focused on clearing the next hallway inside the house. Snipers at the back and front took out whatever guards they could pick off while the rest of them stormed the grounds.

He could have dressed in gear like the rest, but other than a Kevlar vest and leather gloves, Joe hadn't given it much thought. And even the fucking vest had been thrown on him by his father with a harsh, "I am not going to explain that to your fucking mother, thank you."

Joe caught sight of a flash at the end of a hall as he rounded it, and instantly threw his body back around the corner.

Brraaaap.

Bullets peppered the floor.

Joe heard one or two ricochet.

Shit, these guys weren't playing around. Frankly, he was fucking surprised that Rich Earl had access to as many trained guards as he did.

But then again, like the Marcellos had pointed out when Joe mentioned it, anyone's loyalty, time, and protection could be bought with the right amount of cash in their hand. So was the way of a criminal without morals or honor.

Joe waited for the raining bullets to stop.

Then, he waited some more—just long enough to know the guy was probably peeking around the corner to see if he had hit his intended target. Joe stuck his gun around the corner first, and then his face second.

His finger was already wrapping tight around the AR-15's trigger when he saw the guy peer around his side of the hallway, and there was no hesitation when Joe cocked his finger back twice in quick succession.

One bullet plugged into the guy's throat.

The other, between his eyes.

The man with the ski mask-covered face dropped to the ground like a sack of rotten potatoes.

"Clear," Joe uttered.

As he stepped down the hallway, he could hear the crackling picking up on the bottom level of the large estate. One of Rich's fucking idiots had managed to shoot some kind of decorative oil burner that was a little too close to drapery.

It went up like a dried Christmas tree.

Nothing to stop it.

Nothing to help it.

The smoke was rising, now, and he was kind of pissed off that it had happened at all. Unnecessary complications, really.

Something else to worry about.

Joe moved into the hallway, and several men followed behind. Lucian and his son, John, quickened their steps just enough to head past Joe as they came to a staircase. One that lead to the downstairs, to the upstairs, and down another hallway.

"Fuck," Joe muttered.

"We'll go upstairs," he heard Lucian say.

"We'll begin clearing out and checking rooms downstairs," Dante said from behind Joe, although he heard him just fine in his damn ear.

"We'll take this hall, and check the rooms," his uncle, Theo, said.

"Everyone out in ten."

Lucian glanced back at his brother just as he had started climbing the stairs. "Dante—"

Dante was already moving downstairs with Giovanni on his heels. "Ten minutes is all we can afford, Lucian. There's security on this house. It's burning down. Someone is *coming*—they have to be. We can't be here when they get here, okay? *Ten minutes.*"

"You can be gone in ten minutes if I don't have her," Joe said, done with any pretense that he gave a fuck about someone giving him orders, "but I will be here until I find her."

Because she *was* here.

Liliana had to be.

Joe saw the dinner for two in the dining room, and the lipstick stains on the glass of water next to the nearly-finished plate of salmon. They'd found the dance studio set up specifically for a ballet dancer shortly after they stormed the house.

She was fucking here.

Somewhere.

He just had to find her.

The group split into three smaller ones, and separated to their respective areas. No one said goodbye, but occasionally, the comm in Joe's ear would buzz with someone muttering something to their partner.

"I'll start on this side," Damian said.

Theo headed past the two men in the hallway. "I'll hit the end first."

Joe was already rearing back, and letting his foot slam into a door just below the knob. He didn't think they needed a fucking update on what he was doing.

Kind of seemed obvious, didn't it?

An empty bathroom stared back.

Fuck.

He moved on.

It was an office, next.

Then an empty room altogether.

He was getting fucking nowhere. And by the sounds coming from his ear, everyone else was in just about the same predicament. The rising upset continued between the men as more empty rooms stared back at them.

Joe was just getting progressively more and more pissed off. So, maybe when he came in front of the next door, and expected that room to be empty, too, he kicked it a little harder than was necessary to get it open.

And his whole world stopped.

Because there she was.

At first, Joe blinked at the sight in front of him. The grip on his gun loosened as he took in Liliana's sobbing form—bruised, welted, and bleeding face, her dress a mess of blood, and rips, and the pointe shoes on her feet. She hadn't seemed to notice the door open, or that he was standing right there.

Ready to save her.

Joe took in the man on the ground, too. The belt tight around his neck, and the back of his skull beaten in with a broken lamp beside him.

Apparently, she hadn't needed him to save her.

She fucking saved herself.

"Liliana," Joe said.

To him, it was a murmur.

To everyone else listening in the comms, it must have been a shout because they all quieted at once. Like they weren't even there to begin with.

Or maybe that was just his world tilting back on its proper axis.

Who was he to say?

"Liliana."

Joe set his gun aside, and rushed into the room. She was finally looking at him then—all bruised eyes, and bloodied lips. He reached for her, but she was already reaching back. She held on to him for dear life—it was in those moments when he couldn't breathe from how fiercely she was hugging him that he finally learned what that *really* meant.

But he got it.

And it was okay.

Because he was holding her like that, too.

"I'm sorry, I'm sorry," he murmured against her bruised cheek, dotting soft kisses to the same spot. "Sorry it took so long; sorry it happened at all. I'm so sorry, *Tesoro.*"

Liliana just kept shaking her head.

Shaking all over, really.

His hands found welt marks on her jaw and throat in the same shape as the width of the belt around Rich's dead neck, and the man was *fucking lucky.*

Lucky that he was dead.

Lucky Liliana had done it.

Lucky he never had to meet Joe when he was fucking inspired, and had a damn good reason to kill.

Oh, the rosary around his throat never felt as light as it did in those moments. He wouldn't even have apologized or confessed for that one. There wouldn't have been a need.

"Get them off," Liliana mumbled in his neck. "Please get them off."

He didn't know what she was talking about, but her hands were fumbling between them, and her legs kicked against his form. He figured it out then when she sobbed, and shuffled her feet like she was trying to kick off the goddamn pointe shoes.

"*Get them off?*"

"Okay, okay," Joe whispered.

He made quick work of removing the satin ribbons tied around her calves and ankles before he pulled the shoes from her feet. As soon as they were gone, Liliana sucked in a deep, ragged breath of air.

It sounded like freedom.

"We have to go."

It shouted in his ear.

It also came from the doorway.

Joe didn't even mind being rushed, now.

He got what he came for.

"Let's go over this again, Miss Marcello."

"There's nothing to *go over,*" Joe heard Lucian's lawyer snarl.

The speaker on the chair in front of Joe and Lucian crackled with the volume of the lawyer's irritation. A simple wire tap had been placed in Liliana's hospital room so that Joe and Lucian could listen in from a nearby room while the detectives made their rounds.

"It's okay," Liliana said.

Joe flinched.

Beside him, Lucian stiffened.

Her voice was faint—it had been like that since he pulled her from that room. She didn't want to talk, and when she did, it was like she wasn't there at all. It was going to take time for her to absorb what happened, and adjust accordingly.

Or, that's what people kept telling him.

Joe wanted to tell those people to fuck off.

"You're saying you have *no memory* of the home Rich Earl purchased in Vermont—no memory of being there, or how you got away from there?"

Joe had to give the detective credit, really. He kept hounding on this line of questioning like it was going to get him somewhere. And maybe with a woman who wasn't Liliana—one who hadn't grown up in the life—he might have tricked her in to saying something of use.

She wasn't so dumb, though.

She wasn't falling for it.

"The last thing I remember is looking up and seeing the emergency room sign above my head," Liliana said, repeating the one line of her story that wouldn't—because it *couldn't*—change. "I'm sorry I don't have the answers you want."

All it took was a few documents, and a good look around the mansion in Vermont for the police to suspect someone else had been there with Rich, and his men. They found the women's clothes, and all the other things he had set up for Liliana. They found his papers linking himself to the place, and then the information he had been gathering on Liliana, too.

It didn't take geniuses to figure it out.

She showed up at a hospital the same night Rich's estate was attacked, and partially burned. She arrived battered, and broken.

They put two and two together.

It made four.

It also made a fucking media circus, and a shitshow for the rest of them.

"I think if maybe you tried a little harder," the detective started to say.

"You're edging closer to a harassment suit with every word," the lawyer warned, "and you know it."

"We are trying to piece together this investigation, sir."

The lawyer scoffed. "Is that the line you're going to play with me?"

"I beg your pardon?"

"*Look at her.*"

Joe cleared his throat, and glanced away from the speaker. He didn't need to be in the room—he couldn't be anywhere near someone who might see his face, and connect him to what had happened—to know what the lawyer meant.

Liliana was *hurt*.

Bad.

She'd not just been hit, no.

She'd been beaten like a dog.

"How many hits to the head does she have to take before you believe that she *can't* remember what happened, detective?" the lawyer asked. "How many drugs need to show up in her system before you realize she was not an accomplice, but a victim in all of this? How many bruises and split-open welts do the doctors need to describe for you to understand she was a survivor of a man who she has a violent history with?"

"I—"

"Why are you trying to make a victim in to a criminal, sir?" the lawyer murmured.

Lucian rested back in his chair, and stared up at the ceiling. For a moment, Joe wondered if the man was praying because that seemed to be a popular thing with the Marcello family. Family, and God.

One always came before the other.

He respected it, really.

"Had they just handled this the first time," Lucian said under his breath, "then she wouldn't need to do this all over again. She wouldn't have to justify *why* she's a victim. This wouldn't have needed to happen at all."

Yeah, Joe knew that.

Got it, too.

"It's over, though," he said. "The bastard's not coming back."

Lucian shook his head. "But she *knows*. She's always going to know, Joe. People didn't protect her—the system failed her."

"Or it's going to make her more amazing," Joe returned, shrugging.

His companion glanced over at him. "You think?"

"How could she not be?"

Joe didn't know what was going to happen from here on out. He didn't know what Liliana's plans were for her life, or for them.

Was she going to keep dancing?

Was she going to be as vibrant?

Was she going to love him?

He didn't have those answers—despite wanting and needing them like nothing else—but that was okay, too. He didn't need to have the answers for those questions. They weren't *his* answers, and this wasn't about him.

It had never been about him.

This was Liliana's life, and her choices from here on out could only reflect what she wanted and needed the very most. He was going to be there—or not, if she didn't want him to be—to support whatever in the hell she wanted to do.

And that was okay, too.

That's what love had taught him.

He still hadn't gotten to tell her yet, though.

"My wife wanted me to thank you," Lucian said quietly.

Joe nodded. "You really don't have to."

"She'd like to have you over for dinner, too, but …"

Yeah, the media.

His face.

Separation of church and state, so to speak.

Joe had to go underground, and keep his name out of it. He needed to go back to his life, and pretend like he hadn't left it. He needed to let the hell this had caused blow over so the trail went cold, and the case was closed. Or, as closed as it could be, all things considered.

How long was that going to take?

He didn't know.

"Maybe someday," Joe told Lucian.

Lucian smiled faintly. "There's definitely going to be a someday, Joe."

Liliana was sleeping when Joe finally slipped into her hospital room. The clock on the wall showed it was just past one in the morning, but this was the safest time. The nurses were focused on their work, the detectives were gone, and the families of other patients had left, too.

Well, *mostly.*

"Wondered when you were going to sneak in here," Lucian muttered in the corner.

Joe shrugged one shoulder. "Have to be careful."

"I appreciate the effort, Joe."

Beside the man, his wife slept peacefully covered in her husband's suit jacket. Joe had drifted around—although made sure to stay out of sight— the hospital and grounds enough to watch people come and go for Liliana all day.

Her sisters.

Brother.

Cousins.

Aunts and uncles.

Grandparents, too.

Even friends, and the owner of the ballet company.

She had a steady stream of guests, and her room showcased it with all the flowers, cards, and helium balloons filling one corner. She certainly hadn't gone without attention and visitors which made him feel somewhat better.

And entirely lonely.

Because he hadn't been one.

He was sure she noticed it.

"Jordyn," Lucian murmured, carefully waking his wife from her sleep. "W-what?"

The woman blinked sleepy eyes at her husband, but didn't seem to notice Joe standing just beyond the closed doors.

"Let's step out for a minute, Jord."

"Why would we—"

Her words cut off when her gaze landed on Joe.

"Oh," Jordyn said quietly. "About time you showed your face, don't you think?"

Joe smiled a bit. "My apologies."

"She asked about you."

Joe nodded. "I figured she would."

Jordyn said nothing else, but allowed her husband to help her from what looked to be the most uncomfortable place to sleep that he'd ever seen. Then again, it probably felt like a fifty-thousand dollar mattress when someone was exhausted enough to not care.

Who was he to say?

Lucian and Jordyn passed Joe by quietly, but not before the woman reached out and patted his cheek with a soft touch.

A *mother's* touch.

He recognized it because of his own mother.

Joe was not the type to let someone else touch him—certainly not someone he didn't know very well, and hadn't spent much time with on a personal level.

And yet, Liliana's mother felt familiar.

Fine, even.

"Thank you," she whispered.

"Please don't thank me."

He really hadn't done very much at all.

Nothing worthy of praise, or thanks, anyway.

Jordyn smiled, and shook her head. "Have a good visit, Joe. I'm sure we'll be seeing more of you."

Lucian gave Joe a look. "Someday."

"Yeah, someday," Joe echoed.

Joe only moved once the two had left the room, and the door hissed as it closed. He pulled a chair away from the wall, and dragged it close to Liliana's bedside. Her eyelids didn't even flicker with a realization that he was there. Not even a twitch of her muscles. He had been told she was medicated—probably morphine—and that would force her to rest whether she wanted to or not.

In a way, he was grateful.

She needed to rest, and he didn't want to wake her up just because he was selfish.

In another way, he wanted to see her.

Speak to her.

Tell her.

Tell her everything.

Joe settled himself on sitting in the chair, and imprinting her image to his memory. Her bruised face, and the bandages that had been carefully placed over welts that had broken the skin. Each mark made his heart heavier, and every bruise left his rage festering something awful. She hadn't suffered any broken bones except for her foot—two toes, and a bone on the side of her foot, apparently. Or, that's what had been told to him. Two to three months of recovery for that, and absolutely no dancing.

But it was done.

It was *over*.

Joe slid his hand in with Liliana's beside the tucked in, stark-white hospital blanket. His fingers interwove with hers, and he stroked his thumb along the side of her hand. The only spot on her fucking hand that wasn't bruised.

Jesus.

"You look sad," he heard her whisper.

Joe glanced up, and found pretty hazel eyes watching him, although still a little sleepy. "Hey, *Tesoro*."

Liliana managed a smile for him. "Hey."

"I'm not sad, Liliana."

"No?"

"No," he promised, "not now."

"Why the frown, then?"

Joe laughed. "Don't I always frown?"

"Not like *that*."

Yeah, well …

"Sorry I couldn't come in today," he said, reaching up to cup her cheek in his palm. "Too much going on, and I have to lie low for a while."

Her smile faltered. "What does that mean?"

Now or never.

"Until all of this blows over with the media and cops, I have to go away. Back to Chicago, and make sure I'm seen, and whatever else."

"You're ... not staying?" she asked.

So faint.

It *killed* him.

"I'm sorry," was all he could say.

No excuse would be good enough.

Nothing was going to make it better.

"I'm sorry, Liliana. This was how it was supposed to go before you and me ... yeah," he said lamely. "And everything else made it worse. None of that matters, though, because you're good and you're *here*. Right?"

"Matters to me, Joe."

Yeah, he bet.

It mattered to him, too.

"What if I give you a promise," he offered.

Liliana sniffled. "What kind of promise?"

"That I'll be back. And we can start this all over again, if you want. We can do this different the next time—do it *better*, if you want. We can be Joe and Liliana without business, and everything else. Because I *will* be back as soon as I can. If you want me to, I'll call, and we'll figure shit out that way, too."

She was quiet for a long time.

He didn't say a word, either.

She broke the silence first. "Calls would be nice."

He chuckled, and leaned over to press a quick kiss to her lips. "Every day, I promise."

"Are you going to stay until I get out of the hospital?"

No.

"My flight leaves in the morning," he said.

"Oh."

"I'm sorry."

Sadly, she whispered, "Won't you love me, Joe? Don't you love me? I love *you*."

He blinked.

His words failed.

His heart *ached.*

How could she not know?

How could she not *know* that she was everything to him?

"I love you more than anything," he told her. "I am always going to love you, Liliana. Won't you let me show you?"

"When?" she asked.

Joe didn't even have to think about it. "Forever."

TWENTY

Four months later …

LILIANA DRAGGED THE cloth over the back of her neck to wipe away any sweat, and help her cool down. Even though the studio was a no-go zone for phones—they had to be silenced, or shut down entirely—she snuck hers out of the bag she'd left in the corner while her back was turned to Gordo.

It wasn't like the man could see her.

And he'd been going easier on her since she started back a month ago. For the most part.

Besides, it was worth the risk to check—

Liliana blinked at the blank screen in front of her. No calls, and no texts to show. She was starting to wonder if she should get worried. It wasn't like Joe to not call her. He always did—first thing in the morning, and a text before he knew she was going in to dance since she wouldn't have her phone, and another call before bed.

He kept his promises.

All of them.

Which also meant she hadn't seen him in months.

Why hadn't he called today?

"Liliana, I know you're not looking at your phone when you're supposed to be rehearsing for tomorrow's show."

Gordo's tone was half-teasing, and half-chiding. She saw the looks in some of the other ballerina's eyes whenever she got away with a misstep or a slip that he would never let them off on, but nothing could be done about it.

She told him she was fine.

And she was.

Mostly.

She grinned, and quickly slid the phone back into the bag before turning to face the room again. The strange thing was, she didn't look forward to this as much as she once used to. She didn't get a sense of dread or fear now when she put on her pointe shoes—a feat she overcame by talking for hours to a therapist her father called in—but something wasn't right about this place for her anymore.

Or maybe it wasn't the place at all.

Maybe it was *her*.

And ballet.

She could move, and she could still dance like she always had, but it didn't have that same freeing feeling it used to. She didn't love it deep in her bones the way she used to. Sometimes, that scared her more than anything.

Sometimes, that made her more determined than anything else could, too. Determined to *dance*, regardless if Rich Earl had taken it from her. Determined to get on the stage at least one more time and *be* the ballerina who lived and breathed ballet.

She could do it.

She *would* do it.

She just didn't know why she was doing it anymore.

"Let's start again from the top," Gordo said when Liliana rejoined the others.

From the top it was …

"Have you just come from the studio?" Cara asked.

Liliana nodded, and took a sip from her to-go cup of coffee. "I did."

"And how was it today?"

"Same as usual."

"Try descriptive words," the therapist urged.

Liliana laughed under her breath, but thought about what she had been told, too. Cara Rossi had walked into her hospital room two days after Liliana arrived, and explained why she was there with a smile that could make anyone feel comforted.

She had a therapist before, but Cara was not the same.

She was entirely different.

A woman like Liliana, in a life like hers, with a husband much like the rest of the men Liliana had grown up in. The woman hailed from Chicago, but lived in Toronto, Canada with her husband, Gian, and their five boys.

She specialized in helping women—addicts, or victims of domestic violence, specifically. She could make Liliana talk for hours, but it only felt like minutes. She never once looked at Liliana with pity, or judgement for anything she said.

Yeah, she was something else.

Something special.

"I guess you could say I just haven't regained my old love for it, yet," Liliana said, "or maybe it's that I haven't found what I'm looking for in ballet, if you get what I mean. I used to dance and feel like nothing else mattered. It was just me and the stage, but now it's me and … nothing."

Cara raised a brow as she took in Liliana's words. "Why do you think that is?"

"I think ballet took something from me once, and then he used it against me again. So, instead of having this deep love and respect for what ballet gave me, and what I can do with it, I am stuck feeling like it's a weight I would rather rid myself of before it pulls me back down."

"Use his name. He doesn't get the power to make you silent."

Liliana smiled. "Yeah, I know."

"You feel like *ballet* took something from you. That's the first time I've ever heard you say that. Why?"

Well, that wasn't so easy to explain.

That was complicated.

Cara waited her out.

She always did.

"Rich watched me dance once … it's what made him seek me out, and brought him into my life. Now, I've got this strange place in the back of mind that I keep going to every single time I have to think about getting back out on the stage."

"Like someone else is going to be waiting."

"Someone like him, yeah."

"Someone else was waiting once," Cara said softly. "Didn't you tell me that? Someone else watched you dance once, and he was nothing like Rich, Liliana."

Yes.

She had told Cara that.

She told her everything.

"Joe," Liliana murmured.

"You haven't seen him in a while, I suspect," Cara said. "Your father tells me it wasn't possible, so that must be difficult, too."

"He calls. We talk."

"Not the same, though, is it?"

Liliana frowned. "No, not at all."

"When will you get to see him?"

That, Liliana didn't know.

"Soon, I hope."

Cara nodded. "Have you thought about what you might want to do *besides* ballet?"

Months ago, Liliana would have said nursing. She only had a little bit of schooling left to finish to actually get her degree for that, but now, she wasn't so sure.

So was her life.

Suspended.

Upended.

Confusing.

"I still want to work in a hospital setting," Liliana said, "but I'm not sure in what department, or whatever."

"You know, the first place to see a domestic violence case *is* the hospital, Liliana. There are also shelters who employ nurses and counselors, on top of them having separate jobs at the hospital. I mean, if something like that was … in your thoughts."

She stiffened a bit.

That had never crossed her mind.

But now that it was *there* …

"And you could always see ballet like this," Cara said, smiling in that way of hers, "maybe Rich didn't take something away from you as much as he gave you the chance to find something different when you might not have gone to look for it yourself."

Cara leaned forward, and pointed a finger at Liliana, adding, "But don't even thank him for it, though. He gets nothing, now—not your fear, your pain, or even your success. He gets *nothing*. Not even in death."

Yeah.

Liliana would make sure of it.

"Are you ready for tomorrow?" Cella asked.

Liliana set her napkin down on the empty plate, and nodded. "For the most part, yeah."

"Nervous?" Catherine asked from two seats down.

"Not really." Liliana shrugged. "My foot is good—everything is healed. The doctor gave his okay a month ago, and I haven't really had any pain but for the usual blisters and bruising from just *dancing*."

"Reason number fifty-two why Cella never stayed in ballet," her sister muttered.

Liliana laughed. "Hazard of the job?"

"Listen, nothing about feet is very fucking pretty to begin with, Liliana. But I am not going to go about helping it along with something like ballet."

"Truth," Catherine agreed.

"Did you see Cara when she was here today?" Liliana asked her cousin.

Catherine glanced over. "I did, yeah."

She hadn't known that the same therapist helping her was also helping her cousin for an entirely different set of reasons. It wasn't something they talked about because frankly, they didn't want or need to. Everybody deserved their privacy, too. She knew now that Cara worked with her cousin, though.

"Shouldn't swear at the table," Lucia said with all the attitude she could muster.

The girls grinned, giggled, and went back to their plates. It probably wasn't the swearing that bothered her little sister as much as it was the fact *nobody* was talking to her. Lucia was pretty obvious in that way even if she wouldn't admit it.

The clang of metal hitting crystal quieted the family filling the long Marcello dining table. All of her family was there—apparently, they needed to gather and celebrate her show tomorrow as a unit.

She loved them all for it, really.

All her uncles and aunts, cousins, grandparents, and her own mother, father, and siblings. Cella sat on one side of Liliana, and little Lucia—although, being a teenager, she wasn't so little anymore—sat on the other side of her. Her brother, mother, and father sat across from her at the table while everyone else was spread out the rest of the way.

Still, they felt close.

It was kind of strange how that worked sometimes. They were always there when she needed them, and never too far away. Yet, they didn't smother her or drive her crazy. They never voiced opinions on her choices after what happened, and they let her live.

If that wasn't love, what was?

She had been so busy for the last month desperately trying to get up to par for her role in the show—not the lead, but the second, which was good enough for her—that she had kind of let her family fall to the wayside.

Not intentionally, of course.

They hadn't said a thing about her doing it, either, but she knew they had to be wondering. Was she doing okay? Was she overworking herself? Was she lonely when she came home to her studio apartment night after night with no one to greet her but her thoughts?

She wished they wouldn't worry at all, but trying to tell them not to was pointless. It was just what family did.

Liliana hadn't realized she needed this—a moment to get away from everything else in her life, and just spend time with her family. They were her happy place, if she ever had one.

Well, them … and Joe.

At the head of the table, her uncle stood with a smile as his gaze landed on her. "Liliana, we are all so very proud of you for what you've been able to do, and what you are *yet* to do. And we certainly can't wait to see where you go from here."

Her father raised his own glass, and the rest of the table followed suit. "To a Marcello *principessa*," her father murmured. "To one of *mine*."

"*Principessa*," the word echoed from several voices.

To her, being a mafia princess had never really felt like the weight around her throat that some liked to claim it to be. No, to her, being in this family was all she had ever known, and she was grateful for them.

Sure, they could be a little overbearing, and a touch too loud. Oh, they didn't know how to mind their own business, and they could bicker like nobody's business, too. But that was also *family*.

And all they ever gave to her was unconditional love, and a constant flow of adoration and support. Who could say they had all of that?

Because she could.

And she loved them for it.

She always would.

This was the moment Liliana had once loved the most about ballet. When the curtains closed, and the applause roared. When she bowed with the rest of the dancers, and she could hear thousands of feet rising from their seats. When the lights became brighter, and she could truly appreciate just how out of breath she actually was.

These were those moments.

Instead of feeling what she used to feel, all Liliana could bring forth was a sense of … completion.

Not even resignation, or sadness.

That heaviness was gone, too.

There was no weight around her neck, and no wishing to find something she used to have when she put on her pointe shoes, and moved like air. There was no rush of adrenaline in every fast beat of her heart, and gone was the longing to get it back.

It just felt *done*.

Liliana didn't have time to think on it for long because the curtain was pulling open again, and the dancers were stepping forward. Her arms were linked with the two women on either side of her, both dressed in similar pearl-white costumes with their hair slicked back into tight buns, and their faces painted identically.

Yet, she knew her family would be able to pick her out easily.

She found them in the front row easily enough. Her mother sitting beside her father, and the trail of her siblings next to them. Just behind their row sat her uncles, aunts, and the rest who had been able to come.

But it wasn't all of them her gaze was drawn to. It wasn't them who made a tangible, visceral clenching sensation start to grab at her chest, and her stomach.

It wasn't their gazes who met hers, and pinned her in place even as the dancers moved to bow again.

It wasn't them.

Because it was *him*.

Joe.

Then, her heart jumped.

And *stopped*.

Joe grinned in that way of his—something she found he liked to save just for her. A simple tilt of the edge of his lips that spoke of sin, love, and darkness. It made her hands tremble, and her knees weak.

He raised his hand a bit to wave two fingers at her, and winked, too.

The cheeky bastard.

Now, his missing calls had made a hell of a lot more sense. He didn't like to lie to her, or even omit things in their conversations. She bet he had been ignoring her calls to avoid having to do just that.

It wasn't Joe's style.

"Time to move," she heard someone call behind the curtain.

Shit.

No, what she wanted to do was stand right there, and keep staring at the love of her life. She hadn't gotten to look at him for so long, and now he was there.

The rest of the night could wait.

Surely.

Apparently not.

Liliana let the ballerina next to her drag her off the stage. God knew if she didn't let her do it, Liliana was never going to go willingly. As usual, the dancers were flooded by the crew and people from the studio the moment they stepped behind the curtains. Flowers were handed out, and compliments given.

Another successful show.

And Liliana felt like it was her last, too.

She wasn't really thinking too hard on that if only because her mind was somewhere else entirely. Overwhelmed, spinning, and fucking reeling.

Thinking about a man she hadn't seen face-to-face in months who was only just a few feet away separated by nothing more than a—

"*Tesoro.*"

Oh, *his voice.*

Liliana spun around to find Joe standing right behind her still wearing that grin of his. And a fucking tailored three-piece suit that made him look like every woman's walking wet dream. Like sin in the flesh, but covered by five-thousand dollar Armani. His blue gaze drifted over her features like he was waiting for her to say something.

To say *anything.*

She didn't know what to say, or where to begin.

Behind him, her parents waited patiently.

But they let him go first.

They let her see *him* first.

Liliana didn't even think about it before she launched herself at him. Joe's arms were already open and ready to catch her. With a laugh, she grabbed his jaw, and pulled him in for a fast, burning kiss that had her heart rate picking up speed all over again.

And *tight* ...

God, he held her so tight.

Dragged her *so close.*

The world drifted away when he was kissing her. The now-familiar dance of their lips melding together while he coaxed her mouth open for him was as comforting as the way she dragged in a heavy, ragged breath.

The ache in her chest ...

The happiness in her heart ...

All for him.

Joe pulled back just enough to gaze at her again as his thumbs stroked her cheekbones. "You look beautiful, and you were amazing."

Liliana smiled. "I missed you."

"I know, my girl. Me, too."

"Aren't you forgetting something?"

His last promise.

He only had one more to keep.

She didn't need him to, but she wondered if he would remember what he told her that he would do when they met up again.

"I don't think I need an introduction, but for you ... It's Joe Rossi," he murmured, dotting kisses to the seam of her smiling lips all over again. "It's far more than just nice to meet you again, Liliana."

TWENTY-ONE

"THAT FELT LIKE a goodbye," he heard Liliana murmur against his neck.

Joe held her a little tighter. "Not my kiss, I fucking hope."

He swore his heart had jolted for a second. This goddamn woman was going to be the death of him, he was sure of it.

Liliana laughed a little, and then pulled back just enough to stare him in the eyes. "No, not you. *Never* you."

"Then what?"

"The show, I guess. Dancing. Ballet."

She shrugged, saying nothing else.

Joe didn't really need her to. "It doesn't feel the same, then."

"I did it, though," she said quietly, "and that's what I wanted to do the most."

He stroked her cheeks with the pads of his thumbs, and then dipped his head down low enough to catch her lips with a sweet kiss. "Then, that's all that matters."

"I don't know what to do with my life now."

Joe chuckled. "You've got all the time in the world to figure that out. That's the best part about being young, *Tesoro*."

And if she wanted him there—as long as she wanted him there with her—he would be right beside her to help her figure it out. Whatever she needed, Joe would be there to give it to her every step of the way.

A throat cleared behind them.

Ah, yeah.

Shit.

He'd almost forgotten about everyone else.

As much as Joe didn't want to let Liliana go—not even for a single second—he stepped aside because he knew others were waiting to congratulate her. This whole night had been huge, even if she wasn't going to say so out loud. Her first time back on a stage since everything had happened, and of course, she was amazing.

"You looked wonderful," Lucian told Liliana.

She took the hug from her father with a wide smile, and the same from her mother, too. A kiss from both, as well. Joe hung back a little but only because he didn't want to intrude on their moment together.

"We're so proud of you," Jordyn added.

"Thanks, Ma."

Liliana seemed determined to bring Joe into their conversation one way or another when she glanced over her shoulder at him. "I see you were all keeping secrets from me."

Lucian chuckled when his gaze met Joe's. "We have to keep some tricks hidden up our sleeves, don't we?"

Sure, Joe had known about Liliana's upcoming show. She had told him about it over the phone, although she never went in to any great detail about it. He'd never been able to quite tell if she was excited, or not.

She just *talked*.

But when Lucian called Joe with the suggestion that he come to attend the show, he practically stumbled over every word he said to agree. It had already been four long months since he'd been out of New York and away from Liliana. It wasn't like he wanted to spend one more damn minute away from her.

He figured shit was still hot and heavy in the city because of the whole Earl thing, but he did his best to keep his head down, and his attention away from any news about New York. A watched pot never boiled, as the saying went.

"Joe," Jordyn said, drawing his attention to Liliana's mother.

"Yes?"

"I hope you're going to join us later."

"I didn't know something was happening, actually."

Lucian chuckled. "Ah, I forgot. Just consider it *your* surprise, then."

"Oh, the *party*," Liliana said, turning with a smile to face Joe. "They're throwing me a party at the mansion."

Lots of people.

A family he wasn't a part of.

Attention.

The spotlight being with her.

None of that would have been Joe's thing had someone asked him months and months ago. Yet, he was quick to nod and agree.

"Sounds fun," he said.

And he meant it.

"You know," Liliana said, finishing her second glass of champagne, "your brother has texted or called me at least once a week since you left."

Joe's gaze drifted from the gathered Marcello family back to Liliana tucked into his side. "Is that so?"

Cory hadn't mentioned a thing.

Joe wasn't exactly surprised.

"Yep, he did."

"And did he annoy the hell out of you like he does to me on a daily basis?" Joe asked.

Liliana snorted, and then smacked Joe with the back of her hand lightly to his chest. "You know your brother *loves* you. Be nice."

Joe rubbed the spot she'd hit, although it didn't actually hurt. "Hey, this is me being nice. Trust me, Cory wouldn't expect anything different."

"Yes, I remember. You two show your affection through kicking the shit out of each other."

He tipped his head to the side a bit, saying, "That, and apparently by Cory calling my girl to check in with her, and make sure she knows the rest of my family hasn't forgotten about her in the meantime."

Liliana stilled beside him. "Yeah, I guess that's exactly what he was doing."

Joe reminded himself to thank his brother. And maybe sign off on buying another business with him—one he'd been holding off on for a while because it meant more time spent away from the happiness and privacy of his own company.

Cory would like that.

Always pushing Joe out of his comfort zone.

It seemed in a very short span of time, his family had managed to get quite attached to his little ballerina. They were fully willing and ready to welcome her into the folds of their family whenever Joe got back around to bringing her home with him.

He just didn't know when that was going to happen.

"And your mom, too," she added.

"Probably not my dad, though."

Liliana grinned. "Damian Rossi *is* kind of quiet."

"That he is."

"He did say hello whenever your mom called, though."

Joe smiled faintly to himself. "Seems like his style."

"I miss them."

His arm tightened around her waist, saying, "They miss you, too."

"Yeah?"

"Why wouldn't they?"

Liliana shrugged a bit. "It's not like we know each other very well, or—"

"They don't have to know everything about you. They only need to know *one* thing that matters to them above the rest."

"And what's that, Joe?"

Their gazes met.

He leaned in and kissed her—soft, slow, and sweet.

"How much I love you, Liliana. That's all they care about."

She smiled against his kiss. "I love you, too, Joe."

"Sorry I was gone for so long."

"Yeah."

"It won't happen again."

Liliana's gaze darted up to meet his—green fire in a blink.

God, he loved this girl.

"Promise?" she asked sweetly.

"You know it."

Liliana's grin turned a little sly as she peered around the room at her family. Some were fully engaged in conversations, while others were looking at something on a tablet, and laughing. They had finally given Joe and Liliana a little room to breathe, and be alone. He appreciated it, but he also didn't mind being there with her and her people, either.

This was good.

"Everybody is … busy," Liliana said.

Joe nodded. "Seems so."

"I don't think they would notice if we skipped out for a few."

"*Liliana.*"

She pressed her lips tight together at his dark warning.

"What?"

Far too innocent.

She wasn't at all innocent.

"You're supposed to be celebrating with your family."

"And I am!" Liliana smiled brightly. "And we'll come back in a bit. What, you don't want to get me into a coat room somewhere and see what's under this dress, Joe?"

He eyed the tight, bodycon dress she had on—royal purple, with silver rockstud heels to match. She'd let her hair down in loose waves, too. His favorite because he could wrap his hands in the strands, and pull while he fucked her.

"*Jesus,*" he muttered under his breath. "I'm trying to be good here."

"Yeah, but you're not. So, let's go."

He didn't even try to refuse.

He all but *let her* sneak him out of the room.

Liliana tasted like tart, hot candy under Joe's tongue. He couldn't bury his face deep enough between her thighs to sedate the fucking hunger he felt for this woman. Every tremble of her legs, and every squeeze of her cunt around his fingers as he fucked her with his hand and his mouth drove him insane.

Every gasp …

Every plead …

Every-fucking-thing.

They had ended up in a coat room. Or something like that. He really hadn't paid too much attention because he had been far too distracted by the sight of Liliana on her knees as she sucked him off the very second he closed and locked the door.

That was a justifiable reason to be distracted.

Nobody ever looked as hot like that as she did.

And then he couldn't fucking take it anymore, knowing he was going to blow his load if he didn't stop her right then and there, so he got Liliana on her back instead. On a table—or a coat table, whatever in the hell they used this thing for.

It was sturdy enough.

Liliana was just panting her way through her third orgasm as her fingers threaded in Joe's hair began to tug and pull. It stung like nothing else, but he fucking loved it, too. Her back was arched high off the table, and her dress was pushed up around her hips. He wasn't sure where in the hell her panties had landed when he ripped them off.

That's all delicate lace like that was good for anyway—to be seen, and then completely *ruined.*

Like pretty wrapping paper before the prize.

"Again," Joe murmured, lapping at the inside of Liliana's thigh. "You're going to come for me again, Liliana. And then *again.*"

"I *can't*—"

Wrong.

She could.

He would just *show* her.

"You won't even need my mouth on you this time," he said, ignoring his painfully hard erection rubbing against the side of the table. He was practically fucking dry humping it anyway just to give him some goddamn relief. If it got any thicker, his dick was going to punch through his boxer-briefs considering he hadn't bothered to do anything more than tuck it back in after he'd pulled her mouth off his dick. "Just my fingers, my girl."

Liliana shuddered. "Lies. I can't come again."

"You can."

She shook her head.

Joe just smiled.

Game on.

"God, I love a challenge," he murmured.

He soaked in the way her sex clenched hard around two of his fingers when he eased them back inside her wet, tight walls. She hissed low, and those fingers of her came back to find his hair when she lifted her back off the table again.

So pretty.

So *responsive.*

Her body had to be fucking sensitive. A little too sensitive, maybe.

He started a massaging rhythm against the upper, fleshy part of her cunt that he knew was going to make her come, and come fucking *hard.* And with each stroke of his digits against her G-spot, Liliana started to shake a little more.

"Oh, my *God,*" she breathed.

Spun.

So breathless.

High, even.

He lived for her sounds.

"Are you going to give it to me?" he asked.

Her green eyes flew wide, and he saw the way her pupils blew open when her gaze landed on him. Her pretty pink lips—all that lipstick was long gone, now, stained on his cock—fell open in to an O-shape and her chin trembled.

"I think so," he said.

The sound that came out of Liliana when she came a fourth time was unlike anything he'd ever heard. Raw, and harsh. Yet, still so fucking sexy and beautiful. Like she couldn't believe what she was feeling, but he bet it was worth it, too.

Christ.

She was worth it.

"Fuck," she mumbled.

Sobbed was more like it.

Joe chuckled as he kept massaging her G-spot even through her orgasm. He felt her arousal soak his fingers, and slick down his hand. Jesus, she was so wet, it was crazy. He didn't stop his intent to make her come again like this. Even as she sobbed her way through yet another G-spot stimulated orgasm.

The *most* beautiful thing he had ever seen.

Joe stood straight, flipped Liliana over, and pulled her to the edge of the table so that her feet could touch the floor. It took two quick smacks of his hands against the back of her thighs for her to open her legs for him. She had made a wet spot on the back of her dress, and probably left one on the table, too.

Damn.

As hot as that was ...

Well, they'd figure out how to hide it later.

She shuddered and shook when he rubbed his hands over her ass, and then moaned hard and deep when he fished his cock out, and stroked it through her folds. Every touch of his dick against her cunt made her whine, and jerk.

"Sensitive," she whispered.

Yeah, he bet.

"This is all mine, isn't it?" he asked.

He heard her swallow thickly. "All of me, Joe."

"You trust me, don't you?" he asked, letting his dick slide into her pussy and soak his length. Then, he dragged his cock higher until it came to rest at her ass. Liliana didn't even tense, but let out a sweet laugh. "You're so fucking wet right now—let me fuck you like this. *Trust me.*"

"Are you going to make me beg for it?"

"I won't even have to."

"So cocky."

"Confident, actually."

Because it would be better like this. Better when she was strung out on sex, and feeling thoroughly fucked. Better when all she would want to do is beg to be filled and stretched out to her max like nobody else could do for her.

Just *better.*

"Please," Liliana whispered.

Jesus.

Yes.

That was all he needed to hear.

He used his cock first to tease her, and test the ring of her tight ass with just the head. When he felt her trying to back onto his cock, he pulled away, and got his fingers wet instead. He'd never heard her moan like she did when she had two of his fingers—and then three—filling her ass, and stretching her open.

It was only when her wild eyes looked back to find his, and he could see the beads of sweat starting to form on her backside, that he put his cock back where he wanted it to be the most.

Slow going.

One fucking inch at a time.

Halfway, she tensed, and sucked in a sharp breath. He felt those inner rings of muscles bear down hard on his length, enough to take his own air away.

"Shit, relax," he uttered.

Liliana wet her lips. "Just *fuck me*, Joe."

"Demand and beg when *I'm* ready, babe."

She cursed.

He laughed.

And then he was sliding all the way in because her little distraction had been enough to let her body relax. Once his cock was seated balls-deep into her ass, he pushed his hands hard against her lower back, and kept her pinned to the table.

He couldn't have her moving.

Fuck, not right then.

He'd bust a nut, and ruin *everything*.

"Joe?"

He eased up a bit on his hold. "Fucking killing me here, Liliana."

"Not nearly as much as you're killing me."

Yeah, he bet.

"Won't you fuck me now?" she asked.

God, yes.

And he did.

Harder than fucking ever.

Joe paced the length of the alleyway for what felt like the hundredth time.

At *least*.

His father kept his calm tone on the other end of the phone, and while Joe usually appreciated Damian's laidback demeanor, today wasn't quite the same. It wasn't helping with his nerves at all.

"Joe," his father snapped.

It brought him back to reality in a blink.

"What?"

"How long have you been pacing now?"

Joe's gaze narrowed as he looked around the alleyway. "How do you know I'm pacing?"

"I can hear your feet making a permanent path in the concrete, Joe."

Oh.

Well …

"I'm trying to calm down," Joe muttered.

"You don't need to calm down."

"You don't know. You're not here!"

"Joe, come on, now."

"I am *coming on*, Dad. I'm freaking out."

"He likes you," Damian murmured, "and you know he does. You have no reason to be acting like this."

"Says *you*."

"All right, you know what? You call me when you've talked to Lucian."

"Why?"

"So, then I can tell you that I told you so, son."

His father hung up the call.

Without a goodbye, too.

Asshole.

Joe shoved his phone back into his pocket, and then wiped his sweaty palms along his pant legs. Jesus Christ, this should not be such a nerve-wracking thing. He wasn't even the type of man who got nervous about this kind of shit.

Then again, he'd never done this before.

So, what did he know?

Fuck, fuck, fuck!

All right, that was enough of that. Joe sucked in a breath, and refused to sit out here and panic anymore than he already had. At most, this meeting could end one of three ways.

One—very well, and he got what he wanted.

Two—badly, and he was refused.

Three—Lucian could just kill him.

Maybe the last one was a little dramatic, but they had their things. Joe went to the worst-case scenario first, and worked back from there.

That was *his* thing.

Stepping up to the back exit door of the restaurant, Joe knocked on it and stepped back to wait. Not two seconds later, the door was opened up, and a Marcello enforcer poked his head out.

"Hey, Rossi."

Apparently, his face was familiar, now.

People even knew his name.

Or … his last name.

"Is—"

"Yeah, boss is waiting for you," the man said.

Joe blinked.

What?

He hadn't told Lucian he was coming because this had all been a little last minute. He'd been in New York for a week, but had to get back to Chicago for some work that needed to be done. He'd stayed long enough for Liliana to finish her shows for the week, but now she was done, too.

Done entirely, she said.

Ballet was no longer a need or want for her.

She was flying out to Chicago with him tomorrow. She missed his family, and God knew they missed her if the many texts and calls to him were any indication. They would like his little surprise when she showed up to dinner with him tomorrow evening.

"You coming, or you gonna stay out here looking foolish?" the enforcer asked.

Joe shot the man a look. "Nice."

"Yeah, well, I try."

Joe followed behind the enforcer, and let the man direct him through a busy, bustling restaurant. Lucian was seated in his usual area—the private dining section. The man had a host of papers and files spread out on the table, and didn't even glance up when Joe approached.

"Have a seat," Lucian said.

"Do you ever take vacations, or break from … this?" Joe asked.

Lucian shook his head. "Rarely."

"Your wife must love that."

A smile curved Lucian's lips.

"My wife *is* my break and vacation, Joe."

Ah.

Okay, then.

"How long were you planning to pace and talk on the phone in the alleyway before you gained enough courage to come in here and speak with me?" Lucian asked.

Joe blinked. "How did you know—"

"I know everything, or the cameras tell me."

Again … *ah.*

"Ask," Lucian said quietly, still going through his files.

"You don't know if I came here to ask anything."

"Yes, I do. You probably feel like you waited too long to ask as it is, Joe. Frankly, *I* would not have waited as long as you did, but I appreciate that you were able to hold yourself back. So, please, put yourself out of this misery, and just ask me what you came here to ask."

Joe bit his inner cheek.

He glanced down at his clenched hands.

He had never been more sure of anything in his life than *this.*

"I want to ask for your blessing, Lucian."

Finally, Lucian glanced up from his work to stare at Joe. He didn't know what he expected to see staring back at him, but the calm assuredness in Lucian's gaze was not it. *That* took him by surprise more than anything else.

"To marry her," Lucian clarified.

Joe nodded. "Yeah."

"When do you plan to ask?"

"I don't know … just that I *will*."

Lucian leaned back in his chair, and stared out the window at the passing people on the sidewalk. "She'll say yes, Joe. I hope you're not worried about that."

He wasn't.

Much.

"And what about you?" Joe asked. "Do I get a blessing from you?"

Lucian smirked. "Joe, I would have given you my blessing months ago—the first night you met her, actually, and noticed that she was a dancer just by the way she walked. What kind of man notices that sort of thing about a woman, anyway? I suspected … the kind of man who would notice everything else about her, too."

"You heard that?"

Because they had all seemed rather distracted at the table.

Lucian chuckled. "I told you—"

"You see and notice everything."

"Exactly. I'd like a call before you ask so that I know, and can let her mother know."

Joe nodded. "Will do."

"And give her something more than asking her in bed," Lucian grumbled. "That's *not* the story I want to be told."

Glancing away, Joe smirked. "I will keep that in mind."

"You better."

EPILOGUE

Three months later ...

"*YES*, CELLA," Liliana huffed into the phone, "I will meet up with you before I head to Chicago next week."

"Promise?"

"You know I'm not even moving there yet."

"Feels like it," her sister said sadly.

Liliana slowed her rushed movements to finish getting dressed—she was already late to class, and didn't want to miss the whole damn thing. Still, she also didn't want to hear her sister sounding like Liliana had just kicked her fucking puppy.

"Chicago isn't *that* far away, Cella."

"Far enough."

"Yeah, I guess, huh?"

"Lucky I like Joe," Cella grumbled.

Liliana smiled. "He's hard not to like."

She had another couple of months left before summer break was there, and then she would be heading to Chicago to live full-time with Joe. Next year, she would start her second to last year of school before she could move onto counseling domestic violence victims within hospitals and shelters.

She wanted to do this more than anything. She knew her sister—and her littlest sister, too—was going to miss her, though.

That kind of made it hard.

"I'll be over," Liliana said. "Promise, Cella."

"Okay. And you know, even though I'm sad that you're moving, I'm also really happy that you're happy, Liliana."

"Yeah, I know. Love you, huh?"

"Love you, too."

The knock on Liliana's door made her say goodbye quickly to her sister. She knew what it was going to be before she even moved to open the door.

Every Friday—it never failed—Joe sent her flowers.

Roses.

Lilies.

Carnations.

A different flower for every Friday with a little note from him. Unless, of course, he was in the city to visit with her, then he was there, and she didn't need flowers. She still liked his reminders that he was always thinking about her, though.

She didn't even try to hide the smile when she pulled open the door to greet the delivery man, but she froze in place when she saw Joe on the other side.

Tiger lilies in hand.

Leather jacket and dark-wash jeans.

Down on one knee.

Joe smiled.

Liliana grinned.

"Thought you might like to get them delivered personally this week," he said.

Liliana's gaze caught the beautiful solitaire diamond sitting in a white-gold setting, resting on the top petal of the tallest flower.

Where it couldn't be missed.

"This *is* nice," she said.

A quake colored up her words.

Just a little.

"Liliana."

Her gaze darted back to his.

Joe looked like everything to her.

Life.

Love.

Forever.

That's what he looked like kneeling there.

"I'm not very good with words—not the type, *Tesoro*."

"You don't have to be, Joe."

"But I hope you know that you're my *one*, Liliana. You had me captivated from the first second, and you'll have me stuck that way until the last one, too. I don't want it any other way."

And he was hers, too.

"Marry me, my girl."

Did he expect any other answer?

"*Yes.*"

THANKS!

Thank you so much to all the ladies who helped me during the process of writing this book. London, for the cover design, and of course, being the first to read Joe and Liliana's tale. Eli, for your editing and support. Tracy, Mia, Tori, and Felicia for finding all (hopefully, haha) my typos. Your work and love is so appreciated, truly.

I would be remiss if I didn't also mention Michael Stokes, and his photography which provided the image for the cover of this book. Antoni Bialy will forever be my Joe, and seeing that shoot come up on Twitter was, by far, a highlight of my month. So, thank you.

To my readers—thank you for still being on this journey with me. I love you all.

To my family … one more down. A million more to go.

Hugs, loves.

Bethany-Kris

ABOUT THE AUTHOR

Bethany-Kris is a Canadian author, lover of much, and mother to four young sons, one cat, and three dogs. A small town in Eastern Canada where she was born and raised is where she has always called home. With her boys under her feet, a snuggling cat, barking dogs, and a spouse calling over his shoulder, she is nearly always writing something ... when she can find the time.

Find Bethany-Kris at her:

WEBSITE: www.bethanykris.com
BLOG: www.bethanykris.blogspot.com
FACEBOOK: www.facebook.com/bethanykriswrites
TWITTER: @bethanykris
INSTAGRAM: @bethany.kris

Sign up to Bethany-Kris's New Release Newsletter here:
http://eepurl.com/bf9lzD.

OTHER BOOKS

John + Siena

Loyalty
Disgrace

Cross + Catherine

Always
Revere
Unruly
The Companion

Guzzi Duet

Unraveled, Book One
Entangled, Book Two

DeLuca Duet

Waste of Worth: Part One
Worth of Waste: Part Two

Standalone Titles

Effortless
Inflict
Cozen
Captivated

CAPTIVATED

Donati Bloodlines

Thin Lies
Thin Lines
Thin Lives
Behind the Bloodlines
The Complete Trilogy

Filthy Marcellos

Antony
Lucian
Giovanni
Dante
Legacy
A Very Marcello Christmas
The Complete Collection

Seasons of Betrayal

Where the Sun Hides
Where the Snow Falls
Where the Wind Whispers
Seasons: The Complete Seasons of Betrayal Series

Gun Moll Trilogy

Gun Moll
Gangster Moll
Madame Moll

The Chicago War

Deathless & Divided
Reckless & Ruined
Scarless & Sacred
Breathless & Bloodstained
The Complete Series

BETHANY-KRIS

The Russian Guns

The Arrangement
The Life
The Score
Demyan & Ana
Shattered
The Jersey Vignettes

Find more on Bethany-Kris's website at www.bethanykris.com.